"I'm leaving Tur  **New York," Haz**

Ward felt everything
you're taking your annual trip early?" Hazel had family
there that she visited regularly.

"No. I mean I'm moving to New York permanently."

Turnabout without Hazel's vibrant presence? It was
unthinkable. Trying to absorb the impact of what
she was saying, he raised a brow. "This seems a bit
sudden."

"Not really. Aunt Ellen has asked me several times
to work in her fashion-design business. I've finally
decided to accept her offer."

"I see." Except he didn't. Why would she do such a
thing? "Exactly how soon do you plan to make this
move?"

"I talked it over with Verity before she and her family
headed out on their vacation and I promised her I
wouldn't leave until she returns." Hazel shrugged.
"They're due back in about three weeks."

So soon! The sick feeling in the pit of his stomach
deepened. "And you've made up your mind?"

She nodded. "But for the next three weeks," she said,
"I'll do whatever I can to help with Meg."

He forced a smile. It was the second time today she'd
touched him that way. He found he liked it. He had
to remind himself to keep things on a just-friends
basis. But unfortunately it didn't seem like he'd have to
worry with that for much longer…

Winnie Griggs is the multipublished, award-winning author of historical (and occasionally contemporary) romances that focus on small towns, big hearts and amazing grace. She is also a list maker and a lover of dragonflies, and holds an advanced degree in the art of procrastination. Winnie loves to hear from readers—you can connect with her on Facebook at Facebook.com/winniegriggs.author or email her at winnie@winniegriggs.com.

Books by Winnie Griggs

Love Inspired Historical

Texas Grooms

Handpicked Husband
The Bride Next Door
A Family for Christmas
Lone Star Heiress
Her Holiday Family
Second Chance Hero
The Holiday Courtship
Texas Cinderella
A Tailor-Made Husband

Visit the Author Profile page at Harlequin.com for more titles.

WINNIE GRIGGS

A Tailor-Made Husband

HARLEQUIN® LOVE INSPIRED® HISTORICAL

If you purchased this book without a cover you should be aware
that this book is stolen property. It was reported as "unsold and
destroyed" to the publisher, and neither the author nor the
publisher has received any payment for this "stripped book."

LOVE INSPIRED BOOKS

Recycling programs
for this product may
not exist in your area.

ISBN-13: 978-0-373-42527-3

A Tailor-Made Husband

Copyright © 2017 by Winnie Griggs

All rights reserved. Except for use in any review, the reproduction
or utilization of this work in whole or in part in any form by any
electronic, mechanical or other means, now known or hereinafter
invented, including xerography, photocopying and recording, or in
any information storage or retrieval system, is forbidden without
the written permission of the editorial office, Love Inspired Books,
195 Broadway, New York, NY 10007 U.S.A.

This is a work of fiction. Names, characters, places and incidents are
either the product of the author's imagination or are used fictitiously, and
any resemblance to actual persons, living or dead, business establishments,
events or locales is entirely coincidental.

This edition published by arrangement with Love Inspired Books.

® and TM are trademarks of Love Inspired Books, used under license.
Trademarks indicated with ® are registered in the United States Patent
and Trademark Office, the Canadian Intellectual Property Office and in
other countries.

www.Harlequin.com

Printed in U.S.A.

I waited patiently for the Lord;
and He inclined unto me, and heard my cry.
—*Psalms* 40:1

Dedicated to my fabulous agent, Michelle Grajkowski, who is not only a great advocate for my work but also a great friend. And also to my wonderful brainstorming partners, Amy, Christopher, Joanne and Renee, who helped me figure out what direction to take my story when I lost my way.

Chapter One

Turnabout, Texas
June 1899

"I think he's sleeping. We prob'ly shouldn't bother him."

Sheriff Ward Gleason opened one eye and tilted his chin up enough to see from under the lowered brim of his hat. Sure enough, the child on the train seat in front of him had turned around and was kneeling up facing him. She had her doll propped up on the seat back facing him as well.

"Is there something I can do for you, Half-pint?" He mentally winced as soon as the words left his mouth—it was the nickname he'd used for his younger sister. Bethany was on his mind quite a bit right now. And this child, with her curly blond pigtails and freckled button nose, had her look.

The girl giggled. "My name's not Half-pint, it's Meg." She held up her doll. "And this is Chessie."

That much he already knew. The youngster, who couldn't have been more than four or five, had chattered almost nonstop since she and her companion, whose name was apparently Freddie, had boarded the train about an hour ago.

Not that he minded. Sleep had eluded him on this long, mournful trip and he would prefer not to be left to his own thoughts.

Ward straightened and tipped his hat back off his brow. "Pleased to make your acquaintance, ladies."

"Did you hear that, Chessie?" Meg half whispered to her doll. "He called us ladies."

Then she looked back his way and pointed to his companion. "Why do you have that puppy with you?"

Ward glanced at the dog sleeping on the seat beside him. At four years old, give or take, Pugs wasn't a puppy anymore, but he was lapdog-sized, so he understood her confusion.

"He's my sister's dog. But I'm going to be taking care of him now."

The little girl frowned. "How come your sister didn't want him anymore? Was he bad?"

"Not at all. But I'm afraid she's no longer able to take care of him."

"Oh." The little girl studied him thoughtfully for a moment. "Is she sick?"

His throat constricted but he nodded. "She was. And now she's gone." Bethany's casket was aboard the train two cars back—he was escorting her remains back to Turnabout to lay her to rest beside their parents. He was finally bringing his sister home. Just not in the way he'd wanted.

Did the little girl understand the concept of death?

But Meg nodded solemnly. "My momma and poppa are gone too. It's just me and Chessie and Freddie now." She gave her doll a tight squeeze. Then she looked at the dog. "What's his name?"

"Pugs."

She smiled. "That's a good name for a doggie." The child's smile turned hopeful. "Can I pet him?"

Ward shrugged. "Sure."

The child turned at once to her companion. "Freddie, can I pet the puppy? Please?"

Freddie, who appeared to be about sixteen, turned to stare at Ward, obviously reluctant. Ward didn't take offense. In fact, he approved of the young man's caution.

Then the youth glanced back at Meg. "You shouldn't be bothering folks. Turn around and play with Chessie."

Ward frowned. The youth didn't sound so much protective as irritated. He'd gathered from earlier chatter that the two were siblings, and he would have expected a more caring attitude. Then again, he knew from personal experience what it was like to be thrust into the role of parent at that age. Twelve years ago, he and Bethany had become orphans as well. He'd been sixteen at the time and Bethany almost thirteen. And though he'd tried to be a parent to his little sister, he'd failed her, with tragic results.

Which was why he itched to give Meg's brother a lecture about just how precious a little sister was and how he should cherish her while he had her. Maybe he *would* say something to him at some point if he could do so without Meg overhearing.

But now was not that time.

A moment later he realized the train was slowing. They must be approaching Kittering. After this stop, there were only two more before the train would pull into the Turnabout station. It would be good to get home.

Would Hazel be waiting for him at the depot?

Hazel Andrews, Turnabout's seamstress, had been Bethany's best friend when they were children and the only other person who had visited her from time to time these past twelve years. She'd been a true friend to his sister.

And to him.

Hazel had been the only person he'd been comfortable discussing her with since Bethany had been installed in that private asylum—his worries and concerns over Bethany's mental state and care, his memories of happier times.

The only things he didn't discuss with Hazel were his feelings of guilt.

Ward pulled his thoughts back to the present as Meg's brother leaned forward to speak to the passenger in the seat in front of him, a matron who was trying to watch over two fussy children. One of the children chose that moment to let out a loud, petulant whine. Whatever Freddie had been saying to the child's mother was met with a firm *no* as the harried woman tried to quiet her little one.

Freddie plopped back against his seat as if in defeat.

"Please, can I pet the puppy?" Meg asked again.

Freddie glanced back at Ward, an assessing gleam in his eye. "Are you sure it's okay with you, Mister?"

Ward shrugged. "Pugs would probably be glad to get some attention and I certainly don't mind."

Freddie stood. "The thing is, I need to get off to send a telegram. Would you mind watching Meg till I get back?"

Ward hesitated, not sure he wanted that responsibility. Then again, it was just for a few minutes and they were in a confined space—it wasn't as if the child could run off or get into trouble. "I suppose I can do that."

With a relieved smile, Freddie turned to Meg. "You behave yourself and do what this man says, you hear?"

The little girl nodded, obviously more interested in the dog than her brother's departure.

Without another word, Freddie quickly headed for the exit.

Ward gave the girl a smile. "Meg, why don't you sit here with me and Pugs until Freddie comes back."

The child eagerly scrambled from her seat to join him.

Meg and Pugs took to one another immediately. Before long the little girl was the giggling recipient of canine kisses and face licks.

Ten minutes later, the flow of passengers exiting and boarding had finally trickled to nothing and still there was no sign of Freddie. He thought about going in search of the youth, but thoughts of having to drag Meg and Pugs along gave him pause.

For the first time Ward wondered if he should have taken Hazel up on her offer to make this trip with him.

But if they'd taken this trip together, she might have read more into it than he intended. Hazel had been making it obvious for a while now that she had more than a casual interest in him, though he'd done nothing to encourage her. He didn't have any interest in forming that kind of relationship with any woman, not so long as he was sheriff. A man couldn't be responsible for the welfare of an entire town and also give a wife the attention she deserved.

Though, to be honest, on the rare occasions when he allowed himself to think about it, if he ever did want to find himself a wife, Hazel would likely be his first choice. Not that he'd ever let her know that.

So instead of inviting her along, he'd asked her to take care of the things that needed to be done in preparation for the funeral. And she'd graciously agreed. As she always did when he asked a favor of her.

The whistle sounded, bringing him back to the present. The train would be pulling out of the station soon and Meg's brother still hadn't returned.

Ward stood. He picked up Pugs and reached for Meg's hand with his free one. "What do you say we go get some fresh air?"

She nodded and trustingly took his hand.

As they stepped out on the loading platform, Ward scanned the area for any sign of Meg's brother, but the youth was nowhere to be seen. What could be keeping him?

The conductor yelled a long, drawn-out *all aboard*. Ward immediately marched over to him.

"You can't leave yet, you're missing a passenger."

The conductor frowned. "We have a timetable to keep to. Whoever's missing had better hurry."

Ward nodded toward Meg. "It's her brother." He kept his voice pitched for the conductor's ears only.

The man looked down at Meg and his expression lost some of its officiousness. Then he grimaced. "I can give you ten extra minutes, but that's the best I can do."

Ten minutes—that wasn't much time. "Do you know where the telegraph office is?"

The conductor nodded to his left. "Inside the depot."

At least he didn't have far to go. "Come on, Half-pint, we're going for a little walk."

He managed to get the three of them inside the depot, then looked around. Freddie was nowhere to be seen. His feeling that something was seriously wrong deepened.

Ward marched to the counter and got the clerk's attention. "A young man came in a little while ago to send a telegram. Did you see where he went afterward?"

The balding man didn't bother glancing up. "Can't help you. Hadn't been anyone send a telegram all afternoon."

The train whistle sounded again and Ward's pulse kicked up a notch. What would he do if Meg's brother didn't return before the train departed? He couldn't abandon Meg but he couldn't take her with him either.

His best option was to stay behind with Meg until they located her brother. Which meant sending Bethany's casket on without him, the mere thought of which set a silent howl of protest pulsing through him.

But he had to tamp that down. He was a lawman and his duty to help others had to override his personal desires.

Decision made, Ward returned to the train just long enough to collect his and Meg's bags. Taking firm hold of his two charges, he watched the train pull away without him.

It appeared Bethany's remains were going to make the last leg of her trip home without him.

He'd failed her all over again.

Hazel Andrews closed the door of the Fashion Emporium and hurried down the sidewalk. She'd had a busy morning making certain everything was taken care of for Bethany's funeral this afternoon. It was the last thing she would be able to do for her childhood friend and she wanted to make sure she'd given it her best.

Now she was headed to the station to meet the morning train. She wanted to be there when Ward stepped off. This couldn't have been an easy trip for him and he would need a friend right now.

And it seemed that was all she was destined to be to him—a friend.

"Oh!"

"Pardon me." Hazel had been so lost in her own thoughts she'd practically run into Cassie Lynn Walker. "I'm so sorry, I wasn't paying attention. Are you all right?" She bent to pick up the package the very expectant mother-to-be had dropped.

Cassie gave a self-deprecating laugh. "I'm fine. And thank you," she said as she accepted the package. "It was as much my fault as yours. I'm clumsier than a toddler learning to walk these days." She rubbed her protruding stomach ruefully.

"You have good cause to be." Hazel did her best to force down the pang of jealousy. It seemed every other woman of marriageable age in Turnabout had found a husband and started families.

Was it so wrong of her to want the same thing?

Cassie touched her arm, smiling sympathetically. "I hear the sheriff's sister was a good friend of yours. I'm awful sorry for your loss."

Cassie's words pulled Hazel out of her self-pitying thoughts. Unlike Bethany, she still had the opportunity to change her circumstances. And that's what she intended to do.

In the most decisive way she could imagine.

"I hear tell the sheriff didn't make it in yesterday afternoon as planned. I hope nothing serious has happened on top of his loss?"

Hazel shook her head. "He's assured me he'll be on this morning's train." It wasn't an answer, exactly, but it was the best she could do. "In fact, I'm on my way there now. If you'll excuse me."

As Hazel resumed her march to the train station, she wondered exactly what had delayed Ward. The telegram he'd sent had only stated that he'd been temporarily detained and would arrive this morning.

It wasn't like the always serious-to-a-fault sheriff to get sidetracked easily, so it must have been something really important.

A few minutes later Hazel stepped onto the station platform and saw the plume of smoke in the distance that signaled the train approaching.

She knew she shouldn't *still* get this little tingle of anticipation at the thought of seeing Ward. After all, she'd given up on her hopes that he would someday return her feelings. Truth to tell, she wasn't even certain what her own feelings were anymore. Sure, she still liked and admired him, but she wasn't certain she loved him, at least not in the romantic sense. She wasn't even sure she knew what that kind of love was.

And right now she had other problems to deal with. Her financial situation was such that she needed to make some radical changes in her life. Saying goodbye to Turnabout and all her friends here was going to be difficult, but accepting her aunt's invitation to move to New York and work with her seemed like the best answer to her financial woes.

And perhaps it would give her a fresh start in other areas of her life as well.

On the heels of that thought, she saw the train rounding the curve that brought it fully into view. Her lips curved in a self-mocking smile as she realized her hand had gone up to her hair to make certain none of her unruly tresses had come loose. Old habits were hard to break, it seemed.

Hazel stood well back on the platform as the train pulled in, wanting to avoid the steam and soot it trailed in with it. She eagerly scanned the few passengers who stepped from the train and smiled as soon as she saw Ward's tall, familiar form emerge.

Then her brow went up. He wasn't alone. He had Pugs with him, thank goodness. But there was also a small girl holding tightly to his hand. Who was this child and why was she with Ward? Did she have something to do with why he'd been delayed?

Hazel didn't step forward immediately, trying to take in the implications of what she was seeing.

Ward scanned the platform, as if looking for someone. When his gaze finally connected with hers, the smile that lit his face warmed her in spite of her earlier resolution. Was it pleasure or relief that she saw reflected there?

Then she noticed how tired and harried the normally unflappable sheriff looked and rushed forward, all her nurturing instincts bubbling forth. "Welcome back. I see you brought some friends with you."

Ward nodded. "I did. This is Meg." He turned to the little girl. "Meg, this is Miss Hazel, the nice lady I told you about."

He'd spoken of her? "Hello, Meg."

The little girl moved closer to Ward. "Hello." Then she held out her doll. "This is Chessie."

Meg's attachment to Ward and his protective attitude toward her in turn touched something inside Hazel. She'd always thought he'd make a good father someday.

Smiling at that thought, she stooped down to get a better look at the child's doll. "Well, hello, Chessie. I'm so pleased to meet both of you."

Hazel met Ward's gaze, dozens of questions swirling in her mind, but none she wanted to ask in the presence of the child.

"Meg is going to be in my care for a while," he said cryptically.

Hazel waited a moment for more information but none was forthcoming. Finally, she straightened and turned a smile on the little girl. "Well then, welcome to Turnabout, Meg. I hope you're going to enjoy your stay here."

Meg nodded. "Is Mr. Gleason really the *sheriff*?"

Hazel cut a look Ward's way. "That he is." She gave him a teasing smile. "And a very good one too." She was rewarded for her praise with a faint upturning of his lips.

"Sheriff Gleason's sister died," Meg stated forlornly.

The words jolted Hazel's attention back to the little girl. "Yes, I know." She studied the child, her curiosity growing. Apparently Ward had told Meg something of Bethany. Or had she already known?

Yes, the child favored Bethany slightly, but that didn't mean anything. If someone had tried to pass Meg off as his sister's daughter, surely Ward knew better—

As if sensing something of her thoughts Ward raked a hand through his hair and then turned to Meg. "Half-pint, why don't you take Pugs and sit on that bench over there. I need to speak to Miss Hazel for a few minutes."

Half-pint. That's what he used to call Bethany. Hazel again felt that tug of both curiosity and denial.

What was going on here?

Chapter Two

Ward had hoped to put off this conversation at least until after the funeral, but he could see now that that had just been wishful thinking. Hazel had never been able to hide her emotions and her expression practically screamed with the questions playing out in her mind.

Besides, he needed her help, so the sooner he gave her the explanations she wanted, the sooner he could make his request.

The thing was, he'd felt off balance ever since he'd realized Freddie wasn't coming back. He was certain that was why he'd experienced such an unexpected flood of relief when he spotted Hazel waiting for him on the platform earlier.

At least relief was how he chose to describe what it was he'd felt.

Not that she was hard to spot—she tended to stand out even in a crowd. And it wasn't just her red hair. As a seamstress she took full advantage of the skill and materials at her disposal. Even though she wore a dark colored dress today, a departure from her usual bright colors, she hadn't resisted adding what he thought of as "Hazel touches" to it. The elegant bits of ribbon and lace she added to her frocks and the feminine fit were part of her trademark style.

Shaking off those wayward thoughts, Ward took Hazel's arm and drew her a few feet away from where Meg sat, making sure he could keep an eye on the child in his periphery. Ignoring the familiar scent of orange blossoms that always seemed to cling to her, Ward launched immediately into a quick explanation. "I know you have a lot of questions, but there's not really much to say right now. The short version is that Meg and her brother boarded the train a few stops past mine, then the brother slipped away at the very next stop, abandoning his sister. I'm looking out for Meg until I figure out what to do with her."

Hazel's eyes widened and he saw the genuine sympathy reflected there. "Oh my goodness. That poor baby." She glanced toward Meg. "How awful for her. I hate to contemplate what could have happened if you hadn't been the one to take charge of her. But how—"

He raised a hand to stem the flow of words. "I'll answer all your questions, or at least tell you as much as I know, after the funeral."

"Of course." She bit her lip a moment. "You called her Half-pint," she said softly.

He rubbed the back of his neck, feeling unaccountably self-conscious. What was wrong with him? "It sort of slipped out the first time." He shrugged. "It's just a silly nickname." But they both knew it was more than that.

Hazel studied Meg thoughtfully. "She does favor Bethany just a little."

"So you see it too."

Hazel nodded. "I think it's the freckles and pigtails."

Then she turned and gave him a probing look. "But she's *not* Bethany."

Did she think he was being overly sentimental? "Of course not." Then he quickly changed the subject. "Is everything in place for the funeral?"

Her raised brow said quite clearly that she knew he was avoiding the subject. But she followed his lead. "Yes. Reverend Harper will preside at a graveside service at one o'clock, just as you requested."

Before he could say more than a quick thank-you, they were interrupted.

"Sheriff Gleason, glad to have you back in town."

Both he and Hazel turned at the hail.

Ward straightened when he realized it was Mayor Sanders. The man wouldn't be here unless there was town business to discuss.

Hazel spoke up first. "Good day, Mayor. Are you here to meet someone?"

Ward was surprised to hear a slightly confrontational tone in her voice. Was she at odds with the mayor over something? That thought brought out his protective urges.

"Actually, I came to see Ward." The mayor tugged on the cuff of his shirt. "Official town business."

She pursed her lips. "Surely whatever you have to discuss can wait. Sheriff Gleason just returned from his sister's deathbed. And now he has to get ready for her funeral."

He relaxed, realizing she'd gotten her back up on his behalf. She was certainly a magnificent sight when she got riled up, all flashing eyes, ruddy cheeks and battle-ready posture. But in this instance her well-intentioned interference was unnecessary. This was his job. "I assume there was some kind of trouble while I was gone?"

The mayor turned from Hazel back to him with a relieved nod. "I'm afraid so. There's been another incident and it's likely the same scoundrel who hit the Lawrences' and the Carsons' places. Only this time they've moved right into the heart of town."

Hazel spoke up again, her foot tapping impatiently. "Pardon me, gentlemen, but this seems to be a discussion that can wait until after the funeral."

Mayor Sanders shot her an apologetic look. "I'm sorry. I certainly don't expect the sheriff to do anything about this today. But I wanted him to hear about it straight away in case he runs into some talk or complaints from other townsfolk."

"Quite right." Ward gave Hazel a firm, not-your-business look before he turned back to the man who was, in effect, his boss. "Let's go to my office so you can fill me in on the details." Then he hesitated, looking over at Meg, remembering he wasn't as unencumbered as he'd once been.

He shifted his gaze to Hazel, hoping she could read his unspoken request.

And of course she did. Taking her cue, Hazel smiled down at the child. "Meg, why don't you come with me while Sheriff Gleason and Mayor Sanders take care of a little business?"

But Meg popped up from the bench and clutched at Ward, her eyes wide with apprehension. Poor Half-pint, being abandoned by her brother had obviously made her anxious about any hint of being cast aside again.

As usual, Hazel rose to the challenge. Without further prodding from him she stooped down to get on eye level with Half-pint. "We can take Chessie and Pugs with us too. And I'll introduce all of you to Buttons."

"Who's Buttons?"

Hazel's eyes widened as if she couldn't believe Meg didn't already know. "Why, Buttons is just the prettiest and smartest cat you've ever seen."

Ward refrained from rolling his eyes at that clearly overblown description and placed a hand on the child's head, trying to reassure her. "It'll be okay, Half-pint, it's just for a little while." Wasn't that the same promise Freddie had made to her? "I'll come on by to get you later on my way to the funeral."

Ward ignored the startled look on the mayor's face— a sign of what he could expect from his fellow townsfolk over the coming days, no doubt—and turned to Hazel. "Thank you," he said, touching her arm. "I'll come by the dress shop as soon as I'm able."

She nodded, her eyes widening slightly. He pulled his hand away quickly, wondering if she'd felt that same spark of awareness.

What was wrong with him?

She recovered quickly and her eyes flashed a warning. "Then we're going to talk."

"Of course."

He watched as she bent to pick up Pugs. Then she took Meg's hand with her free one and began regaling the little girl with tales of her cat's exploits.

Once again Hazel had stepped in to help without the least hesitation. Strange how he'd gotten used to always having her to count on. And she never let him down.

Then, shaking off thoughts of the usually-flamboyant-but-always-dependable seamstress, he shifted into his businesslike frame of mind and turned back to the mayor. "Let's go over to my office and you can give me the details."

As Hazel led the child away from the station she silently chided herself for that unguarded reaction to Ward's touch. Hopefully she'd recovered quickly enough so that he hadn't noticed.

Pushing those unwanted thoughts aside, she turned her focus to the little girl at her side. It was so like Ward to take personal responsibility for a lost child's welfare. He could have turned Meg over to the sheriff in Kittering. Or contacted a children's asylum. Or done any one of a dozen other things that would have shifted responsibility for the little girl to someone else. And no one would have thought any less of him if he had, especially given the mournful errand he was on.

But that wasn't his way.

If she wasn't careful, she'd find herself falling for the overly serious, secretly tender-hearted sheriff all over again. And she had to guard her heart against that, at all costs. She'd made her decision to leave and she couldn't let sentiment hold her back now. It had become painfully obvious to her that there was no future for her in Turnabout, either financially or emotionally.

Because, by her reckoning, if nothing changed to bring customers into her shop, she'd be out of funds in about three months.

This was for the best, no matter how difficult taking that first step would be.

"Is it very far?"

Meg's question drew Hazel's thoughts back to the present. She'd planned an impromptu stop as a treat for the little girl, but she realized Meg looked sleepy. "Actually, I thought we'd make one stop along the way, but if you'd rather go straight to my place we can do it another time."

"Where do you want to stop?"

"There's a little shop called The Blue Bottle, where they sell the most delicious sweets. They also have a selection of wonderful wooden toys. Would you like to visit there?"

Meg's face lit up and she nodded enthusiastically. "Oh yes. And Chessie would like it too."

"Then that's what we'll do. And since you're probably tired from that long trip, I'll let you pick out whichever sweet you like."

"Can we get one for Sheriff Gleason too? He's tired from the trip too."

Hazel looked at the child's earnest expression and her heart melted a little more. Meg really had developed an attachment to Ward. "I think that's a splendid idea."

How could this sweet child's brother have just abandoned her? There had to be more to this story than what Ward had told her in those few seconds. Surely it was some dreadful mistake and Meg's brother would come looking for her soon. To believe otherwise was just too sad to contemplate. And if she knew Ward, he wouldn't rest until Meg's situation was put to rights.

But if the brief time she'd spent with Meg was any indication, if and when the brother returned, it might be difficult for the sheriff and the little girl to part ways.

Ward sat at his desk in the sheriff's office, waving Mayor Sanders to the chair in front of him. He had hoped the string of incidents—part vandalism, part schoolboy pranks—plaguing the community had run their course and things would have settled down by the time he returned, but from the sounds of things, that wasn't the case.

Before Ward had gotten word of his sister's passing, there had been several incidents that seemed the work of overzealous mischief-makers. The hooligans had visited Enoch Lawrence's place three times, trampling the garden, splattering paint, stealing laundry from the clothesline. Then they'd moved to a neighboring farm, opening the paddock gate and letting Saul Carson's horses out, causing the rancher to lose a full day rounding them back up.

The one rather vague eyewitness account he'd gotten had come from Enoch's daughter Hortense, who said she thought she caught a glimpse of two youths racing away after one of the incidents. All of which led him to believe it was the work of rambunctious kids who'd gone overboard with their pranks. But that didn't make it any less unlawful and when he caught the culprits they would be dealt with severely.

"So let's have it," he said to the mayor.

"Last night someone broke a window in the back of the mercantile, pulled some of the canned goods from the shelves and took fistfuls of rock candy from the display case."

It was sounding more and more like some fool kids with too much time on their hands. But they were getting much braver and more criminal with each incident. "You keep saying *they*. Do we have any idea how many?"

"No, in fact, no one's seen anything since Enoch's daughter reported what she saw. I'm just assuming it's the same culprits." He rubbed his chin. "There's some as think it was the Lytle boys, though no one can agree which ones."

Elmer and Orson Lytle were cousins but there'd been hard feelings between them for years. He wasn't sure even they remembered the reasons anymore. Both men had two sons who were unfortunately beginning to follow in the footsteps of their fathers.

"Why the Lytle boys?"

"You mean besides the fact that they're wilder than badgers and twice as ornery? The four of them started a brawl in the middle of the mercantile. Doug had to throw them out for disrupting his business and they were none too happy about it."

"That's not really proof that they're the ones who broke into the place." Though it sure gave them a strong motive.

The mayor shrugged. "Of course you should do your own investigating. I'm just letting you know what folks are saying."

Then he gave Ward a pointed look. "The main thing you need to keep in mind is, folks are getting really stirred up about this, demanding something be done." He grabbed the edges of his coat and gave them a tug. "And quite frankly, I agree with them. I know this isn't a good time for you, what with your sister's passing and all. But it may mean some extra patrols and late-night vigils from you until the perpetrator is caught."

There was the hint of a warning in those words.

Ward wasn't opposed to putting in extra hours to catch these lawbreakers; it was his job after all. But what did that mean for his ability to look out for Meg?

The mayor gave him a calculating look. "Not to pry into your personal business, but that little girl you had with you at the train station…"

He paused a minute as if expecting Ward to fill in the blanks. But Ward refused to make this easy for him and held his peace.

After a moment of awkward silence, the man continued. "Mind if I ask where she's going to be staying while she's here?"

"That hasn't been decided yet." Ward met the man's gaze steadily, daring him to say anything else on the subject. While looking after Half-pint might not be part of his job, it was definitely a responsibility he felt strongly about. He hoped he wasn't going to be put in the position of having to choose between the two duties.

Finally, Mayor Sanders nodded and took his leave.

Ward remained at his desk, fatigue dragging at him like an anvil. He hadn't slept well since he'd received word of Bethany's passing, and it was all starting to catch up with him.

The news of the break-in at the mercantile had only added to that feeling of bone-tired weariness.

Ward pushed away from his desk, mentally throwing up his hands. It was time to get ready for the funeral and nothing was going to make him late for that. He hadn't been there to escort Bethany's remains on the last leg of her trip home. Sure as the sun came up in the morning, he would be there to see her laid to rest.

As he walked the short distance to his house, a small structure next door to the sheriff's office, he wondered how Hazel and Meg had fared. He had to admit, for all Hazel's unorthodox ways, it was good to know he had someone like her whom he could count on to help out in a pinch.

Sometimes it felt as if he were taking advantage of the warmer feelings she had for him, especially since he didn't return those feelings. But then again, he'd never led her on or gave her reason to think he considered her anything more than a friend. Better if they both just looked at it as one neighbor helping another.

Maybe she'd have some idea of what he should do about this whole unexpected situation with Meg. After all, Hazel's mind seemed to work in ways he'd never been able to fathom—she might see something he was missing.

Could he impose on her to take in the little girl until the matter was resolved? He certainly couldn't keep Meg at his place—if for no other reason than that his cramped living quarters weren't a fit place to house a little girl.

But first he'd have to answer Hazel's questions about Meg's situation.

It didn't take him long to get cleaned up. He pulled out his Sunday suit and paid meticulous attention to how he dressed. He would do his sister proud today.

As he pulled on his freshly shined boots, he glanced toward his bed. It would be so good to lie down for just a few minutes but he resisted the temptation. If he lay down now, he might not get back up until tomorrow morning.

Besides, Hazel and Meg would be waiting for him.

When he reached the dress shop he was surprised to see Hazel had the Closed sign in the front window. His conscience niggled at him. Was it in honor of Bethany's funeral? Or because he'd taken advantage of her generosity and left Meg in her care?

He'd just raised his hand to knock when the shop door opened and Hazel and Meg stepped out.

The dark blue—nearly black—dress Hazel wore should have looked severe on her. But somehow it didn't. Instead it highlighted the coppery gold of her hair and set off her green eyes to perfection. And her smile, as always, softened her sharp features. It was a mystery to him why some other bachelor hadn't claimed her hand by now. Seeing her with Meg drove home just how suited she was to be a wife and mother. If only he was the settling-down sort—

Better he not let his thoughts go there.

Before he could greet them, Meg rushed over and hugged his leg. "Sheriff Gleason! You came back!"

The strength of relief and delight in the little girl's voice caught him off guard. His anger toward her brother resurfaced. It was wrong that such a young child should be made to worry about being abandoned.

"Of course I came back, Half-pint. I told you I was going to look out for you."

"Miss Hazel and I got this for you," she said, holding out a small parchment-wrapped parcel. "It's a piece of brittle. I had one, too, and it's very good."

"Why, thank you." He turned to Hazel. "Both of you."

Hazel nodded. "You're welcome. But it was all Meg's idea."

Meg cast a worried look at the closed door. "Do you think Pugs and Buttons will be okay while we're gone?"

"Absolutely." Hazel slid the key in her pocket. "Buttons will simply find a shelf or tabletop to settle on if Pugs gets too rambunctious."

Meg turned back to him. "Buttons didn't seem to like Pugs very much. But Miss Hazel says that they're gonna learn to be friends."

He took her hand. "Well let's hope Miss Hazel is right, shall we?"

As they walked down the sidewalk with a happily chattering Meg between them, Ward found his thoughts turning to the funeral service that lay ahead. Thoughts and emotions he'd been able to hold at bay while dealing with Meg's tumble into his life were trying to break free. His sister's life, such as it had been, was over and she was at peace now.

He mourned her passing and he mourned that he'd never been able to make things up to her. His guilt was still there, coloring all those other feelings, and it was only made worse by the faint but real undercurrent of relief he felt at her passing.

Ward cleared his throat, trying to refocus his thoughts. "I want to thank you again for taking care of all the funeral arrangements. I know that was a lot of work to drop in your lap."

Hazel's expression softened. "You're more than welcome. I was honored to be able to do this for Bethany."

Would she be up to doing him one more very large favor? Having her take Meg in until he could come up with a more permanent solution for the little girl seemed an ideal solution, at least from his perspective. There was no one he'd trust with Half-pint more. And she, of all people, would likely agree that he wasn't the best caretaker for a child. After all, she'd been there when Bethany had had her accident, the day everything changed.

When they reached the churchyard Ward could see the small crowd gathered for the funeral. He was surprised by how many were there—he hadn't realized so many people remembered his sister.

As they reached the graveside, he steeled himself once more against the flood of emotions threatening to break free. He knew his sister was in a better place now, but the guilt he felt for having made her last twelve years in this world so troubled was something he'd never be able to forgive himself for.

He tried to focus on something other than the yawning hole in the ground. Jacob White stood to one side, softly playing his fiddle—a hymn that Ward couldn't quite place. There were flowers on the closed casket— mostly irises, which had been Bethany's favorite. He had no doubt Hazel was responsible for those little personal touches. He would have to remember to thank her again later.

Hazel stayed at his side during the service, which seemed fitting. She was almost as much family to his sister as he had been. And there was no one in his life he felt closer to.

Throughout it all, he maintained a rigid control over his own expression, not daring to look anywhere but at the casket and that yawning hole in the ground that lay waiting to swallow up what was left of his little sister's earthly remains.

Reverend Harper, who had known Bethany before her accident, gave a touchingly personal eulogy. The words of God's love and promise of everlasting life were a balm to his own troubled spirit.

Once the service ended, Hazel touched his arm for a moment, the gesture oddly consoling. Then she withdrew with a restless Meg to one of the benches that were tucked under an ancient oak near the edge of the cemetery.

Strange how he missed the comfort of her presence.

As the mourners disbanded, many of them paused to offer condolences. Among them were Enoch Lawrence and his daughter, Hortense. Enoch's voice was overly loud and gruff as he assured Ward he would hold him in his prayers. The man's hearing loss seemed to be getting worse by the day and he compensated by raising the volume of his own voice.

Then Hortense, or Tensy as she preferred to be called, spoke up, her eyes moist with emotion. "It was a lovely service," she said. "Just the sort your sister would have wanted."

Tensy was closer in age to him than his sister, so the words were probably mere platitudes, but he appreciated the thought. "Thank you, I believe she would have as well."

"Please, if there is anything at all I can do for you over the coming weeks, don't hesitate to let me know."

"Thank you." He'd received many such offers today. While he was certain they were all sincerely meant, he didn't intend to take anyone up on them.

After all, what could anyone do to ease his guilt?

Chapter Three

Hazel helped Meg hop up on the sturdy but worn bench. Meg had been remarkably well behaved during the service, fidgeting much less than Hazel had anticipated, but by the end it had been clear she needed something to distract her.

It warmed Hazel's heart to see so many folks gathered for the service. Did Ward realize they were all there to support him?

The soft strains of "What a Friend We Have In Jesus," Bethany's favorite hymn, had added an air of reverent sweetness to the gathering. Had Ward felt it too?

But she could tell that he'd withdrawn into himself. There was an air of rigid control about him, as if he were trying to hold back some unwanted emotion. It was his way, of course. But she couldn't help but wonder if it wouldn't have done some good for him to mourn outwardly as well.

What was he feeling? Grief, of course—but there was more to it than that. Guilt? Sorrow for what could have been? A touch of relief that his sister was at peace now? Probably a combination of all of them. She knew because she felt some of that as well.

Meg swung her legs and chattered away to her doll, pointing out a squirrel scampering up a tree, a butterfly flittering around and any number of other things that caught her eye.

Earlier, when the three of them had walked through town, Hazel had imagined that they must look the very picture of a happy family. Oh, how she wished that were true.

But she had to stop thinking like that. She looked around and realized she and Meg were on the receiving end of a number of curious glances but thankfully no one approached them. She had no answers to give them where Meg was concerned.

The questions she had about just who Meg was and what the future had in store for the little girl were growing. Could Ward really find Meg's brother if the youth didn't want to be found?

Hazel had briefly considered questioning the little girl herself earlier but that just hadn't felt right. So far Meg seemed to be adjusting to the situation remarkably well, but there was no sense in needlessly stirring up potentially painful memories.

She'd have no such compunction with Ward, though. As soon as she could get him cornered, he would definitely have some explaining to do.

Then she glanced his way and her resolve faltered. He looked so weary, so weighted down. Maybe she wouldn't press him today.

Tomorrow would be soon enough.

When the last of the townsfolk had left, Ward turned to see Hazel and Meg already heading his way. The two of them made a sweet picture together, a welcome contrast to the dreariness of his thoughts.

"Have you had anything to eat today?" Hazel asked as they reached him.

Ward's lips turned up slightly. She was bound to be near-to-bursting with questions about Meg, but leave it to her to focus on more immediate needs.

"We had breakfast before we boarded the train this morning," he answered.

She shook her head with pursed lips. "That's what I thought—you skipped lunch. Come along, let's get you something to eat."

He shot her a questioning look. "Come along where?" Hazel herself was the first to admit she wasn't the world's best cook. When the church held the annual picnic hamper auction fund-raiser, hers was usually one of the last baskets bid on.

"Daisy's restaurant. I haven't had time to do any cooking of my own."

"All right. But I'm buying."

She raised a brow, as if that was a given. "Of course."

"And then we'll talk." Though he wasn't certain how he would give her the full explanation with Meg listening to the conversation.

"Yes, we most certainly will."

Then she smiled down at Meg. "You should know, this restaurant we're going to is very special."

"It is?"

Hazel nodded solemnly. "Do you know what a library is?"

The little girl shook her head.

"Well, a library is a place that's full of books, all kinds of books—" her tone changed as if revealing a great secret "—including picture books."

"I like books with pictures," Meg said hopefully.

"Well then, you're going to really like the library. It's located inside the restaurant. I'm sure Miss Abigail, the lady who runs it, will be happy to let you borrow one."

Ward was impressed. It seemed Hazel had thought far enough ahead to find the child a distraction while they chatted.

Once in the restaurant, Hazel asked Abigail to show Meg the picture books. As soon as they were out of earshot, Hazel rounded on him. "Are you up for a discussion, or would you rather wait until you've had time to rest up a bit?"

He was surprised she was giving him a choice. "Ask your questions and I'll answer them as best I can."

"What do you know about Meg other than her name, and what are your plans to see that she's cared for?"

Ward quickly and succinctly explained what had happened up to the point where he decided to step off the train with Meg in Kittering to search for Freddie.

When he paused, Hazel, who'd been making sympathetic and amazed noises by turns during his recitation, finally spoke up. "But this is awful. That poor little lamb. Did you learn what happened to Freddie?"

Ward again felt that burning anger over what Meg's brother had done. "I contacted the local sheriff and he gathered up some folks to help search. After nearly an hour I finally looked through Meg's bag and found this."

He withdrew an envelope from his pocket and handed it to Hazel. He watched as she began to read. He had no need to look over her shoulder. He'd read and reread the stark missive enough times that he now had it memorized.

If you are reading this letter, then Meg is now your responsibility. It's my hope that you will provide a good home for her, but that is up to you. Meg is my sister but I never asked to be left in charge of her. I have my own future to look out for. I can't give Meg the kind of home she needs and she would not be happy or welcome in the new life I'm starting, so please don't try to find me.

Here are some things you need to know. Her name is Megan Lee, but everyone calls her Meg. She is four years old and her birthday is August 10. She likes to talk a lot but a sharp word will usually settle her down, for a while at least.

We don't have any other family to speak of so it won't do any good to go looking.

Good luck.

Freddie

Hazel raised her gaze from the sheet of paper and looked at Ward, her expression one of disbelief and dawning outrage. "This is terrible. How could anyone, most especially her brother, be so heartless as to dump her in the hands of a complete stranger with such disregard for her feelings and safety?" She glanced toward Meg. "That poor little girl—does she know?"

Ward rubbed the side of his jaw. "I'm not certain how much she really understands. When I asked her about the trip they were on, she said Freddie told her only that they were going to find a new family for her. Apparently there was no familial affection on either side. Meg doesn't seem unduly dismayed that her brother is no longer around."

"What's going to happen to her now?"

That was a good question. "For the time being I'll keep trying to locate Freddie. I also plan to search for any other relative or family friend who might be able to shed some light on this situation."

Hazel's forehead creased in frown lines. "What if you do find her brother? Surely you can't place her back in his charge. There'd be nothing to prevent him from abandoning Meg again. And next time Meg might not be so lucky in who she winds up with."

He was in total agreement with her on that score. "No, Freddie won't get his hands on Meg again, even if he does decide he wants her back. But I need some answers, and Meg's brother is the best one to give them to me." His jaw tightened. "For all I know, Freddie may have stolen Meg away from another family member who is frantically searching for the child even now."

"Oh, I hadn't thought of that." She plopped back in her seat. "I suppose anyone who would toss aside a child so callously is capable of anything." She gave him a searching look. "How do you plan to proceed with her in the meantime?"

That was the sticking point. "I haven't quite figured that part out yet. Any suggestions?"

"She's obviously formed a bond with you. It would be a shame to hand her off to a stranger yet again."

Not the answer he'd been hoping for. Where was that eagerness to help him she'd always displayed with such annoying tenacity? "The trouble with that plan is that I'm not exactly in a position to offer her a proper home."

She traced a circle on the table with her finger, not quite meeting his gaze. "Oh, I don't know. Other than being a trifle small, there doesn't seem to be anything wrong with your home."

"That's not what I meant." Was she being deliberately obtuse? "For one thing, my work is not the sort where I have regular hours or that allows me to have a child tagging along. For another, I'm hardly the kind of caretaker a four-year-old needs."

Hazel's expression regained some of that familiar softness as she met his gaze again. "She could certainly do a lot worse."

Her answer surprised him given what had happened to Bethany. But Hazel had always been a look-on-the-bright-side kind of person.

"You seemed to have managed all right last night," she added, as if that settled matters.

"I wasn't on my own. Reverend Mills, the preacher over at Kittering, offered us a room at his place for the night and Mrs. Mills took care of Meg."

Hazel nodded slowly, nibbling on her lower lip as if trying to puzzle something out. What was going on in that rather unorthodox mind of hers?

Then she seemed to come to a decision. "If it'll help you, I'll be glad to watch Meg for a few weeks, but first there's something you need to know."

Relieved that he'd gotten a commitment of sorts from her, Ward smiled. A few weeks should be sufficient time for him to figure things out with Meg. But why had she put a time limit on it? Had she started some new project while he was away—it seemed Hazel *always* had a project or cause to champion.

He spread his hands, inviting her to continue, confident it was something he could deal with.

She lifted her chin, giving him an almost defiant look. Why was she being so melodramatic? Surely, whatever it was wasn't so—

"I'm leaving Turnabout in a few weeks and moving to New York," she finally blurted.

Chapter Four

Ward felt everything inside himself suddenly go still. Surely Hazel hadn't meant that the way it sounded? "You mean you're taking your annual trip early?" Her mother had come from New York and Hazel still had family there that she visited regularly.

"No." She tucked a stray tendril behind her ear. "I mean I'm moving to New York *permanently*."

Turnabout without Hazel's vibrant presence? It was unthinkable. Trying to keep his demeanor matter-of-fact while he absorbed the impact of what she was saying, he raised a brow. "This seems a bit sudden."

She studied her hands on the table. "Not really. Aunt Opal has asked me a number of times over the years to work in her fashion design business. I've finally decided to accept her offer, is all."

"I see." Except he didn't. Why would she do such a thing? And why now? She'd always said on her return from her trips back east that it felt really good to be home again. "Exactly how soon do you plan to make this move?"

"I haven't set an exact date, but soon. I talked it over with Verity before she and her family headed out on their vacation and I promised her I wouldn't leave until she returns." Hazel shrugged. "They're due back in about three weeks."

So soon! The sick feeling in the pit of his stomach deepened. And if she'd been planning this since before the Coopers left, why was he just now hearing of it? "I see," he said again, not that he did.

Why had her decision unsettled him so much? "And you've made up your mind?"

She nodded, looking down as she brushed at her skirt. "So you see, I can only help you with Meg for that long."

This was so much bigger than not helping with Meg. How could she just leave like this? How long had she been contemplating this move? Was she so unhappy with her life here, or was there something in New York drawing her there? Could she have met someone on her last trip? Was—

Hazel reached across the table and touched his wrist, bringing his thoughts back to the here and now.

"But for the next three weeks," she said, "I'll do whatever I can to help with Meg."

He forced a smile. It was the second time today she'd touched him that way. He found he liked it. Perhaps a bit too much. He had to remind himself to keep things on a just-friends basis. But it didn't sound like he'd have to bother with that for much longer.

"I appreciate that," he said, responding to her offer. "And we'll just have to hope I have some answers about Half-pint by then."

He glanced toward the library area, forcibly shoving aside his feelings about Hazel's defection to deal with later. Right now he'd have to figure out how to best let Half-pint know she wouldn't be staying with him after all.

As if understanding what he was feeling, Hazel followed his gaze. "She probably won't understand why you need to hand her off to me."

"I'm not exactly handing her off," he protested.

She gave him a stern look. "That's not how she'll see it." Then she glanced Meg's way. "The news would be best coming from you, I believe."

Ward nodded and caught Abigail's eye, signaling that she should bring Meg back to the table.

Meg skipped back to them, a large book clutched in her hands. "Miss Abigail said I can borrow this one," she told Ward proudly. "We can read it together."

The trusting way she looked at him made Ward feel even more guilty for what he was about to do. But it was for the best. He lifted her up on his lap. "That sounds nice. But I have some good news for you. Miss Hazel has said you can stay with her at her place for now."

The little girl frowned. "But you said I could stay with *you*."

He kept his smile firmly in place. "I know, but being sheriff means I sometimes have to work long hours. Besides, Miss Hazel's place is bigger and much nicer. And I promise I'll visit with you every day."

Meg's lips trembled slightly. "Don't you *want* me to stay with you?" She tightened her hold on her doll. "I promise I'll be good," she said desperately. "Freddie says I'm a lot of trouble but I promise I won't be if you give me a chance."

The child's pleas touched Ward's heart and he again wanted to strangle Freddie. He brushed the hair from Meg's forehead. "I don't think you're any trouble at all, Half-pint. In fact, I think you're a bright little ray of sunshine. But I don't have a lot of room at my place and you'll be much more comfortable at Miss Hazel's."

She gave him a wobbly smile. "I don't take up much room."

He had to work to keep his encouraging smile in place. "True, but it's not just the space. I also have to work, and I'm afraid I can't take you with me when I do."

"I can stay at your house while you work. I'm big enough to stay by myself—Freddie said so. And I can clean things for you while you're gone. Freddie taught me how to sweep and dust, at least the things I can reach. Please." Her lower lip trembled as if tears were imminent.

Ward's chest tightened. He wouldn't be able to bear it if she started crying. Her words, as well as her desperation not to be handed off again, spoke of what her life must have been like under her brother's care.

How could he tell her no? Yet how could he not?

Almost without conscious thought, he turned to Hazel for help.

Hazel wasn't certain how she'd expected Ward to react to the news that she was leaving Turnabout, but she definitely felt let down. Not that she'd expected him to beg her to stay, not exactly anyway. But she'd certainly expected more from him than the mild curiosity he'd displayed.

She supposed his reaction, and her disappointment over it, was just one more indication that it was indeed time for her to move on.

But there would be time to mull that over later. Right now there were more important matters to attend to. Responding to Ward's what-do-I-do-now look, Hazel refrained from saying *I told you so*. Instead, she reached over and lightly touched Meg's wrist. "I have a very nice guest room at my place and would love to have you stay there with me. My very best friend, the lady who usually works at the dress shop with me, is out of town for the next several weeks and it would be nice to have you to keep me company."

But Meg wasn't swayed. "You have Buttons to keep you company," she said earnestly. "Sheriff Gleason doesn't have *anybody*." Meg's voice had a desperate tone to it and her lower lip trembled again. She swiped at her eyes with the back of her wrist. "He lost his sister so he needs me to be his new family."

Hazel heard Ward's sharp intake of breath but for the moment she didn't dare meet his gaze. The emotions swirling around in the aftermath of that statement were both too strong and too fragile for that.

She finally took a deep breath and glanced at Ward, studying his now closed-off expression, silently gauging his needs against Meg's. Normally she'd do just about anything to put a smile on his face. But this was bigger than what he needed, or rather what he *thought* he needed.

Making a decision, Hazel met Meg's gaze again and took both of her hands. "You're absolutely right," she said firmly, "and families *should* stay together."

She ignored Ward's involuntary movement, keeping her focus on Meg, warmed by the child's blossoming smile. "So how about we do this? You can stay with me during the day while the sheriff is at work and keep me company at the dress shop. And then in the evenings, Sheriff Gleason can fetch you and take you home with him."

She sensed Ward's displeasure but ignored him for the moment.

Meg seemed to think about her words for a minute. "You mean, sort of like I was going to school?"

Hazel squeezed her hands. "Exactly! Only you'd be coming to the dress shop instead of school."

"All right." Meg hugged her doll tightly. "I guess that would be okay."

"Good girl. We're going to have fun together, I promise."

Hazel straightened and turned to Ward, noting his look of betrayal. She hoped, once he thought things over, he would see that this was the best solution. And not just for Meg.

To do him credit, he refrained from argument and smiled down at the little girl. "All right, Half-pint, we'll give it a try. But don't say I didn't warn you. Instead of a nice bed at Miss Hazel's, you're going to have to sleep on the couch in my parlor."

Meg didn't seem the least bit concerned. "I'm going to be a good little sister, I promise."

Hazel saw something flash in his eyes—something that seemed part pain and part tenderness. Which only strengthened her belief that underneath his closed-off exterior was a man with a very big heart. A man who needed someone to lavish his affection on. And if it couldn't be her, she was glad he had Meg.

But he squeezed the little girl's shoulder and helped seat her in her own chair. "I'm sure you will."

Did Ward know how much Meg had already changed him, breached his defenses?

As they ate their meal, Ward was relieved to see Meg return to her sunny, chatty self. He felt much less satisfied with the way they'd settled matters.

His mind was reeling from the double blow Hazel had landed him. First saying she was moving away—his mind still shied away from that one—then giving in to Meg's pleas to let her stay at his place. Both seemed like betrayals, though he refused to think about which stabbed deeper.

How could Hazel have done this to him? Especially after he'd given her all the reasons why Meg staying at his place couldn't work. And it wasn't just the demands of his job, though that should have been enough to make his point. Didn't Hazel know about the added demands that dealing with this town hooligan had placed on him?

But he wasn't fit to be caretaker of a little girl under any circumstances, especially one who was so young. He'd thought Hazel understood.

Was her sudden defection due to the fact that she was moving away? Was it so easy for her to leave everything she'd grown up with behind? Leave every *one* behind?

Things seemed to be changing so fast. He still hadn't gotten used to the loss of Bethany. And then being thrust into the role of caretaker for Meg. Now Hazel up and announced she's leaving. It was just too much to take in.

After the meal, he escorted them back to Hazel's place, feeling acutely conscious of the curious looks they were receiving from the folks they passed. He supposed it was difficult for his neighbors to see him in the role of a child's guardian as well.

As soon as they stepped inside the dress shop, Meg went in search of Pugs and Buttons.

Taking advantage of the opportunity to speak freely, Ward turned to Hazel. He wanted to ask her not to leave. But he had no right. And nothing to offer her if she stayed. So he focused on Meg instead. "You realize I know nothing about being a parent to a little girl."

She moved to the shop counter. "You did okay with Bethany."

"Bethany was twelve, not four, when our father passed. And we both know how badly I failed in taking care of her."

She spun around, her expression dismayed. "Don't say that. It wasn't your—"

He interrupted her before she could finish that statement. "Spare me your platitudes." He waved a hand, silencing whatever protest she seemed poised to make. "But that's beside the point. As sheriff, I'm likely to get called out in the middle of the night. How can I do my job if I'm playing nanny?"

Her lips pursed in exasperation. "You won't be *playing* anything. And you'll be a father to her, not a nanny."

He jerked his hand, dismissing her explanation. "Those are just words. I'm not qualified to be either."

But she didn't relent. "You'll figure something out. And as you've said yourself, this is just a temporary situation. Once you get the answers you're looking for, you'll be able to turn Meg over to the proper parties. Until then, yes, perhaps as sheriff you'll be slightly less responsive in the evenings than normal." She straightened. "And, if the worst happens and you really need to be out, you can bring her here to me, any time of night or day."

He could tell she meant that. But he wasn't certain how practical that solution would be given the kinds of situations he might be called on to respond to. For now, though, he'd have to accept her terms. "I warn you, I start making my rounds very early in the mornings."

"That won't be a problem—I'm an early riser as well."

It seemed she had an answer for everything.

They just weren't the answers he was hoping for.

Hazel gave him a breezy smile. "You undoubtedly have some things you need to attend to. Why don't you just go about your business. I'll bring Meg to your place at, say, half past five?"

Was she actually *dismissing* him? He wasn't at all a fan of this new Hazel, the one who was looking ahead to leaving Turnabout rather than trying to claim his attention. This was going to take some getting used to.

Of course, since she was leaving soon, there wouldn't be a "new Hazel" to get used to much longer.

But she was right, he did have some things to attend to. He nodded, then turned to Meg. "I'll see you later, Half-pint. Be good and mind Miss Hazel."

As Ward marched out of Hazel's shop, he jammed his hands in his pockets. Why was Hazel pretending she didn't hold him accountable for what happened to Bethany? She'd been there that day, after all, had seen what had happened when that rotten board in the loft gave way.

Of course she didn't know the full extent of his guilt. Bethany had fallen out of the barn loft because he had neglected to make the needed repairs, even though he'd known it needed tending to.

And why had he put it off? Because he'd been busy mooning over a girl. He'd spent so much time that week trying to figure out how to ask Lucy Brick if he could walk her to church the following Sunday that he hadn't gotten around to doing all the maintenance work he'd set for himself.

And because of his lack of discipline, Bethany had fallen and never been quite the same again.

It had been his first and most tragic lesson in how costly such distractions could be. He'd almost forgotten that last year, had let his guard down again because of a desire to get closer to someone. He'd begun to think just maybe he could relax his guard a bit around Hazel, could perhaps look at her as more than a friend.

Then that Walker girl had been kidnapped right under his nose. That incident had ended on a happier note than the one with Bethany, but her rescue had been no thanks to him.

It just proved, once and for all, that he couldn't do his job, a job where others depended on him, if his loyalties were divided.

It was as simple, and as hard to swallow, as that.

Hazel stared at the door Ward had just exited through. Somehow, telling him of her plans to move had made the whole thing seem much more real, more inevitable. Almost as if she'd reached the point of no return. His lukewarm reaction to the news, however, had bothered her more than she'd like to admit. There'd been a couple of times today when she'd thought he'd looked at her with a warmth that was based on more than mere friendship. But apparently that had been wishful thinking.

One thing Ward had made obvious was that he was not happy with the way she'd handled the matter of Meg's living arrangements. Well, that was just too bad. She'd done what she thought best.

And speaking of Meg...

Pasting on a smile, Hazel turned to the little girl. How was she going to entertain her for the next several hours? In spite of Ward's obvious assumption that she would be a better caretaker for Meg, she had very little experience with children. True, Verity's little girl, Joy, spent a lot of time with them in the emporium, but she'd never been left alone with the six-year-old for more than a short time.

Then she realized Meg's chattering had slowed down and her eyes were getting droopy. Poor lamb, she'd had a trying couple of days, and she was probably used to napping after lunch.

Hazel held out her hand. "What do you say we go upstairs and read one of the stories from that book Miss Abigail loaned you?" There was really no point in opening the shop for the few business hours left to the afternoon. It was a sad fact that with the amount of ready-to-wear clothing available through the mercantile, demands for her services had dwindled considerably. It was the reason for her current financial woes, the reason she'd accepted Aunt Opal's invitation to move to New York.

Hazel settled Meg on the bed in her guest room and opened the book of fairy tales. She only made it through one page before the child was fast asleep.

Feeling at loose ends and wanting to occupy her thoughts with something other than Ward's reaction to her news, or lack thereof, she focused on what might be needed to make Meg's stay at Ward's place more comfortable. Uncertain what a bachelor like Ward might have on hand, she decided the first order of business would be to gather up some extra bedding. That done, she turned to more personal needs.

Ward had mentioned that there was hardly anything in the girl's travel bag—a change of clothing, a wooden toy, a nightshirt.

She looked through her own things and came up with an extra hairbrush, a sweet-scented bar of soap she'd purchased last time she was in New York and a soft washcloth.

She studied the still-meager collection, feeling dissatisfied with the result. A trip to the mercantile was definitely in order. They'd go as soon as Meg woke from her nap.

The little girl slept for nearly an hour but when she woke she was once more a bubbly chatterbox. When Hazel explained about the trip to the mercantile, Meg seemed to look on it as an adventure.

There were three other customers in the store and Mr. Blakely was behind the counter when they arrived. All heads turned and conversation ceased when she and Meg walked in. Meg turned suddenly shy and moved closer to Hazel's side. Hazel placed a hand protectively on her shoulder.

"Good day, Mr. Blakely," she said cheerily. She introduced Meg merely as a new friend, then straightened. "We're just here to pick up a few necessities."

"Of course." The mercantile owner nodded. "Let me know if you need help with anything."

Hazel led Meg down the middle aisle where she found a toothbrush and toothpaste, which had been conspicuously missing from Meg's things. She also found some ready-made undergarments and a nightshirt that looked to be about the right size. A little tin horse that Hazel noticed had caught Meg's eye rounded off her purchases. She brought everything back to the counter for Mr. Blakely to ring up. While he took care of that, she smiled down at Meg. "Should we add a few lemon drops to our purchases?"

Meg's eyes lit up and she nodded enthusiastically.

Mr. Blakely reached into the display case and added the candy to the pile of items. "On the house," he said with a smile. "As a welcome to Turnabout gift."

Once they were done, Hazel paused a moment. "I was wondering, Mr. Blakely, if you'd mind if I borrowed one of your handcarts."

The shop owner waved a hand. "Of course. You can bring it back in the morning if you like."

Hazel loaded their purchases in the cart, then smiled at Meg. "Would you like to ride?"

A few minutes later Hazel was walking down the sidewalk pushing the cart with a giggling Meg riding inside.

When they arrived back at Hazel's place, Hazel loaded up all the other things she'd gathered for Meg and added them to the cart as well.

Meg looked it over and frowned.

"What's the matter," Hazel asked. "Is there something I forgot?"

"What about Sheriff Gleason?" the little girl asked. "Shouldn't we do something for him?"

That was unexpected. "What would you suggest?"

Meg was quiet for a minute, her face scrunched in thought. Then she smiled. "Maybe some flowers to make his home pretty."

Hazel hid a grin as she pictured Ward's reception to such a gift. "I think that's an excellent idea. Come along, I have a rose bush in my backyard."

Candy this afternoon. Flowers this evening. Yep, Meg was going to be very good for the stuffy sheriff.

Chapter Five

W ard opened his door to see Meg and Hazel standing there. Meg had her doll under one arm and a small jar filled with flowers in her hands. The three of them were accompanied by an overflowing handcart and squarely perched atop the mound of goods was Pugs, his stubby tail wagging. It definitely appeared Meg was moving in.

Hazel waved to the cart. "Meg and I gathered up a few things we thought she might need while she's staying here."

Apparently he and Hazel had different concepts of how many items "a few" entailed.

"And I picked these for you." Meg held out the flowers.

"Why, thank you." Ward took the proudly offered bouquet, not quite certain what he should do with it. No one had ever given him flowers before.

From the corner of his eye he noticed Hazel eyeing him and Meg with a touch of amusement. So she found this funny, did she?

Hazel cleared her throat. "Meg's already had her supper along with a nice warm bath." She waved to the overflowing handcart. "Mr. Blakely said we could keep the cart overnight. So you can either return it yourself in the morning or leave it with me when you drop Meg off and we'll return it."

He set the jar of flowers on the bench that sat just inside the door and then stepped past her to roll the thing into the house. "I'll take care of it."

"Well then, I'll bid the two of you good evening." She stooped down to bring her face level with Meg's. "I'll see you tomorrow, sweetheart. Make sure you help Sheriff Gleason take care of Pugs."

"Yes, ma'am. And don't worry, me and Sheriff Gleason will be okay."

Ward hoped she was right. Then he frowned at Pugs. "Wait a minute. You're not leaving the dog here, too, are you?"

Hazel straightened. "Of course. He needs to get used to being with you since…" She glanced Meg's way. "Since I already have a pet."

He understood her reluctance to let Meg know she was leaving. No point in giving Half-pint something new to worry about. He still couldn't quite accept the idea of Hazel's imminent departure himself. In fact, he'd decided it was probably just another of her not-quite-thought-through schemes and that she'd give up on it eventually.

Still, there was a nagging voice inside him that said he was wrong.

"Don't worry," Meg said, giving him a reassuring look. "Pugs won't be any trouble and I'll help take care of him."

Hazel straightened and, with a final wave, turned and left him alone with the little girl and the dog. He tamped down the cowardly urge to call her back.

What did he do now?

Shaking off his uncharacteristic uncertainty, Ward brought Meg the rest of the way into his house and watched as she took it all in. Which didn't take long, given the small size of the place. This first-floor level was really just one large room—to the left was the kitchen and dining area and to the right was what passed for a parlor. There was also a small washroom just behind the kitchen.

A set of stairs led up from the parlor to the second floor, which was where his bedchamber was located, along with a small room that served as storage in lieu of an attic.

That was it. It had always been more than enough for him, especially since he didn't entertain guests here. But right now it felt exceedingly small.

He'd seen Hazel peeking inside when she thought he wasn't looking. What had she thought of the place? Not that that mattered, he told himself irritably.

Meg moved to the sofa, drawing his attention back to her. "Is this where Chessie and I are gonna sleep?"

"I'm afraid so." Was the child having second thoughts about the arrangement? He certainly was. "It's not too late to go back to Miss Hazel's place if you want." He did his best to keep the hopeful note out of his voice.

Meg sat down on her soon-to-be bed with a bounce. "I like it here." Then she looked around. "Where will Pugs sleep?"

"Over there on the floor by the stove." He hoped Halfpint wasn't expecting him to turn any of his linens into a dog bed.

Meg popped up and went to the cart. "Me and Miss Hazel made him a bed, we just need to decide where to put it."

Of course they had. "That was right thoughtful of you."

"Uh-huh. And it's pretty too." She drew out a large, lumpy-looking pillow made of a yellow-and-blue-striped fabric. "Pugs already tried it out and he likes it."

"As he should." He hoped Meg didn't hear the note of sarcasm in his voice.

Fortunately, the child seemed oblivious to any undertones. She nodded agreeably. "We're going to make another one for him to use at Miss Hazel's house when we're there with her."

"Sounds like Pugs is going to be a very pampered pooch."

She nodded. "Miss Hazel says Pugs took very good care of your sister and that he probably misses her a lot. So now we need to take extra special care of him."

Leave it to Hazel to put such a sentimental spin on it. Still, he couldn't find it in himself to fault her for it. "Miss Hazel is right." Ward looked at the cart full of things Hazel had delivered along with Meg. Apparently she had indulged in a bit of shopping this afternoon. He'd have to remember to reimburse her.

Having to stow all of this stuff made Meg's moving in feel much more permanent than it had seemed earlier. Where was he going to find the room? He looked around at the sparse furnishings of his place. There was really only one choice.

He moved to the large bookshelf situated on the far end of the room. He quickly cleared off one of the lower shelves. "Let's stack your things here for now. We'll find something better tomorrow."

"Yes, sir." Meg carefully placed her doll on the sofa and came over to help him.

Nestled in one corner of the cart, he found what looked like a miniature bird cage, complete with a metallic bird perched inside. "What's this?"

"It's a music box. Miss Hazel gave it to me. Isn't it the most beautiful thing you ever saw?"

"It's mighty pretty, all right." He examined the delicate brass contraption.

Meg nodded. "She has a lot of them and she let me pick out whichever one I wanted." The child took it from him and turned the key affixed to the back of the box. "This one was my favorite." As soon as she released the key, a lilting tune began to play, filling his home with its happy sound.

"I never had anything this special before," she said dreamily.

They finished unloading Meg's things to the strains of the delicate tune.

He finally leaned back on his heels, studying the results of their labor. Maybe he could come up with a couple of crates or an old trunk tomorrow. Perhaps Hazel had something he could borrow.

He paused on that thought. He'd have to stop relying on the accommodating seamstress for those sorts of things.

Was she really leaving? She'd said it was because she wanted to work with her aunt, but he suspected there was more to it than that. What wasn't she saying? It shouldn't bother him so much that she wasn't confiding in him, but for some reason, it did. She'd always been so open with him before. If truth be told, she often over shared. He couldn't remember now why that had irritated him.

Meg tugged on his pants leg, reclaiming his attention. She had retrieved the book he'd just put away. "Would you like to read me and Chessie a story?" she asked.

He stood and dusted his hands. "All right, but let's get your bed fixed up first."

Hazel had been supremely confident that he could handle this. It suddenly seemed quite important he proved her confidence in him was not misplaced.

Hazel had been up since dawn. How had Ward and Meg gotten on last night? It had been difficult to leave yesterday evening, especially when she'd seen the I'm-not-ready-for-this-yet expression on Ward's face. But it had been the right thing to do. That little girl had her heart set on being Ward's family and Ward needed someone in his life to show him that kind of devotion.

And it obviously wasn't going to be her. As she sipped on her morning cup of coffee, she bowed her head and offered up a heartfelt prayer.

Heavenly Father, I don't know how long or short a time Meg will be under Ward's care, but I do believe that You brought them together for a reason. Please help these two hurting souls find solace and healing in each other, for whatever time they have together.

After she'd put out some food for Buttons and spent time cooing over him as befitted his temperament, she straightened and looked around her for something else to do. "I really should spend some time sorting through my things and packing the items that can be shipped ahead," she told the feline absently. "Then again, Ward did say he was an early riser so maybe I'll just go downstairs to the emporium and open the doors now. What do you think?"

The cat continued eating without acknowledging her words.

"Downstairs it is." She turned toward the stairs and descended to her shop. She unlocked the door and turned the sign from Closed to Open. Mr. Hill had already turned out the town's streetlamps so it wasn't quite as early as she'd thought. But even so, hers was the first shop on her block to open for a change.

Hazel had just finished raising the shades on the display window when Ward escorted Meg and Pugs into the place.

"Good morning," Ward greeted her. "I see you're as good as your word about rising early."

She noted the hint of surprise in his voice. "Of course. No point in letting the cool of the morning go to waste."

Meg's pigtails were slightly uneven but at least all the hair was contained and she seemed to be in a sunny mood.

"Did you two have breakfast yet?"

Meg nodded enthusiastically. "Sheriff Gleason and I had some bread and fig jam. It was very good."

Ward looked sheepish. "It was all I had. I'll pick up some groceries before she returns to my place this afternoon."

Did he even know how to cook for a four-year-old?

Wanting to have a word in private with Ward, she smiled down at Meg. "If you and Pugs would like to go say good morning to Buttons, he's right over there by the button bin."

With a nod, Meg skipped over to greet the cat.

Hazel immediately turned to Ward. "So how did things *really* go last night?"

He grimaced. "It could have gone better. But we both survived so I guess that's something."

"Was it really so terrible?"

He shrugged. "One thing I figured out pretty quick

was that I'll have to do something about our sleeping arrangements."

"Why? Did you have trouble getting Meg to settle down?"

"Not at all. From what I can tell, Meg slept like a hibernating bear cub all night. Problem is, she goes to bed so early, I have to do the same or risk waking her. And I realized that if anyone comes knocking at my door needing help, they'll disturb her before I can so much as get out of bed. And even if they don't, it doesn't seem right my being upstairs and her being downstairs by herself."

"Oh, I hadn't thought of that." She frowned "But didn't you say you don't have a guest room?"

"I don't. Which means I'll have to turn my room over to Half-pint. And I'll sleep on the couch."

"That doesn't sound very comfortable." Hazel resisted the urge to once again offer to let Meg sleep in her guest room. He had to figure out how to make this work without her. Instead she made another suggestion. "Edgar Crandall would probably let you use one of the hotel's portable beds. It wouldn't be the same as your regular bed but it would be more comfortable than the sofa."

She saw what looked like consternation in his expression but it disappeared quickly. He merely said, "Good idea. I'll check into it."

She smiled sympathetically, trying to be supportive while not taking on more than she should. "I know it's a bit awkward while you're getting used to the situation. But things will get better once you're both able to form a routine."

"I don't think it will come to that. I hope to have a

more permanent solution for her predicament before long."

What kind of solution did he hope to find? "Whatever happens, you need to make sure Meg has a good home. It breaks my heart to think of all she's been through."

He stiffened as if she'd insulted him. "Of course. I don't intend to turn her over to just anyone. That's why I need to do some digging, to find out as much as I can about her situation and what options we have."

"And just how do you plan to accomplish that?"

He arched a brow. "You're certainly curious about the details for someone who's leaving us all behind soon."

Even though his words stung, Hazel tried not to take offense. "My leaving is beside the point. I care about Meg and what happens to her."

He nodded in acknowledgment. "To answer your question, I'll start with what I know. They boarded the train at Adler's Bluff. And if the note Freddie left is to be believed, their last name is Lee. I'll wire the sheriff of Adler's Bluff and see if he knows anything about them."

She placed a hand on his arm. "You do realize she's growing more attached to you by the day. Even if you find family members who want to take her in, it's going to be a difficult separation for her."

"We'll just have to deal with that when the time comes. She'll be better off with someone else, someone who can be a good parent and will give her the kind of loving home she needs. You and I both know I'm not that person."

That again. "I know no such thing."

He gave her an exasperated look, as if her words

were nonsense. Then he crossed his arms. "Regardless, you won't be around to see how it all unfolds, will you?"

She stiffened, brought up short more by the hint of accusation in his tone than the words themselves. "My future plans are not up for discussion. Meg's future is what we need to concentrate on."

Why in the world did he keep bringing that up and in such an accusatory way? Was he more bothered by her plans to move away than he'd let on yesterday? If so, was it because he'd truly miss her or was it just the inconvenience of not having her to help with Meg?

The shop bell jangled, interrupting their conversation.

Eunice Ortolon, the town's biggest busybody, breezed into the shop, chin up at a disapproving angle. Hazel had no illusions she was here to make a purchase.

Nevertheless, she stepped forward with a smile on her face. "Good morning, Eunice. Is there something I can do for you?"

"I came to speak to the sheriff. I saw him step inside here."

Ward straightened and spoke up. "What can I do for you?"

"I wanted to make certain you'd been made aware of the incident at the mercantile."

He nodded. "Mayor Sanders and I discussed that when I arrived in town yesterday."

"Does that mean you'll be arresting the Lytle boys?"

"If I find proof that they are indeed the perpetrators, I certainly will."

"Proof? I would say it's obvious that they're guilty."

"Unfortunately, suspicion and talk don't constitute proof." He placed his hat back on his head. "Now if you ladies will excuse me, it's time for me to make my rounds." And with a tip of his hat, Ward made his way unhurriedly through the door.

That was one of the many things Hazel admired about Ward: his ability to remain calm even when provoked.

Eunice's lips pursed in a sour line for a moment, then she caught sight of Meg, playing on the floor with Pugs. Her expression quickly changed to one of speculation. "So that's the little girl the sheriff's taken in."

Hazel nodded, feeling suddenly protective of both Meg and Ward. "Her name is Meg." Then she gave the same explanation she'd heard Ward give when pressed. "Her family placed her in Sheriff Gleason's care temporarily. I'm merely helping out during the day while he's at work." All of which was true.

Eunice, however, wasn't ready to let the subject drop. "I would think anyone who knew the sheriff well enough to leave their child in his care would know about the loss of his sister. This hardly seems an appropriate time for him to be taking on such a responsibility."

Hazel's protective instincts shifted to include Ward. "On the contrary, it seems the *perfect* time. Sheriff Gleason needs such a distraction right now to keep him from dwelling on his loss."

Eunice sniffed disdainfully. "Distraction? Hah! I would think finding this hooligan who's been running amok through our town would be enough to keep him busy."

"I'm sure he's working hard to discover who the culprit is."

"Well, I don't know why it's taking so long. Everyone in town knows one of the Lytle boys is to blame. The only thing Sheriff Gleason needs to do is find some proof as to which one and then arrest them."

Hazel pressed her lips tightly closed to keep from saying something she'd regret. She crossed her arms. "Are you interested in ordering a new frock today?"

Eunice made a quick excuse about not being quite ready to decide, then made her exit.

Which was just as well. Much as she needed the business, she wasn't sure she could deal with Eunice's sanctimonious airs right now.

Once Eunice left, Hazel had an idea. "Meg, how would you like for me to make you a new dress?" The little girl's wardrobe had been pitiably lacking. And remedying that was a good way to keep her and Meg occupied while they spent the day together.

The child's eyes rounded. "Brand new? Just for me?"

Had Meg never owned a new dress before? "Of course. And you can help me pick out the fabric."

Meg held out her doll. "What about Chessie? She only has this one dress and it's getting raggedy."

Hazel smiled approvingly. "What a wonderful idea. Why didn't I think of that? We can even make it to match yours if you like?"

Meg returned Chessie to the crook of her arm and clapped in delight. "Oh yes! Me and Chessie would really like that."

They spent the next hour or so picking out the proper fabric and trims, pausing occasionally as customers showed up.

In fact, more ladies found their way into her shop that morning than she'd seen in the past few weeks. But none of them ordered anything. The visits seemed to all be thinly veiled excuses to get a better look at Meg and to try to find out more about the child. Thankfully, the little girl seemed oblivious to the stir she was creating.

When pressed, Hazel used the same explanation

she'd given Eunice. And for the most part, folks left it at that.

As Hazel and Meg studied fabrics, she had to gently steer the little girl away from the more inappropriate fabric choices, but at last they found something both of them liked. It was a bright yellow cotton fabric with tiny white and orange flowers scattered throughout.

Hazel was getting excited about the project. She'd never made children's clothing before so this would be something new for her. It would be easier than a lady's garment, but she could already envision ways to make it special for Meg. She would make a fairly simple jumper first, just so she could produce something quickly. But then she'd make a couple of additional garments and do something extra special—maybe some pin tucks or even smocking.

"And I think we'll make a white ruffled pinafore that you can wear over it."

"And one for Chessie too?"

"Of course." The little girl certainly loved her doll.

Meg tilted her head, studying Hazel thoughtfully. "Can you make clothes for a man too?"

The little girl's question brought up an image of Ward's broad shoulders and lean, athletic build. She could make him a shirt in a crisp fabric, perhaps a smoky blue color to match his eyes.

Before she could answer Meg's question, the shop bell jangled, signaling the arrival of yet another visitor. Hazel turned toward the door and braced herself for more prying questions. This time it was Hortense Lawrence standing there. Surprising, since Tensy had never set foot in the emporium before.

Had it taken the promise of gossip to get her into the shop?

The young woman stood at the threshold of the dress shop as if not quite certain whether or not to come the rest of the way inside and Hazel's heart softened. Tensy had always been somewhat shy and awkward.

"Why, hello. Please come in. Is there something I can do for you?"

"Yes, that is, I was just wondering..." Tensy's stammering response tapered off as she glanced Meg's way. But rather than being interested in Meg's presence, Tensy seemed disconcerted by it, as if she hadn't expected Meg to be there.

Hazel chided herself for jumping to conclusions. It didn't appear Tensy was here to pry about the little girl after all.

Hazel smiled down at Meg. "Sweetheart, you see that display of ribbons over there? Why don't you go pick out one for you and one for Chessie while Miss Lawrence and I talk?"

After Meg skipped off to examine the ribbons, Hazel gave her visitor a bracing smile. "Now then, was there something you wanted to discuss with me?"

"I'm sorry, I wasn't certain what the child's relationship was to you and I didn't want to say anything to upset her."

"Oh?" What did she have to say that would upset Meg?

Tensy hesitated, as if uncertain how to proceed. But then she squared her shoulders and gave Hazel a self-deprecating smile. "Forgive me for prying, but I heard a rumor that you're moving away and I wanted to find out if it was true."

So it was a different sort of gossip Tensy was trying to dig into. Though she wasn't sure why Tensy should care about her leaving town—the two of them weren't particularly close. Hazel was glad she'd sent Meg out of earshot. No point in giving the little girl something else to worry about. "That's not a rumor, it's the truth. I'll be moving to New York in a few weeks. I have an aunt who lives there and she's invited me to work in her fashion studio. It's all quite exciting." At least that was what she kept telling herself.

Tensy nodded with an approving smile. "I thought it must be something like that. You've always been such an inspiration to me."

Hazel was slightly taken aback. She'd never realized Tensy had even noticed her before. "What a lovely thing to say. Thank you."

"Oh, I mean it." Tensy sighed. "It's so uplifting to see a woman who's not afraid to spread her wings and go where her talents can really shine." She fingered her collar. "I don't think I'd be able to summon the courage for such a move myself. But you're going to do well in New York, I just know it."

It seemed at least one person was happy for her.

Then the woman hitched her shoulder slightly. "I apologize if it seems I came here just to pry into your personal business, but I do have a reason for asking. I wanted to see if the rumor is true because I'd like to have a very special dress made, and there's no one in Turnabout who can do it better than you."

Hazel perked up at that. Even if she'd be closing her shop soon, it would be nice to have a paying customer again, some money coming in to help her stretch her dwindling funds. "I certainly have time to take care of that for you before I leave. Tell me what sort of dress you're looking for and what sort of occasion you'll be wearing it for."

The woman actually blushed. "I'm hoping to wear it when I get married."

"Married! Oh, Tensy, that's wonderful!" And totally unexpected. Hazel hadn't been aware that the woman was even walking out with anyone. It seemed there was much more to Tensy than she'd realized.

It also reinforced the notion that she herself really *was* destined to be the last woman of her generation in Turnabout to find a husband.

Oh yes, it was definitely time to move on with her life.

Chapter Six

Hazel pushed aside her self-pitying thoughts. This was about Tensy, not her. "Who's the lucky man?"

Tensy's blush deepened. "I'm afraid I can't say. I'm being premature because he hasn't actually asked me to marry him yet." She wrung her hands. "But we have an understanding," she added quickly, "and I have high hopes that the proposal will come soon. The only reason I'm confiding in you this way is because you'll be leaving soon and I had my heart set on a special dress…"

Hazel sincerely hoped Tensy wasn't headed for heartbreak. But it wasn't her place to preach caution. "Say no more," she said, raising her hands. "I'm honored to have you share your secret with me. Now, let's pick out a style first and then we'll discuss fabrics. Do you have anything in particular in mind?"

"I want a dress special enough to make me feel like a princess."

Hazel hid a smile at her customer's hyperbole. "I'll do my very best. It's my personal belief that every bride should feel like a princess on her wedding day." She drew out the latest copies of *Harper's Bazaar* and *Vogue*

Magazine that she had on hand and the two women began poring over them.

Tensy eagerly looked through the magazines, pointing out everything that caught her eye. These tended to be ostentatious gowns with lots of lace, ruffles and beading. Hazel mentally winced. She had nothing against embellishments, but these could be taken too far and one had to be conscious of how it would look on the individual. Tensy was much too squarely built to be able to wear such styles with grace.

When Hazel diplomatically mentioned the cost of the materials involved in such elaborate creations, Tensy's expression turned to one of dismay.

"Actually," Hazel said with a conspiratorial smile, "I prefer something less elaborate myself. There's something so elegant about a simple, understated design, especially when it's paired with just the right fabric. And we can certainly add a few extras to give it that regal look you want."

Tensy perked up a little at that. "You always look so fashionable, whatever you're wearing," she said wistfully. "I suppose I should trust that you know best."

It was a half-hearted acceptance, but Hazel gave her an approving smile. "I promise you won't be disappointed. Your future husband will have eyes only for you on your special day."

That brought a more genuine smile to Tensy's lips and they quickly picked out a design that Hazel felt would be much more flattering for the bride-to-be. As they turned to the selection of fabrics and trims, Hazel found her mind drifting to what it would be like to be designing her own wedding gown. Ward would make such a handsome groom. To walk down the aisle with him waiting at the altar, she'd be the envy of every woman in town.

Firmly pulling back on those thoughts, Hazel turned her focus back to Tensy and studied the girl thoughtfully. "I think a soft pastel would set your hair and complexion off to the best advantage. I have a couple of selections over here that I would recommend you choose from."

After much discussion, they settled on a pale pink satin with a bit of ivory lace trim for the cuff and waist.

Hazel made short work of getting Tensy's measurements and preferences on trim. While she put away her things, Tensy drifted over to say hi to Meg.

The shop bell rang just as Hazel returned from the workroom and Ward walked in.

Tensy straightened. "Sheriff Gleason, how nice to see you."

Ward tipped his hat. "Miss Lawrence."

Meg ran up to the sheriff with a broad smile. "Miss Hazel is going to make me and Chessie new dresses."

"Is that a fact?"

"Uh-huh. You want to see the pretty fabric we picked out?"

While Meg chattered away to Ward, Tensy turned to Hazel. "I'd best be heading back home to get Pa's lunch cooking. Thanks for your time today."

Hazel smiled. "My pleasure, and don't worry, your secret is safe with me." She'd pitched her voice low so that Ward wouldn't hear.

Tensy gave her a grateful smile, then with goodbyes for Meg and Ward, quickly made her exit.

Hazel watched the woman retreat, her movements those of a mouse scuttling away from a cat. It was hard to imagine that someone as timid as Tensy had found a beau. She hoped whoever the gent was, he treated her well.

Ward reclaimed Hazel's attention, drawing her thoughts from her new customer. "So how have you ladies passed the morning?"

"It's been unusually busy," Hazel said drily, "but not with actual customers, I'm sorry to say."

Ward glanced toward Meg, a sign that he knew just what had drawn the townsfolk in this morning. Then he changed the subject.

"I sent that telegram to the sheriff over in Adler's Bluff. I'm hoping to hear something back soon."

"And in the meantime?"

"In the meantime I do my job, namely to tackle the problem of whoever has set the town on its ear this past couple of weeks."

There was something in his tone that caught her attention. "Do you have any leads?"

"Nothing firm. I plan to go back and talk to the victims and see if I can dig out any additional information that might lead me to identifying the culprit."

"Do you think whoever is doing this will strike again?"

His jaw tightened. "I'm hoping to resolve this quickly so we don't have to find out."

"And when you do identify him?"

"Or them. I'll make the arrest. After that it's up to a judge to figure out the fines and any other consequences."

Then he smiled. "But right now, I'd like to take you two ladies to lunch."

"That's quite generous. But you don't have to include me. I know Meg would like to have some time with you."

"Nonsense. Meg and I would like to have you join us. Isn't that right, Half-pint?"

Meg nodded enthusiastically. "You can pretend you're part of our family too."

"Why, thank you, Meg. I think I would enjoy that." She would enjoy it more if there was any chance it would become real rather than pretend.

After lunch, Ward escorted Meg and Hazel back to the dress shop, then headed out for the Lawrence farm. This was where the first incident had taken place. There had to be some significance to that, even if it was just a matter of convenience.

Tensy answered the door, wiping her hands on her apron. As soon as she recognized him, she pushed the screen door open. "Why, hello again, Sheriff. Please, come in."

Ward removed his hat. "Thank you. I apologize for the interruption, but I'd like to speak to your father if he's about."

"Yes, of course. He's in the parlor." Tensy led the way the short distance from the entry to the parlor door. "Father, we have a visitor," she called out. Ward tried not to wince at the loudness of her hail as he stepped past her. Had Enoch's hearing got as bad as all that?

Enoch rose from his chair and extended his hand. "I hope you've come to tell me those young hooligans who've been causing all this mischief about town have been caught."

"No, but that's what I'm here to talk about. I know we've discussed this before, but has anything new about those incidents occurred to you? Since it all seemed to start here at your place, is there anything you can think of that might cause anyone to want to do some mischief to you?"

Enoch rubbed his chin. "You thinking it might be personal rather than random."

"It's one of the things I'm looking into."

"I try to treat people fairly, but of course some folks are prone to get their backs up over nothing."

"Anyone in particular come to mind?"

"Charlie Danvers wasn't real happy with that sow he bought from me last month, but old Charlie is hardly spry enough to do this sort of thing. He has a son though."

Andy Danvers was a bit of a hothead. "Anyone else?"

When Enoch shook his head, Ward turned to Tensy. "Miss Lawrence, you say you heard someone the night your garden got trampled, but that it was too dark to see much. So far, you're the only one who has witnessed anything firsthand. Is there anything at all you can tell me? The sound of their voices, their general build, their gait."

"I'm sorry, Sheriff, I really didn't see much other than a couple of shadowy forms running off. I got the impression they were adolescents, but I can't even be sure of that."

"And you didn't see or hear anything on either of the other two instances?"

"I'm afraid not. I wish I could be more help."

"That's okay. Sorry to have bothered you both. The good news for you is, whoever is doing this has moved on to other targets."

Enoch gave a disgruntled huff. "But until you catch them, there's no guarantee they won't return. And it won't get me my shirt and britches back."

Tensy gave her father a reproving look. "Now, Pa,

I'm sure Sheriff Gleason is doing all he can to get this figured out."

Ward acknowledged Tensy's show of support with a smile. Then he straightened. "Well, I'd best be going now. Sorry to have intruded on your afternoon, but if either of you think of anything at all relating to this, no matter how minor, please let me know."

"Of course." Tensy gave him a conciliatory smile. "I just brewed a fresh pot of coffee. You're more than welcome to stay and have a cup with Pa."

"Thank you, but I need to get back to making my rounds." Ward planned to talk to the other three victims as well. Maybe one of them knew something he wasn't aware was important.

Two hours later he was feeling more frustrated than before. Unfortunately, those visits yielded even less information than his visit to the Lawrences. There seemed to be no common enemies and no motive except for pure mischief.

Which was going to make his job ten times harder.

Chapter Seven

As Ward escorted Hazel and Meg for supper at Daisy's restaurant that evening, he noticed that while they still received a number of curious glances, they received an equal number of warm greetings. As if folks were getting used to seeing the three of them together.

Once inside, Meg asked to look at the books in Abigail's library again, which gave Ward an opening to speak to Hazel privately for a moment.

"Sheriff Rawley from over at Adler's Bluff finally responded to my telegram. Unfortunately, he's never heard of Freddie or Megan Lee. Which means either Freddie lied about their names or they came from somewhere outside of Sheriff Rawley's jurisdiction."

"So what do you do now?"

"I'm thinking I should press Meg a little harder for whatever information she can remember."

As if he'd asked her opinion, Hazel glanced at the little girl, her expression skeptical. "I'm not certain how much help she'd be. Children that age normally don't know a lot of specifics about things outside their immediate existence."

He raised a brow at that. "And how would you know

the capabilities of children that age?" She'd been an only child and as far as he knew she'd never spent much time around small children.

Hazel's chin came up at that and her eyes narrowed. Had he said something to upset her?

"Well, there's Verity's Joy, who spends quite a bit of her time at the emporium." Her expression and tone were suddenly quite prim.

Apparently he *had* insulted her.

She tossed her head. "And I have lots of little cousins running around getting underfoot when I visit my family back in New York." She moved a fork a half inch to the right. "I wasn't saying don't ask her. I was just cautioning you not to expect too much."

He rubbed his chin. "You don't think talking about her home will bring up bad memories for her?"

Hazel's expression softened. "I think, if she does have unpleasant memories of her previous life, discussing them with you, someone she obviously looks up to, will do her good rather than harm."

Ward wasn't sure whether her words made him feel better or worse. It seemed to assume he was capable of saying the right things, something he wasn't at all confident of.

When Meg returned to the table, he let her crawl up onto his lap and show him and Hazel the new book she'd picked out.

Once their food arrived, though, he set her in her own chair and cleared his throat. "Half-pint, can you tell me what your father's name was?"

"Poppa," Meg responded confidently.

Not very helpful. "What did other people, besides you and Freddie, call him?"

Meg wrinkled her nose thoughtfully as she took another bite. Then she gave him a smile. "Oh. Mrs. Barker at the general store called him Mr. Luther." Her smile broadened. "I like Mrs. Barker, she always gives me a piece of penny candy."

Ward made a mental note—a general store run by a lady named Barker. It might help him pin down a location. But Luther could be a first name or a family name. "She sounds like a nice lady. But your name *is* Megan Lee, right?"

The little girl made a face. "That's what Poppa called me when he was cross. But I like Meg better."

Could Lee be her middle name rather than her surname? "Do you have any aunts or uncles?"

"There were some ants in the kitchen one time. But Poppa got rid of them."

Ward ignored the cough from Hazel that was obviously a strangled laugh. "Tell me about the train ride."

"It was scary at first, but then I met you and Pugs and it got lots better."

"And I'm glad you did. But do you remember how you got to the train from your house?"

She nodded. "Freddie's friend Rory brought us in his wagon."

Another name to look into. "Did it take very long to get to the train station?"

"Oh yes, hours and hours."

The little girl's sense of time might be off. "Tell me about it."

"It was still kind of dark when we got in the wagon and I was still sleepy so I napped part of the time. And we rode forever and ever until Freddie said it was lunchtime. And then we had a little picnic and Chessie and I picked lots of pretty flowers. And then we got back in the wagon and rode some more."

Half-pint certainly had a flair for the dramatic. And she certainly didn't seem particularly upset by any of their discussion so far.

"We came to this town—Rory called it Adler's Bluff," she continued. "Then Rory left us at the train station. But he said he would meet Freddie at Kittering."

Just Freddie. The plan to abandon Meg had apparently been a long-standing one. But that explained how Freddie had managed to disappear so quickly and completely—Rory had arrived beforehand and been waiting to whisk him off as soon as the train pulled into the station. This had indeed been a well-thought-out plan.

At least Ward had a few more names than he'd had before. Her father was named Luther, there was a Mrs. Barker who ran a store in the vicinity of her home and Freddie had a friend named Rory. Perhaps that was enough to help him pin down her former home.

"Were you sad to see Freddie go away?" Hazel asked softly.

Half-pint shrugged and gave her doll a tight squeeze. "Freddie never liked me much anyway. And now I have a new family." She smiled up at Ward. "And that's you."

Ward felt a pang at the child's words and the look of utter trust she aimed his way. How would she react when she discovered her stay with him was merely temporary? Should he say something now to prepare her for what was to come?

Before he could decide, her smile wobbled a bit. "You like me, don't you?"

Had she sensed something of his thoughts? He quickly reached over and gave her knee a squeeze. "I sure do."

That seemed to reassure the child. Then she glanced

Hazel's way. "Can Miss Hazel be part of our family too?"

Ward's gaze locked with Hazel's and for a heartbeat he allowed himself to picture what it might be like to have this family for his very own.

Then he remembered all the reasons why he couldn't let that happen and dropped his gaze.

Later, as he and Meg paused at Hazel's door to bid her good night, she hesitated a moment before going inside. "Tomorrow is Sunday."

"I'm aware."

"I just wanted to say, if you'd like to bring Meg around before church, I'll be glad to help her get ready. I should have one of her new dresses finished by then."

One of them? How many was she planning to make? He glanced down at Meg. "What do you say, Half-pint? Would you like to come by here and get your new dress to wear to church tomorrow?"

"Oh yes."

"Then it's settled."

"Why don't we plan to make a day of it?" Hazel asked. "We can plan a picnic at Mercer's Pond, maybe even find a few late blackberries while we're there."

Meg's face brightened and she turned to Ward. "Oh, can we? I love blackberries."

He nodded. "All right, but only if you allow me to provide the food."

Hazel raised a brow at that. "You're going to cook?"

Did she doubt his abilities? "I'll have you know I'm a more-than-passable cook." Then he grinned. "But no, I plan to stop by Daisy's and ask her to prepare some of her delicious fried chicken."

"Then I'll provide the lemonade and some fresh fruit."

Ward grinned. The woman knew her weaknesses as well as her strengths.

He tipped his hat. "We'll bid you good night then."

Once she was inside, he took Meg's hand and headed to his place. What was wrong with him? It seemed ever since Hazel had announced she was leaving he'd begun looking at her in a whole new light. It was not only unsettling, it was entirely inappropriate.

He'd better get hold of himself before things get out of hand.

Hazel smiled at Ward's chivalry. He'd insisted on waiting until she was inside with her door latched before he and Meg moved on. Was he feeling protective toward her specifically or was he more concerned that the town hoodlum had not yet been caught?

Rather than going upstairs to her lodgings, Hazel went to her workroom to gather up the half-finished dress she was working on for Meg. She spotted the stack of bills waiting on her desk and for a moment melancholy shadowed her happy mood. But then she squared her shoulders. She wasn't destitute yet and had more than enough to cover these notes and keep her going for the next few months. And by that time she would be earning her keep in her aunt's studio in New York. Besides, with the new business Tensy had brought her, she'd have a little extra cushion.

She put thoughts of her change in fortune behind her and scooped up her materials, then headed upstairs. She'd promised Meg to have her new dress ready by morning and she intended to be as good as her word. This first dress would be fairly simple so that she could get it done quickly.

Still, she added a few extra touches as she went—

lace on the collar, a pretty appliqué on the bodice, a brightly colored brocade ribbon around the waist that could be tied in a poufy bow at the back.

As she worked, her mind kept going back to that moment when Meg had asked Ward if their family could include her. The way Ward had looked at her, with something that appeared very close to longing, had thrown her, had made her wonder if perhaps there was a future for them after all.

Of course it could all just be wishful thinking on her part. How could she know for sure?

She still didn't have any answers when she finally finished the dress. But as she stood back to admire her work, she felt a deep sense of satisfaction at what she'd accomplished. It had been quite a while since she'd been able to let her creative instincts have free rein this way.

Remembering another promise she'd made to Meg, Hazel quickly cut and stitched a simple doll-sized shift in a matching fabric for Chessie.

Finally satisfied with her work, Hazel carefully put both the dresses away and prepared for bed. As she turned out the light and slid under the covers, she thought about all the changes that had happened in her life these past few days.

Heavenly Father, thank You for the good things You've brought to me this day. Meg is a treasure and I pray You will help me to do my part to see that things work out for both her and Ward's good.

The renewed joy in employing the talents You gifted me with has been a true blessing. Having the opportunity to create dresses for Meg as well as a lovely gown for Tensy, both of whom show such gratitude, has made me feel useful and creative again. Help me to remember

*that no matter my circumstances, You have me tight in
the palm of Your hand.*

Hazel paused a moment, then added a request to
her prayers.

*And please, help me to understand what Your in-
tentions are for my relationship with Ward and to find
peace with that, whatever it may be.*

Was it presumptuous of her to think God actually
had plans, one way or the other, for her relationship
with Ward?

She decided not. After all, the Scriptures encouraged
you to ask for the desires of your heart and to pray without ceasing. Such a God would most definitely concern
Himself with all aspects of His people's lives.

Satisfied with her logic, Hazel rolled onto her side
and fell asleep almost immediately.

Despite her late night, Hazel was up bright and early
the next morning. In fact, she had her shop door open
before Ward had a chance to knock. "Good morning!
Isn't it a perfect day for a picnic?"

Meg skipped inside but Ward remained on the sidewalk.

"I'm going to leave you ladies here to get all gussied
up," he said with a smile.

Hazel rolled her eyes at the phrase *gussied up.* "We
won't be long," she said.

He waved a hand. "Take your time. You can just stop
by my office when you're ready." With a touch to the
brim of his hat, he turned and headed toward his office.

Taking Meg's hand, she led the little girl to the stairs.
"I hope you and Chessie like your new dresses. I think
they turned out quite well."

She had laid the dress out on the back of her sofa and

when Meg saw it her eyes widened. "This is for me? I never had anything so boo'tiful before."

"A pretty girl like you should have pretty things. And look, here's one for Chessie."

Meg's smile broadened and she held up her doll. "Look at your pretty new dress, Chessie. And it matches mine."

Hazel helped the little girl change clothes and then they dressed Chessie as well.

She gave Meg one of her music boxes to wind up while she brushed the child's unruly tresses until they shone. Rather than putting it back up in pigtails, Hazel let it fall loose and added a simple headband of ribbon that was a daintier match for the one at her waist. In many ways, Meg would be on display today when she walked into the church. And Hazel wanted to do everything she could to make certain the child looked every bit as sweet on the outside as she was on the inside.

Was this what it felt like to be a mother, this caring and worry and pride all rolled together? This aching urge to protect and defend her child and to give her every opportunity to shine?

Shaking off those thoughts, Hazel led Meg to a cheval glass. "See how pretty you look."

Meg preened this way and that, holding her skirt out to show it to best advantage. Then she turned to Hazel. "Do you think Sheriff Gleason will like it?"

"I'm sure he will." Ward had better bend over backward to tell Meg how nice she looked or he'd get what for from her.

She reached for Meg's hand. "Shall we go find out?"

When they stepped inside the sheriff's office a few minutes later, Ward looked up, then leaned back in his chair and let out a low whistle. "Well, now, Half-pint, just look at you. Aren't you just the prettiest flower in the whole garden?"

Hazel relaxed. She should have known that he would say the right things.

Meg twirled around. "Miss Hazel made this just for me."

"Miss Hazel certainly has a wagonload of talent with a needle. And is Chessie wearing a new dress too?"

The little girl was delighted that he'd noticed her doll and Hazel had to admit to being impressed herself. Perhaps she didn't give the prosaic lawman enough credit.

"And doesn't Miss Hazel look pretty too?" Meg added unexpectedly.

Ward turned to Hazel with an assessing look and let his gaze roam slowly from her head to her toes. Hazel grew warm under his perusal but was unable to think of anything to say to diffuse the unexpected tension.

Then he gave a warm, languid smile. "That she does. Why, when I walk down the street with the two prettiest gals in town, every man who sees us is going to wish he was me."

Meg giggled.

Hazel knew just how the child felt. Ward could be quite the charmer when he set his mind to it. And while she knew he was just including her because of Meg's prompting, it still felt nice to be on the receiving end of his compliments.

When they walked into church, Hazel found herself reluctant to leave them to take her place at the front with the choir. For just a heartbeat she considered excusing herself to sit with Ward and Meg. But with Verity and Nate Cooper out of town, the choir needed everyone else to be there.

Much as she tried to concentrate on the service itself, Hazel found her gaze drifting on more than one occasion to the man and child sitting near the middle of the congregation. How easily Ward had slipped into the role of parent. Was he even aware of the bond that was forming between him and Meg?

At one point she became aware that she wasn't the only one casting glances their way. Was it mere curiosity that had captured folks' attention? Or was it something more?

At the end of the service, she was pleased to have Ward wait for her to join them before they exited the church. Had it been his idea or more of Meg's prompting?

They introduced Reverend Harper to the little girl and then they stepped out into the churchyard.

"Is it time for our picnic now?" Meg asked hopefully.

"Very soon."

But before they could get very far, Enoch Lawrence, with his daughter in tow, stopped Ward to ask about the progress he was making in identifying the town's troublemakers.

"Seems to me that it's taking a mighty long time to get this matter resolved, Sheriff." Eunice Ortolon, no doubt attracted by Enoch's overloud voice, had joined the conversation. "You need to find whoever's doing this and lock them up before they attack someone else's place."

The woman said that as if this whole situation was Ward's fault. Hazel immediately stepped forward. "Please, this is hardly the place for such a discussion."

"Well!" Eunice looked as affronted as if Hazel had attacked her personally.

A few more folks had come up to them, including

Saul Carson, the man who'd had his horses turned loose by the criminal mischief-maker.

Ward turned to her, his expression of the don't-argue-with-me variety. "Why don't you and Meg go back to your place and get ready for the picnic?" His tone was more statement than question. "I'll pick up the food and buggy and meet you shortly."

It seemed he was dismissing her. And it probably *was* best to get Meg away from this discussion.

As they walked away, Meg gave Hazel a troubled look. "Why did that man sound so angry? Did Sheriff Gleason do something wrong?"

"Not at all. They were just discussing problems some of the townsfolk have been having that they want Sheriff Gleason's help with."

"I don't like it when people get angry. It scares Chessie."

"I don't like it either. And you can tell Chessie that Sheriff Gleason is just fine so she doesn't have to worry about him."

Poor lamb. Had she grown up in a home where a lot of angry words had been exchanged?

Well, it was time the child replaced some of those memories with happy ones. And today's picnic would be the perfect opportunity for that.

The thought of Ward not having his responsibilities as sheriff to hide behind was also quite nice. Could he become more like that boy she remembered, the confident youth with a ready smile that he had been before his mother's death and before Bethany's accident?

She hadn't seen that Ward in a long time—and she missed him.

Chapter Eight

❧

"This picnic idea of yours was a good one," Ward said as he plopped down on the picnic cloth across from Hazel. "Half-pint had a good time."

Hazel smiled, warmed by the compliment. She would have been more pleased if he'd said he was having a good time as well. But he seemed more relaxed right now than she'd seen him in a while so she'd take that as admission enough.

Meg, tuckered out from chasing Pugs around the meadow and having Ward help her explore the area around the pond, was curled up beside her, fast asleep. Pugs had found a patch of sunshine nearby and was similarly disposed.

"The beautiful weather helped," she said, lightly smoothing the little girl's hair. "And I thought it would be good for Meg to be able to spend time outdoors."

"She certainly does like that old rag doll of hers," Ward observed.

Even in sleep, Meg had Chessie in her arms.

"From what we've learned of her, I imagine Chessie has been her only friend and confidant. I wish Verity and her family were in town. I think Verity's little girl,

Joy, would be a good playmate for her." Of course if Verity were home, Hazel would have no excuse not to leave Turnabout.

She drew her knees up, hugging them through her skirts. While Ward had entertained Meg earlier, she'd found her thoughts straying to another long-ago picnic.

It had been Bethany's thirteenth birthday and her mother had just passed away two weeks earlier. Her friend hadn't felt much like celebrating but Ward had insisted they do something to mark her special day. He'd recruited Hazel's help in planning a picnic, and she'd been the only person invited besides the two of them.

Ward had gone to great lengths to make certain his little sister had something happy to mark the day, treating the two of them as peers whose company he enjoyed rather than his pesky little sister and her equally pesky friend. And at the end of the picnic he'd given his sister a birthday gift—he'd made her a wooden box and placed her mother's cameo inside.

It had been almost comical to see the panic on his face when Bethany started crying. That was the moment when Ward had become more to her than her best friend's bossy older brother.

It was then that she'd fallen head over heels in love with him.

"Penny for your thoughts."

Ward's uncharacteristically whimsical words pulled Hazel's thoughts back to the present.

She felt a touch of heat rise in her cheeks and thought about giving him a breezy non-answer. Then she decided to give him a partial answer. "I was just remembering Bethany's thirteenth birthday."

His expression shifted, sobered. "I wanted to give

her a reason to be happy again but I think I just made things worse."

"Oh no, just the opposite. It meant the world to Bethany that you'd taken the time to do that. In fact, she confided in me later that you'd made her feel like things were going to be okay after all."

He turned to stare across the meadow. "And two months later she had her accident."

She could tell it was time for a change of subject. "How did the new sleeping arrangements work out last night?"

Ward grimaced but then shrugged. "Sleeping on the couch will take some getting used to, but I've had worse beds."

She knew him well enough to know he was downplaying the inconvenience. But Ward had never been a complainer.

He plucked a long stem of grass and stuck it in the corner of his mouth. "You know," he said thoughtfully, "we really didn't have much time to discuss your news the other day."

Hazel felt her pulse kick up a notch. Was he ready to talk about her moving? "What news?" she asked, deciding to make him spell things out.

He cut her a don't-be-coy look. "The news about your packing up and leaving Turnabout. Mind if I ask why?"

She chose her words carefully, not sure how much of her feelings she wanted to reveal. "I told you, I'll be able to work with my aunt Opal. It'll give me a chance to learn new techniques, to grow as a designer, to work with materials I might not otherwise have access to."

He waved a hand, as if dismissing that explanation. "All of that was true last year and the year before. What's changed to make you want it now?"

She was tempted to ask him why he cared but couldn't quite drum up the nerve. Instead she lowered her eyes and picked some unseen lint on her skirt. "If you must know, the emporium hasn't been doing well lately. More and more ladies are purchasing ready-made garments rather than ordering them from me." She shrugged. "Not that I blame them. Ready-made frocks cost less than the ones I make and no one in Turnabout has much need for the really fancy gowns I enjoy working on."

He was silent for a long moment and she peeked at him from the corner of her eye to see his brow had furrowed.

"I hadn't realized," he finally said, his tone sympathetic.

Hazel brushed a leaf from her skirt, trying not to be hurt by his admission that he hadn't paid much attention to her situation. And she certainly didn't want his pity now. "Why should you? But most of the ladies who come into the emporium these days are looking for Verity's hats, not my dresses."

She straightened and put a smile on her face. "Besides, Aunt Opal is not just offering me a job in her design studio this time—she wants to groom me to take over the whole thing when she retires in a few years."

"And that's something you really want to do?"

She shrugged. "To be honest, that isn't the only reason I agreed to move. I've been restless for a while now, feeling the need for some sort of change in my life. Her offer just came at the right time."

"What kind of change?"

This time she decided to be a little more forthcoming. "Even though designing and making clothing is something I enjoy, I do want more out of life. And I've recently come to doubt that I'll find that something more here in Turnabout."

"And just what is it you're looking for?"

Why did he keep pressing? She met his gaze head on. "What just about every feeling human being is looking for—a family to love and be loved by, a home that's filled with joy and laughter, to feel that I'm genuinely important to someone else's happiness." There, let him make of that what he would.

"And you don't think you can find those things right here in Turnabout?"

She stared at him almost defiantly. If she'd had something in her hand, she might have actually chucked it at him. "I used to think there was a chance. But not anymore." Did he really not understand what she was saying?

"But you *do* think you'll find what you're looking for in New York?"

She hoped she would would be a better way to phrase it. "I've done a lot of praying about the matter and I've bent Verity's ear quite a bit as well." She was really going to miss her friend when she moved away.

His eyes narrowed slightly. "And Verity agrees that this is a good idea?"

She felt a touch of annoyance at the skepticism in his tone. "Verity is very much in favor of my making changes in my life and supports me wholeheartedly." Actually Verity had told her it was high time she stopped chasing after Ward Gleason, that any man who couldn't see her worth wasn't good enough for her, and that if it took moving halfway across the country for her to get him out of her system, then so be it.

"And just when did you reach this decision?"

Hazel released her knees and leaned back on her

hands, studying the lone cloud floating lazily across the otherwise blue sky. "About two weeks ago I received a letter from Aunt Opal. She's getting on in age, not that you'd know it as spry and sharp as she is. But she's beginning to think about retiring in a few years and I'm the only family member who has any interest in fashion besides her. In fact, Aunt Opal's the one who inspired me to open my own dress shop in the first place."

She sat up straighter and met his gaze again. "Anyway, in her letter, Aunt Opal said she wanted to give me one more opportunity to join her before she began grooming someone else to take over her business." She knew she was rambling and repeating herself, but she wanted him to understand the choices she was making.

"So that's why you have this now-or-never attitude about making the move?" he asked. "Because you think this is your last chance to step into your aunt's shoes?"

Was he really this oblivious to her feelings? She shrugged. "Actually, it was like a sign, like God was answering my prayer by opening this particular door to me."

"I see."

She couldn't read anything from his tone or expression. Would he miss her at all? She wanted to shout at him, *I'd give it up without a qualm if you'd give me a reason to stay.* But her pride kept her silent. Instead she went to work repacking the hamper.

Ward moved toward the buggy, intending to prepare it for their departure. In truth he needed a few moments to himself to process what Hazel had just revealed. He hadn't realized how tightly he'd held on to the belief that this plan of hers to move to New York was just a passing fancy. Their conversation just now had certainly disabused him of that notion.

How had he not noticed that Hazel's business was struggling and that she was unhappy with her prospects here? Sure, she was always so positive and uncomplaining that it made it easy to believe she didn't have any problems. But that was no excuse. A true friend would have noticed when something was amiss. Was he truly so selfish? Just how bad were her finances?

In the past, every penny he earned went into Bethany's care. Now that that was no longer a concern, he suddenly had earnings he was unaccustomed to spending on himself. Was there a way he could help Hazel out without insulting her pride?

For a start, he'd find reasons to keep buying her meals.

As for the other—he raked a hand through his hair, feeling his gut clench in frustration. He'd been astute enough to recognize the question in her eyes, the hints that her hopes for the kind of future she wanted had been bound up with him. But that was a future he could not allow himself to contemplate.

The twenty-four-hour demands of his job as sheriff didn't leave him time for a family. This job had been the one area of his life where he felt he'd made a positive difference, where he hadn't completely failed those who counted on him. And he'd learned the hard way that he was much better at looking out for the welfare of a town than he was at being responsible for someone totally dependent on his care.

Hazel seemed to believe God was leading her away from Turnabout. Was that truly the case? Or was she just taking the first option that came her way?

Father Almighty, I know You are a God of infinite

*love and that Your plans are for the good of Your chil-
dren. I care about Hazel and don't want to see her unhappy. And, to be honest, I'm not sure moving to New
York is what's best for her. Turnabout is where her
friends, her memories and her roots are. And I would
miss her if she was gone for good, but it's not right for
me to be selfish about this.*

*So I'm going to pray that whatever happens, that You
will help her find happiness and contentment.*

Ward glanced back at the sound of feminine laughter. Hazel had roused Meg from her nap and the two
were sharing a laugh at Pugs's expense. What a sweet
picture they made at that moment, the very image of a
loving mother and daughter. All that was missing was
a father to complete the picture.

*And Lord Jesus, if I had my druthers, I'd have her
find that contentment right here in Turnabout. Amen.*

As Ward slammed the cell door, he decided it was a
good thing yesterday's picnic had been such a success
because today was turning out to be one of those days
full of petty annoyances.

Right after he'd dropped Meg off at Hazel's place
this morning, he'd gotten word that Elmer and Orson
Lytle, two local farmers, were at it again. There'd been
hard feelings between the two cousins for years. Something to do with a land dispute he thought, but he wasn't
sure even they remembered the exact reasons anymore.

He'd tried to diffuse the argument and send the men
on their separate ways, but when the fists started flying
right there in front of the livery, he'd ended up dragging
both of them off to jail.

He glared at the surly pair now incarcerated in adjacent cells. "You're grown men, you ought to be able

to settle your differences without resorting to brawling like a couple of hotheaded schoolboys."

Elmer shook his fist. "If he'd just own up to what he did, none of this would've happened."

And they were at it again, yelling, gesticulating, threatening.

Finally, Ward had had enough. "Quiet! Both of you. If you won't be civil because it's the right way to act, at least consider the example you're setting for your boys. Blakely told me he had to throw all four of them out of the mercantile the other day because they were getting too rowdy."

"Probably started by Larry and Russell."

"Hah! More likely Glen and Bart said something to set them off."

Ward glared them into silence. "I suppose you two have heard about the string of crimes that's been stirring folks up around here."

"Hard to miss it," Elmer said. "Folks haven't been talking about much else lately."

"Did you also hear that there's some folks who think one or more of your boys are responsible?"

"Well, it certainly isn't Larry and Russell. Those boys might be a mite spirited, but they wouldn't let any man's horses out of the pen. They know I'd tan their hides and hang 'em up to dry if they did."

"If you're trying to say it's Glen or Bart, you're dead wrong. Them boys of mine know how to stand up for themselves but they know better than to leave the farm after dark."

Ward looked from one to the other of them. "Are you sure about that? Do you really know your boys as well as you think you do? Maybe it's possible they've seen how little regard you have for other folks' feelings and have begun to believe they can up and do as they please as well? Just think about that next time you feel it's okay to start a ruckus in the middle of town."

Ward tossed the keys on his desk. "Now, I have better things to do than stand here and listen to you two go at each other like mongrels over a bone. I'll be back to check on you later." Maybe if they didn't have an audience, they'd settle down.

Or at least run out of steam.

In the meantime, this dustup had reminded him he had a lot more investigating to do.

Chapter Nine

Ward headed over to the mercantile to talk to Doug Blakely. He'd already questioned him about the break-in, but this time he decided he needed to learn a little more about the commotion the four Lytle boys had caused the other day. Folks seemed to think the two incidents were related, so it bore some additional looking into.

Business was slow inside the mercantile and Doug was more than happy to talk about the incident.

"Elmer's boys, Larry and Russell, came in first," he said as he wiped down his counter. "They needed to pick up some flour for their ma. They were at the counter with the sack of flour and eyeing the penny candy when Glen and Bart walked in."

"And that's when the trouble started?" Ward prompted.

Doug nodded. "I can't say as I know who exactly started it. One of the boys bumped the other and refused to apologize. Next thing I knew they were yelling, the flour sack upended and spilled everywhere, and fists started flying."

Yep, the boys sounded as quick to take offense as

their fathers. "Did you have other customers in the store at the time?"

The shop owner nodded. "Reggie Barr and her youngest kid, Hortense Lawrence, and Hazel Andrews."

Hazel had witnessed it? Why was he just now learning about that?

"In fact, Miss Andrews tried to calm the boys down," Doug continued. "And it almost worked until the flour sack spilled open."

Ward's gut clenched. Didn't the woman have any common sense at all, wading in like that? He didn't believe the boys would have deliberately hurt her, but in the heat of the moment and with tempers flaring, there's no telling what could have happened.

"Luckily Adam Barr and Hank Chandler were nearby and heard the commotion. They helped me break it up before too much damage was done."

Ward already knew about Adam and Hank's role so he let that statement go without comment.

Doug gave him a probing look. "Are you asking about this because you think those boys are to blame for the break-in that happened that evening?"

"I just want to make sure I've checked all the possibilities." He leaned forward. "What do you think?"

The store owner rubbed his chin. "I think, given the timing, those boys are the only culprits that make any sense."

That mirrored his own thoughts on the matter. That, and the fact that the only thing taken was candy, definitely pointed to it having been kids. But which set of brothers? Because he didn't for a minute believe the four of them could work together.

Wanting to leave the adult Lytles to cool their heels a bit longer, Ward decided to check in with a few of the folks who'd witnessed the altercation in the mercantile. Maybe one of them had seen something Doug had missed.

He went over to the Lawrence place first. When he asked Enoch's daughter Tensy to describe what she'd seen, she nodded, her brow furrowed in thought. "I was there but I'm not sure how much I can tell you about what happened. I was by the canned peaches, near the back of the shop, when the boys came in. So I didn't really notice anything until it got loud." She grimaced. "It's a good thing Mr. Barr and Mr. Walker came in to break them up 'cause they were getting mighty riled. In fact, they were still shouting at each other when they were made to leave."

She gave him a troubled look. "You don't think this has anything to do with the break-in that night, do you? I mean I've heard folks talking but I figured that's all it was, talk."

Ward carefully refrained from making any judgments. "I was hoping maybe you could tell me. You caught a glimpse of someone one of the times he was at your place. What do you think—could it have been one of the Lytle boys?"

"Like I said before, I don't know, I only caught a glimpse, and a rather blurred one at that. He was racing around the corner of the barn. But I guess, I mean, I suppose he was about the same size as one of the two older boys, Larry or Glen." She grimaced. "But please don't ask me to say for sure 'cause I couldn't rightly do that."

She seemed to be getting agitated at the idea of being a witness and Ward was quick to reassure her. "Don't worry, that won't really be necessary. I was wondering more if you could disprove the talk based on what you saw then asking you to positively identify someone. I'm sure if you could do that you would have already done it."

She nodded, then frowned. "So you don't think it was one of the Lytles?"

"I didn't say that. It's just it would be easier for you to say it wasn't one of them if the general size or build didn't match than the other way around."

She gave him an admiring grin. "That's very clever of you."

After a few more questions, Ward excused himself and headed back to town. He found Reggie Barr in her photography studio.

"I'll be glad to tell you what I remember of the incident, but to be honest, I was more concerned with keeping Patricia out of harm's way than in noting every detail of what was happening."

"Understandable."

Reggie gave him her version of what had happened, which didn't add anything new to the picture. Maybe he'd get more out of Hazel.

But for now, it was time to check in on the two men he'd left locked in their cells.

Entering his office, Ward was glad to discover that the bickering had died down. He scooped up the keys to the cell doors, then faced the prisoners. "If you two hotheads have settled down enough to go your separate ways without a repeat of this morning's ruckus, I'll let you out. I don't see any need to have the town bear the expense of feeding lunch to a couple of sorry excuses for grown men."

As he inserted the key in the first lock, he paused and gave both men hard looks. "And I suggest you men act like parents and have serious talks with those boys of yours about actions and consequences. Because I aim to get to the bottom of all the trouble that's been happening around town. And if I find proof that any of them were involved, I'll throw them right here in these very same cells. Understand?"

With surly looks tossed at each other, the men mumbled assurances to Ward and he let them go.

When the office door finally shut behind them, Ward leaned back in his chair, enjoying the moment of peace and quiet. Maybe his warning had done the trick and they'd seen the last of these nuisance pranks.

A hint of doubt nagged at him, though, a feeling that he was missing some piece of the puzzle.

Pushing his chair back in frustration, he stood. It was nearly noon, time to take Meg to lunch. And he might as well invite Hazel to come along as well.

After all, she was helping him take care of Meg so the least he could do was buy her a meal.

Which made him wonder yet again, just how serious were her financial problems? And how could he find out without embarrassing her?

As they walked down the sidewalk toward the restaurant, Hazel thought how ironic life could be. Now that she'd decided to leave Turnabout and put thoughts of Ward behind her, she was spending more time in his company than ever before.

Not that I'm complaining, Lord. I'm making some very nice memories to carry with me when I head to New York, and for that I am very grateful.

"So how did your morning go?" Ward asked Meg.

"Miss Hazel is teaching me how to sew."

He met Hazel's gaze over Meg's head. "Is she now?"

Was that approval she saw in his expression?

Meg's head bobbed enthusiastically. "I'm making

a dress for Chessie." She held up the index finger on her right hand, showing him the bandage it sported. "I pricked my finger though."

This time the look he shot her was less approving.

"It bled a little but Miss Hazel said I was very brave 'cause I didn't even cry."

"That is very brave," he agreed solemnly.

The little girl nodded. "Someday I'm going to make beautiful dresses for people," she said earnestly, "just like Miss Hazel."

Hazel was touched by Meg's simple statement. She had a sudden, sharp longing to be the one to raise this child, to help erase any sense of abandonment or un-worthiness she might feel from her previous life. To be the one to help her discover all the wonderful possibili-ties life could bring.

But that was not to be. The new life waiting for her in New York didn't have a place in it for a little girl. Besides, she was coming to believe more and more that God had plans for this little girl that included keeping her close to Ward.

Thankfully Ward seemed unaware of her thoughts and was still focused on Meg. "That sounds like a fine ambition. And you have a good teacher."

"And she says I'm a good student."

They'd arrived at the restaurant by this time and, as usual, Meg went over to look at the books while they waited for their food to be brought out.

"Isn't Half-pint young for sewing lessons?"

"She's old enough to hold a needle and stitch a seam if I mark it for her." More or less. "She still needs a lot of help, of course, but she's a quick learner and what-ever she lacks in skill she makes up for in enthusiasm."

"But isn't it dangerous to give her something as sharp

as a needle? It appears she's already stabbed herself once."

Hazel reached across the table to touch his hand briefly, pulling back as soon as she realized what she was doing. "It was just a shallow pinprick. Don't worry, I keep a close watch on her. And pricking a finger once or twice is a good way to learn how to be careful and how to use a thimble properly."

"Was this her idea or yours?"

Hazel hid a smile. Whether he realized it or not, Ward was already acting like a parent. "She watched me work on a dress this morning and had a lot of questions. I thought it would be best to give her a piece of her own to work on so she could have a way to satisfy her curiosity and gain the pride and confidence that comes with learning a new skill." She sat up straighter. "Besides, it's a skill every girl should learn."

He raised a brow. "At not yet five?"

Hazel shrugged. "She's managing." Then she leaned forward, arms folded on the table. "You should have seen how proud she was when she finished sewing her first seam." It had been uneven and much too loose but that was beside the point.

He turned to watch Meg for a moment while Hazel watched him. Should she tell him that one of the reasons Meg wanted to learn to sew was so she could sew for him? Would that please or worry him?

Before she could decide, he turned back to her and his expression shifted as he changed the subject. "I understand you were at the mercantile the day the Lytle boys caused such a ruckus."

Why the accusatory tone? "That's right."

"And you tried to break things up?"

"Of course. Someone had to do something. I just wish—"

"That was a dangerously fool thing to do. Don't you realize you could have gotten hurt?"

Her irritation at being called foolish was offset by the hint of concern she read into his comment. She waved a hand dismissively. "Oh for goodness' sake, they're just boys, not hardened criminals. They would never hurt me or anyone else. They just need someone to provide them with the right kind of discipline."

"Well, that someone sure as thunder isn't you."

His vehemence set her back. Why was he so angry? "If not me, then who? Their parents certainly aren't doing the job."

"That's not your—"

Meg returned to the table just then, effectively ending their discussion.

But Hazel could tell Ward wasn't appeased.

And a part of her was pleased. Because it showed that he *did* care about her on some level.

But was it enough?

After he left Hazel and Meg at the door to the dress shop, Ward returned to his office. He was still frustrated by his unfinished discussion with Hazel. He had no confidence whatsoever that she wouldn't go barging in again next time a ruckus started. He was even more irritated when he realized he hadn't asked her one question about what she'd actually witnessed that day at the mercantile. Additional proof, if he'd needed it, that he couldn't do his job properly when he got personally involved with someone.

Unable to sit still, he stood and paced across the room. It was a little early, but perhaps making his afternoon rounds would help clear his head. He could also speak to the two men who'd helped break up the ruckus at the mercantile and find out what they remembered.

As it turned out, neither Adam nor Hank had much to add to the picture. Another dead end.

Ward plopped down and leaned back in his chair. He wasn't sure what he'd hoped to gain from those interviews. There was nothing that tied that incident at the mercantile with the Lytle boys to the later break-in, other than loose talk from folks who liked to jump to conclusions.

No, there weren't going to be any shortcuts or easy answers, he'd just have to—

The street door forcefully opened and Eunice Ortolon marched inside, obviously agitated. "Sheriff Gleason, I need to report a crime."

Ward stood and waved her to a seat. "What happened?"

"Someone snatched all of the wash off of my clothesline. In broad daylight, mind you." She fanned herself with her hands. "Whatever is this world coming to?"

So the vandal had struck again. And in the middle of the day. "Any idea when it happened?"

Eunice nodded. "I hung the laundry out on the line around nine o'clock this morning. I went out about thirty minutes ago to check if it was dry and that's when I saw the clothes all scattered on the ground. It wasn't until I started gathering it up, though, that I realized several pieces were missing."

"Anything special about these missing pieces?"

Eunice's face turned an unflattering, blotchy red. "Yes."

He raised a brow, inviting her to elaborate.

"They were my unmentionables." She blurted out the words as if they tasted sour.

Ward didn't give in to the urge to smile. The perpetrator might have a wicked sense of humor but this was criminal mischief, pure and simple. "Perhaps the person who scattered your laundry didn't actually steal anything. A dog or other animal could have come along behind him and carried some of it off."

"Unfortunately, that's not the case."

"How can you be sure?"

She stood. "Follow me."

Uh-oh. He could tell already this was not going to be good.

Chapter Ten

"Mortified. I'm absolutely mortified. Who could have done such a horrid, scandalous thing?"

Ward didn't bother to say anything—he was pretty sure Eunice wasn't expecting an answer.

He stood balanced on the top of a ladder that he'd leaned up against the pecan tree in Eunice's front yard. Dangling from several branches and flapping proudly in the breeze for all the town to see, were Eunice's freshly laundered unmentionables.

It had puzzled him at first as to how the culprit had managed to get some of the white linen underthings so high up in the tree. He didn't believe whoever it was had taken the time to climb the tree in broad daylight to pull off this audacious prank and risk getting caught. But then he'd noticed a number of large rocks scattered around the base of the tree and the puzzle had been solved. The wily criminal had wrapped each garment in a rock and lobbed it into the tree.

As he plucked the last article of clothing from its resting place and stuffed it in the boardinghouse owner's pillowcase along with the others, he couldn't help but think that whoever this prankster was, he had a sly sense of humor. Would any of the Lytle boys have gone to this much trouble, shown this much finesse and ingenuity?

He stepped down from the ladder and handed the pillowcase to Eunice. "Are you sure you didn't see anyone hanging around outside the boardinghouse this morning?"

"I already said I didn't. Believe me, if I'd seen anyone I'd be quick to let you know."

He believed her. Which meant the perpetrator had been able to do this without gaining the notice of the always-on-the-lookout-for-gossip matron. And right under her nose. Quite a feat.

"If you don't mind, I'm going to step back behind your house and check things out."

Eunice clutched the pillowcase to her bosom and nodded. "Just do your job and catch these hooligans. It's a terrible state of affairs when folks no longer feel safe in their own homes."

Ward clenched his jaw at her tone but nodded. "For what it's worth, ma'am, I don't think anyone is in any personal danger from these hooligans, as you call them. But I agree, it's time to put an end to this." And with a tip of his hat, he headed around to the back of her building.

As he'd feared, there wasn't really much for him to see. The ground around the clothesline was well trampled, with most of the footprints obviously belonging to Eunice. Not surprising, especially since she'd apparently raced around picking up her laundry when she'd discovered it scattered on the ground.

There were signs of other footprints that could possibly have been made by the culprit, but they were too distorted to be of much use.

So he concentrated instead on the scene itself. This

side of the boardinghouse was hidden from the main street and faced a wooded area. So it would have been fairly easy to approach unobserved. Again, this was something that had required planning and some knowledge of Eunice's schedule. Not something he could picture any of the Lytle boys doing.

Which meant he was back to square one. Except that now he had a clearer picture in his head of the sort of person he was after.

Someone who was much craftier than what he had at first suspected.

"So first you had to arrest the adult Lytle cousins this morning and then you have to deal with Eunice this afternoon—you've had quite a day." Hazel studied the sheriff's tight jaw with sympathy. While Meg napped, he was helping her carry a large trunk downstairs, one she planned to use for packing the things she would take to New York with her.

Ward grimaced. "I'd say I earned my paycheck today, that's for sure."

"I hear Eunice was madder than a bee-stung polecat."

"A very apt description. But she had every right to be. Whoever made such a spectacle of her laundry deliberately set out to embarrass her." He set the trunk down at the bottom of the stairs. "Now, where do you want me to put this?"

"In my workroom will be fine." No point in leaving this visible reminder of her upcoming departure in the middle of her shop floor.

She held the door open for him. "Are you of the same mind as everyone else, that one or more of the Lytle boys are to blame for all the incidents?"

He set the trunk down and rubbed his chin. "I was. But now I'm not so sure."

"I must say, that's a relief."

His eyes narrowed in surprise. "What do you mean?"

"Just that I think it's not right for folks to place blame like this without any real proof. I know those boys are wild as jackrabbits, but the only time they get really ornery is with each other."

"So you're not basing this on anything other than that you want to think the best of them."

He sounded disappointed. Had he expected her to have a more insightful observation? If so, she was kind of flattered. "Well, I've never seen them take out their anger on anyone else, have you?"

"Can't say as I have." He brushed his hands against his pants. "But that doesn't mean they wouldn't. I know you like to think folks are basically good, but not everyone can live up to your opinion of them."

She saw his gaze drift to the pile of papers on her desk. Why hadn't she put those bills away?

"Thanks for your help with the trunk," she said, drawing his gaze back to her. Then she led the way out of the workroom.

But Hazel wasn't ready to see him leave just yet. "Do you have any theories on who it might be if it's not one or more of the Lytle boys?"

He grimaced and rubbed the back of his neck. "I wish I did. Right now I'd settle for knowing *why* it's happening."

"That makes sense. Knowing why would almost certainly point to who."

He nodded. "But for now, just like everything else about this, it's just one big mystery."

"I have confidence that you'll figure it out." Then she

studied him a moment. "I get the feeling that there was something about the incident at Eunice's place that's bothering you."

That crooked grin she found so attractive lit his face briefly. "I didn't realize I was so easy to read." Then he shrugged. "It just felt different from the others."

"Different how?"

"They didn't just pull the clothing from the line." He leaned against the counter, his expression taking on a faraway look. "They took Eunice's, as she called them, unmentionables, and displayed them on a tree in her front yard. That felt more personal, as if they were deliberately trying to embarrass her rather than just pulling a schoolboy prank that got out of hand."

She loved watching him think through a puzzle this way. "And you think that's significant?"

"I'm not sure. But it certainly does give this whole thing a different angle."

"Eunice can certainly be abrasive at times and she's irritated more than her share of folks around town over the years. Could it be that this incident is separate from the others, that it was done by someone different?"

"I suppose anything is possible." He studied her thoughtfully. "Your mind works in different ways than most."

"Have I just been insulted?" she asked with a mock frown.

His eyes widened in alarm. "Not at all."

His hasty reassurance made her smile.

"I just meant, not many would have made that jump to an alternate solution, at least not as quickly." Then he grimaced. "But I have to say, I hope you're wrong. Because if you're right, that would mean I have two different sets of culprits to identify and capture."

Then he straightened and pushed back from the counter. "Now, unless you have more manual labor to assign me, I need to get back to work at my *real* job."

"That'll do for now," she said with a dismissive wave of her hand.

She watched him leave, then stood at the counter a while longer. Ever since the picnic yesterday, she felt that something had shifted in their relationship, that they'd drawn closer somehow. Did he feel it too?

And what exactly did it mean?

After supper that evening, Ward and Meg took Pugs out for his evening walk. He had enjoyed the discussion with Hazel this afternoon, trying to puzzle things out together. She had a sharp mind and a different way of looking at things that he found inspired him to see things in a new light as well.

What he hadn't enjoyed was carrying her trunk down from the attic for her. And he didn't mean the manual labor part. In fact, he'd rather liked feeling as if she needed him for that.

It was the very physical reminder that her days in Turnabout were numbered, that she was putting plans in motion to leave them, leave *him*, possibly for good.

He'd never really appreciated what a good friend and what a big part of his life Hazel was until he'd learned she was about to leave.

No, that wasn't entirely true. If he was honest with himself, he'd been thinking of Hazel as more than a friend for some time now. He'd just refused to let himself act on those feelings. And after the kidnapping incident with Pru Walker, he'd buried those feelings just as deep as he could.

And now there was nothing he could do about it, was there?

He supposed the bigger question was, was there anything he *should* do about it?

Pushing all of those frustratingly unanswerable questions aside, Ward decided that it was the ideal time to try questioning Meg again. Perhaps he'd have better luck solving her mystery than the one plaguing the town.

Best to start with something fairly innocuous. "Half-pint, I've been wondering, did your brother ever say anything at all about where he and Rory were headed?"

Meg wrinkled her nose. "I don't have a brother."

Ward stopped in his tracks. "You mean Freddie's not your brother?" Had the boy lied about that as well? Had he kidnapped—

Meg giggled. "No, silly. Freddie is my *sister*!" Then she clamped a hand over her mouth. "Oh, I wasn't supposed to tell. Freddie is going to be so mad at me if she finds out."

Freddie was a girl. Probably Winifred or Fredericka then. "Don't you worry about that. I won't let Freddie bother you."

Ward began reevaluating everything he thought he'd known. And it put the role of that Rory fellow in a whole new light as well. How much had Half-pint picked up on? "Do you know why Freddie was running away with Rory?"

"They planned to get married. Freddie said she was gonna be Mrs. Rory Dunkin and start her own family, and now that she had a proper dowry they were going to be able to do it right. She said that I needed to find a new family of my own, too, because there wasn't gonna be room for me in her and Rory's family." She hugged her doll. "I was kinda scared when she told me, but then me and Chessie found you and Pugs and I knew it was going to be okay."

"That's right. There's no need for you to be scared anymore because I'm going to make sure everything is okay for you and Chessie." And he meant it, with every fiber of his being.

The more Ward heard about Freddie, the more heartless she seemed. But he finally had a last name, even if it was Rory's and not Meg's. If he could track down this Dunkin fellow, perhaps he could make the leap to finding out who Meg and Freddie were.

"What's a dowry?" Meg asked, reclaiming his attention.

"It's the money or other goods a bride brings to the marriage." And now that she mentioned it, just where had Freddie come by her *proper dowry*? Could the young couple be thieves? If not, if Freddie had acquired the money through more legitimate means, he had a strong feeling that half of it belonged to Meg.

The little girl appeared to ponder his answer as they continued their walk. Then she looked up at him earnestly. "Will I need to give you a dowry so I can be your new family? The only thing I have is the music box Miss Hazel gave me, but we could share it if you want."

"No, Half-pint, your smile is the only treasure you need to share with me."

"Smiles aren't treasures, silly."

He tapped her nose. "Yours are."

He quickly tried another question, as much to distract her as to gather information. "Did you know Rory before you all made the trip to the train station?"

Meg's pigtails bounced as she nodded again. "He helped Poppa on the farm sometimes. And he liked to pick flowers and give them to Freddie."

Then she surprised him with a question of her own. "Do you like me?" she asked wistfully.

He dropped down to one knee, wanting Meg to see the earnestness in his expression. "Of course I like you, Half-pint. You bring sunshine to my days."

She grinned. "That sounds nice." Then her smile faded. "Freddie didn't like me very much and I'm not sure Poppa did either."

How could those two, who should have been her champions, make her feel that way? "Some people just have trouble letting others know how they feel. It doesn't mean they don't have those feelings."

"Freddie didn't have trouble saying how she felt at all. She told me that I killed our momma when I was borned and that Poppa would never forgive me for it. She said not only that, but that Poppa changed when I came along. He quit laughing and playing with her like he did before. And it was all my fault."

What a terrible burden to have dumped on such small shoulders. He stroked her hair, smiling into her eyes. "No, Half-pint, none of that was your fault. Sometimes things happen that just can't be helped."

Her eyes were huge in her small face. "So it wasn't my fault?"

"No, it most definitely was *not* your fault."

She reached up and hugged his neck. "I wish Poppa was still here so you could tell him. Maybe then he would smile again for Freddie."

Ward tried to hold on to his smile for her sake. But if the man was still here he'd have a whole lot more than that to say to him.

He sent up a silent prayer, thanking God for putting Meg into his care and promising one more time to do all he could to ensure that she had a much happier future than what her past had been.

Hazel had no sooner opened her doors for business on Tuesday morning than Tensy stepped across the threshold.

Hazel greeted her with a smile, wondering what had brought her back so soon. "Hello, Tensy. If you're here for a fitting, I'm afraid I'm not far enough along on your dress for that yet. Perhaps by tomorrow morning?"

Tensy didn't seem at all put off. "Of course." She nervously tucked a tendril behind one ear. "I just wanted to discuss a possible change to the design with you. If it's not too late, I mean."

Hazel braced herself. The girl was so self-effacing that it was hard to get upset with her. But she sincerely hoped they weren't going to have to rehash the bride-to-be's desire for a more fussy design. "What kind of change?"

"I know we agreed that a simple style would be more elegant, but the more I thought on it, the more I felt that what we came up with is just a little *too* plain for the occasion. What do you think about adding a ruffled overskirt below the waist?"

What Hazel thought was that it would be a very bad idea. But she merely smiled, thinking fast. "I certainly understand your wanting to make the dress look special for such an important occasion and of course I want to do everything I can to give you the gown of your dreams. But instead of a ruffled overskirt, why don't we try some lace panels?" She pulled out her sketchbook. "Let me show you what I mean."

Hazel quickly penciled in what she had in mind. Then she went to the back and returned with several yards of a lovely ivory lace. "This shade would look beautiful up against the pink of your gown." She held a length of it next to the partially completed bodice to demonstrate. "See?"

"Oh yes, thank you." Then Tensy's expression shifted. "But will you have time to get this done before you leave for New York? I expect you're anxious to start on your new adventure."

If only Tensy knew—she would gladly trade places with her, preparing to marry the man she loved. That was a perfect adventure as far as she was concerned.

But she smiled and focused on the woman's main concern. "I should have plenty of time to get everything done. I'm not planning to leave until the Coopers return from their trip, and they aren't due back for another two and a half weeks. Besides, even if that wasn't the case, I could take the project with me, finish it in New York and then ship it back."

"Oh, I hadn't considered that." Tensy's whole demeanor had brightened. "This is all so generous of you. But hopefully it won't come to that. I'd hate for you to have to spend your first days in your new role looking back."

Again Tensy's word struck her as unintentionally double-edged. How much looking back *would* she do once she moved to New York?

Meg tugged on her skirt, pulling her back to the present. "My thread got all tangled up," she said woefully.

Hazel smiled down at her. "That happens sometimes, even to me. Wait at the table and I'll help you as soon as I finish assisting Miss Lawrence."

Tensy studied Meg thoughtfully as the little girl walked away. "She certainly seems a lively child. Do you know what Sheriff Gleason's plans for her are?"

Hazel wasn't sure that even Ward knew what his plans were. "He's still hopeful he can find a relative of hers who'll be willing to take her in."

Tensy gave her a thoughtful look. "The child seems rather attached to you. Have you thought about adopting her yourself and taking her to New York with you?"

Hazel was rather taken aback at the intrusiveness of the question.

But before she could figure out how to respond, Tensy placed her elbows on the counter and leaned forward, a dreamy expression on her face. "I hope to have children of my own someday, lots of them."

She gave Hazel a self-deprecating smile. "My ambitions must seem rather small to an independent-minded woman like you."

"Not at all. I think being a good mother is a very noble ambition." Hazel hoped Tensy was less awkward with her own kids than she seemed to be with Meg. But then again, some folks were like that, she supposed, stiff around other people's children but warm and loving with their own.

Hazel glanced fondly at the little girl, who had already found a special place in her heart. She would have no problem at all taking on the role of mother to Meg. But there was no way she would tear the child away from Ward. Because whatever bond Tensy had seen between herself and Meg, Hazel knew Meg's connection to Ward was ten times deeper.

Would she ever have children of her own? Hazel felt that she had so much love to give that she quite literally ached with the need to share it.

She glanced at Tensy, who was lovingly fingering the incomplete dress that was destined to become her wedding gown. There was such a happy glow about her.

That's how a bride should look.

That was how Hazel longed to feel.

Then she gave herself a mental shake. She had to accept that that was not going to be her lot in life, at least not with the man she'd always pictured as her groom. God had opened a different door for her and now she needed to step through with faith and confidence and see what path that led to.

There really wasn't any other choice for her.

Chapter Eleven

That evening, after Meg and Ward had gone to Ward's place for the night, Hazel decided it was time to tackle some of the packing for her upcoming move. Going through her belongings, deciding what to take with her, what to store for later shipping and what to discard altogether was more difficult than she'd imagined it would be.

After several hours of sorting through her things, she decided to head downstairs to go over some legal and financial documents stored there. That, at least, should be less of an emotional drain. Sitting down at the worktable that served as a desk, she began to methodically go through the folders containing the papers. After thirty minutes of staring at figures and legal documents, some of them going back to her parents' time, her eyelids grew heavy.

Just another few minutes, she promised herself, and then she'd set it aside to finish another day.

Sometime later, she wasn't certain just how long, she jerked awake. Her lamp had gone out and she was sitting in the full dark. With a grimace, she rubbed her neck, trying to massage some of the stiffness from it. How long had she dozed?

With a sigh, she stood and headed for the stairs, not needing a light to guide her through the familiar path. Halfway there, she paused. What was that noise?

It sounded as if it had come from next door but that was impossible. Verity and her family weren't due back for more than two weeks. She grimaced at that thought. It meant that was how long she had before her last excuse to delay her departure for New York expired.

Hazel moved to the window. She didn't see anything but there was that noise again. And it was definitely coming from Verity's place.

Could it be the person who'd been causing so much trouble around town? If so, this could be Ward's chance to finally capture the culprit and put an end to it. She just needed to alert him to what was going on.

Hazel quietly slipped out of her front door and then paused. What if the intruder left before Ward could get here? Maybe she should try to get a quick look in the window—perhaps she would see enough to make an identification.

Hazel stealthily moved toward the shop window. The shade was drawn but there was a slight gap on one side. Unfortunately, Hazel couldn't see anything in the dark interior.

She was wasting time. Better to let Ward handle this.

Turning, she hurried down the block and a half that separated her place from Ward's. Clouds hid the moon and stars but the streetlamps provided enough light for her to see by.

She had no idea what time it was, only a sense that it must be quite late indeed. The streets were abandoned at this hour, lending an extra air of eeriness to her scurrying progress and raising the hairs on the back of her neck.

Hazel finally reached Ward's door and knocked, praying he was a light sleeper and that her rapping wouldn't wake Meg.

When he answered the door a moment later, he was fully dressed and fully awake. How was that possible at this hour?

He frowned. "What are you doing here in the middle of the night?" His voice was low and almost angry.

"I heard some noises from the Coopers' place. I thought you should investigate."

Ward immediately transformed from an irritable bear of a man to a businesslike sheriff. "What kind of noises?" He'd already dropped onto the bench next to the door and was pulling on his boots.

"It sounded as if someone was stumbling around inside. I peeked in the front window—"

His head snapped up at that. "You did *what*?"

"I figured it would help if I could see who it was." She couldn't quite keep the defensiveness from her tone.

His jaw tightened and his lips thinned in an angry line. "Of all the fool notions. If whoever was inside had seen you, they could have tried to hurt you."

"Oh pish posh. I assume whoever it is, it's the same mischief-makers who have been running about town causing trouble. Whoever is doing all this isn't violent, he's just trying to stir up trouble. Besides, it doesn't matter. I couldn't see anyone from the window anyway."

He stood. "That doesn't mean they couldn't see you. We don't know what this person, or persons, are capable of because they haven't been confronted. Yet."

She heard the determination in his voice. She wouldn't want to be on the receiving end of his ire.

Ward stood and reached inside a cabinet mounted high on the wall near the door. When he drew out a gun and holster, she gasped.

"Surely that's not necessary."

His expression closed off as he buckled it on. "Let's hope not. But it's best to be prepared."

Hazel began to regret she'd come here. If something happened to him—

She saw him straighten, then hesitate, glancing toward the stairs. His expression shifted into frustration and uncertainty.

"Go do your job," she said. "I'll stay here with Meg until you get back."

He hesitated, then nodded. "I shouldn't be gone long. Lock the door behind me."

Did he think someone would be fool enough to break into the sheriff's home? But she wouldn't bother arguing the point. Instead she nodded and stepped past him into his home.

Before he could leave, she placed a hand on his arm. "Please be careful."

Something flickered in his expression and his hand briefly closed over hers. Then he nodded and quickly made his exit.

Hazel locked the door as he'd requested, then leaned against it with her eyes closed, sending up a silent prayer for his safety.

Ward marched down the street, his lips set in a grim line. It wasn't seemly to leave Hazel in his home, but he didn't have much choice if he wanted to do his job. Under the circumstances, it wouldn't be safe to send her and Meg over to her place.

This was all getting out of hand. Turnabout was a

peaceful town for the most part and it was his job to make certain it stayed that way. It was time to put an end to this little crime spree so things could settle back down into some semblance of normal.

But with all that was changing in his life, he had a feeling that normal would never look quite the same as it had before.

Ward reached Nate Cooper's saddlery shop and slipped around to the back. Sure enough, the rear entrance was ajar, the doorframe splintered where the lock had held it closed. He quietly stepped over the debris and slipped inside. He spotted a crowbar propped against the doorframe. No doubt that was how the intruder had gotten in. It was likely also the noise Hazel had heard.

Things were quiet now, but since the crowbar was still here he figured the intruder was still here as well. Ward moved to the main shop and though he found quite a bit of evidence that someone had been here, the perpetrator was nowhere in sight.

Borrowing a lamp from the shop counter, he lit it and returned to the busted door. There were tracks all right, and from the size of them they'd been made by a youth or a small man.

He returned to the shop area and set the lamp on the counter, deciding to search every possible hiding place.

He spun around when he heard a rustling noise behind him. Then he heard a growled whisper. "Run, it's the sheriff!"

He tried to give chase, but one of them sent a large storage shelf crashing in his path. By the time he made his way over the obstacle, the only sign of his quarry was the sound of pounding footsteps off to his left.

There! He spotted a shadowy form, behind the apothecary shop, sprinting toward Oak Street. Probably planning to cut through the woods and then take one of the half-dozen footpaths that branched off in different directions. If he didn't catch up with him before he got to the wooded area, he'd never catch him in the dark.

The runner was quick—he no doubt had his escape route already planned out. Ward's only chance to catch him was to cut through the schoolyard and try to head him off before he reached the edge of town.

Ward was already moving before the plan had fully formed in his mind. His quarry had disappeared into the shadows again, but Ward was confident he was still out there and hadn't veered course. The faint sound of running footsteps confirmed his gut feeling.

Whoever it was the first intruder had called out to, the two weren't running together. Either they'd split up and the partner had already made his escape or he'd decided to hide in the dark until Ward was gone. But there was no time to worry about that right now; he needed to keep this one in his sights.

He pictured the school grounds in his mind, moving as quickly as he could over the terrain in the dark. Too bad there were no streetlamps in this area. If only this cloud cover would clear so he could get even a glimpse of the runner's face.

Then his foot caught on something that wasn't supposed to be there and Ward found himself pitching forward. He struggled to catch himself, to regain his balance. But his head slammed into something hard and there was an explosion of lights behind his eyes before the darkness overtook him.

Chapter Twelve

Hazel sat in one of the two chairs in Ward's kitchen, her hands in her lap. Her options for seating had been limited. The two chairs here at the table. The bench near the front door. And the sofa that was currently made up to serve as Ward's bed. She'd climbed the stairs to check in on Meg a couple of times now—luckily the child seemed to be a sound sleeper.

This was the first time she'd been inside Ward's living quarters and it felt slightly scandalous, like an invasion of his privacy. Still, she couldn't help but be fascinated by this new glimpse into the man himself.

The place was every bit as small as it had seemed from the outside, and sparsely furnished. Everything was neat and squared away, though there were signs that Meg's presence was starting to add a more lived-in quality to the place.

Otherwise, there was a disappointing lack of personal touches here. But there had been one item she'd noticed when she looked in on Meg. There, on the top of his chest of drawers, was a music box, one that had belonged to Bethany. She knew, because she had given it to her friend on her tenth birthday. She'd saved her money to purchase it and brought it home from her visit to New York that summer. Its presence there, among his own things, had seemed poignant, had brought an unexpected lump to her throat.

There was a sentimental side to the normally nononsense sheriff that few people saw. Not that she'd needed this additional proof. She had seen it in the way he was with Bethany. And it was also there in his interactions with Meg.

Hazel looked at the wooden clock on the mantle. Ward had been gone for quite some time now. What if something had happened? What if this criminal was much more dangerous than Ward had believed? She remembered the weapon he'd strapped on and shivered as she considered the possibilities.

Rubbing her hands over her forearms, Hazel moved to the front window and pushed aside the curtain. Except for a moth circling the nearby streetlamp, nothing stirred, at least not in her line of vision. What was happening? Had he caught the criminal and was busy locking him up and informing the proper parties? Had he given chase perhaps and was even now circling back? Had there been a fight and he was hurt, needing help?

She dropped the curtain and moved back to the center of the room, unable to keep still. Why hadn't she brought some sewing to keep her hands busy or even a book? Just waiting, imagining, was hard on her nerves.

Should she go for help? Even if she could leave Meg alone, who would she go to?

She'd thought for a while now that the town should hire a deputy. Turnabout had grown to the extent that it was too much for one man, even if that one man was Ward Gleason. It wasn't fair for him to be on call twenty-four hours a day, seven days a week. In fact, she would bring it up at the very next town meeting.

Then she grimaced. She wouldn't be here for the next town meeting. How Turnabout handled its peacekeeping needs would no longer be her concern.

Then she reconsidered. Just because she was moving away didn't mean she couldn't say her piece to the town council before she left. Someone needed to stand up for Ward since he wasn't likely to stand up for himself.

And speaking of Ward, what was keeping him?

When Ward woke up, it took him a moment to remember where he was. With a groan he pushed himself up off the ground. How long had he been out? The culprits he'd been chasing were no doubt long gone by now.

As he shifted to a seated position, he saw a coil of rope in the grass. A student's forgotten jump rope perhaps? It was no doubt what he'd tripped over.

He pulled a rumpled handkerchief out of his pocket and dabbed at his head. It came away with blood, but not a great deal. He gingerly got to his feet, testing his sense of balance, then slowly headed back the way he'd come.

He paused at the Coopers' place and secured the door as best he could. He'd check things out later; this would have to do for now. He'd left Hazel alone at his place way too long.

Despite the pounding in his head, Ward approached his home at a fast walk. He'd been gone much longer than he'd intended—from the look of the eastern horizon, it would be dawn soon. It was imperative he get Hazel back to her own place before the town stirred.

He hadn't quite reached his door when it swung open and Hazel stood there, a look of intense relief on her face. Surely those weren't tear tracks on her face?

"Thank goodness you're back. I was getting so worried." The hand she used to push back a tendril of hair trembled slightly.

She *had* been worried. And likely scared as well.

He had a sudden urge to gather her close in his arms and soothe away her worries. It was all he could do to keep his arms down at his sides. "So sorry to have alarmed you. The time got away from me." She didn't need to know about his clumsy accident. But before he could say anything else, her eyes widened and she closed the gap between them.

"What's that on your forehead? Did that villain *hit* you?" Her whole demeanor was an endearing mix of worry and outrage.

Again he had to fight an overwhelming desire to reach for her. All of this unfamiliar emotion must be a reaction to the fall he'd taken.

"I took a little tumble," he said, trying not to worry her. "But it's nothing much. Just a scratch."

She didn't appear the least bit reassured. In fact, just the opposite. "Maybe I should fetch Doc Pratt to have a look at you."

That was the last thing he needed right now. "I'm fine. And you need to get on home. We can talk in the morning."

As usual, she ignored his concerns. "It *is* morning. What happened? Did you catch him?"

Ward shook his head, giving way to his feelings of self-disgust. "No. And I didn't get close enough to be able to identify him either." He was beginning to believe he was as inept as folks were starting to hint at.

She touched his arm, suddenly all sympathy. "Don't blame yourself. You'll catch him soon."

He ignored the platitude, just as he tried to ignore the enticing warmth of her touch. "What time is it?"

"Nearly five."

He *really* needed to get Hazel away from here now. "I think it best if you go on home. I need to clean up and try to get a little sleep myself before I start the day in earnest." Not that he actually expected to get any sleep, but he was trying to play on her sympathy since nothing else was working.

It worked. She was immediately contrite. "Oh yes, of course. I wasn't thinking. I can go get Meg and take her with me now if you like. That way you won't—"

"No, let her sleep. In fact, I'll keep Meg with me or find someone else to watch her at least until lunchtime. So feel free to sleep as late as you like."

"That's not necessary, I—"

"I've kept you up long enough," he said firmly. "We can continue this discussion after we've both had some rest." He rubbed the back of his neck. "I'd escort you home, but—"

"But you can't leave Meg alone. Don't worry—I came here by myself and I can return the same way."

The clouds parted just then, allowing the moon to cast a brighter glow over the town, and Hazel gasped. "Your forehead—that's more than just a scratch. And it's bleeding."

Reaching into her pocket, she drew out a handkerchief and dabbed at his cut. Using her other hand, she brushed his hair out of the way.

How warm and soft her touch felt, how sweetly tender. She'd stepped closer, to better examine the cut in the dim light, and he could feel her breath on his cheek, smell the flowery scent of her soap. Her lips looked soft, inviting. Would they taste as sweet as they looked?

Her gaze met his and she must have seen something of what he was feeling reflected there. Her own eyes widened and her breath hitched. But there was no recoil, no fear, only something very like anticipation. It would take so little effort to close the gap between them that it seemed only right that he do so.

He'd actually leaned in to kiss her before he realized just how close to disaster he was taking them.

The sound of a throat clearing broke the moment. Ward jerked his head around and Tim Hill, the lamplighter, was watching them with a shocked expression.

Ward swallowed a groan. The man was almost as big a gossip as Eunice Ortolon.

He took a step back, trying to keep his demeanor casual as his mind whirled with thoughts of what implications Tim would read into what he'd seen.

Hoping to take control of the situation, Ward addressed the lamplighter. "Tim, would you mind escorting Miss Andrews back to her place? She came by here to report on a break-in at the Cooper place. I'd escort her myself but Meg is asleep and I can't leave a little girl like her alone, even for so short a time."

He sent up a silent prayer that his offhand explanation was enough to nip the gossip in the bud.

Tim closed his gaping mouth and tipped his hat Hazel's way. "It'd be my pleasure, ma'am." But Ward noticed the light of speculation still burned bright in the man's eyes. The man was clearly not entirely satisfied with Ward's explanation.

Hazel, however, smiled pleasantly and fell into step beside the lamplighter. Did she not know how this must have looked? Or did she care so little for her reputation?

Ward watched until they disappeared from view, then turned and went inside. He shut the door, then just stood there, hands jammed in his pockets. What had just happened? How could he have so lost control that he'd actually considered kissing Hazel? Not only considered it but actually started to act on the impulse.

Perhaps that blow to the head had affected him more than he'd thought. Whatever the case, he might have just put Hazel's reputation at risk. And that was something he couldn't just shrug off.

He slowly moved up the stairs to look in on Meg. She still slept soundly, Chessie in her arms.

Pugs glanced up from his pallet on the floor and his tail thumped drowsily.

Ward turned and went back downstairs where he took a seat on the couch. He'd destroyed his sister's life both physically and mentally. It seemed now he was in danger of repeating his careless destruction with Hazel, only in her case it was her reputation he had put at risk.

He bowed his head and began to pray in earnest.

Hazel slowly climbed the stairs to her living quarters, not bothering with a lamp. For just a moment back there it had appeared Ward intended to kiss her. But something had stopped him, even before Mr. Hill had interrupted them.

What did it mean? Why had he tried to kiss her, now, when she'd given up on ever having a relationship with him? And what had stopped him?

The logical, rational part of her mind realized that it was just as well he'd stopped, that there was no sense in starting something that could never go any further. But, oh, the other part of her, the emotional, dreamy side, had wanted that kiss, had wanted to know what it felt like to be held in his arms, even if it was only this one time.

She reached the top of the stairs and wrapped her

arms around herself, trying to somehow hold in all the emotions that were threatening to overwhelm her.

Could it possibly be that now, when she'd given up all hope and resigned herself to moving on, Ward was finally beginning to take notice of her? If so, what would happen if she decided to stay?

Did she dare find out?

Chapter Thirteen

Ward didn't bother trying to get any sleep. He cleaned up and then fixed himself a couple of very strong cups of coffee while he pondered the implications of what Tim Hill had witnessed. If the gossip spread, as it almost definitely would, he would do the right and necessary thing to protect Hazel's reputation.

Marriage. To Hazel. Of course, she'd been hinting for quite some time that she wouldn't be opposed to such a thing. Which meant she probably wouldn't have any big objections, other than on general principles over being backed into a corner to do it.

But how did *he* feel about it? He'd long ago decided that being sheriff would not just be a job to him, it would be both a calling and a way of making amends for the wrong he'd done his sister. He couldn't make things right with Bethany herself but he could do this thing instead. And dedicating himself to the job of sheriff meant putting it first in his life, second only to God. Which left no room for a family. And he'd been all right with that all these years. In fact, it had felt sort of noble to approach it that way.

But what had happened this morning had changed

all that. Just like taking care of Meg when she'd been left in his care had taken precedent over his duty to escort his sister's body home, making sure Hazel wasn't ruined by a scandal of his making took precedent over his vow to never marry.

He would just have to make certain she understood that this was a marriage of necessity, that his dedication to his role as sheriff had to come first.

The bigger issue was whether or not he could maintain that kind of discipline himself. His ability to resist Hazel's unique brand of charm was being sorely tested lately.

Downing the last swallow in his second cup of coffee, Ward carried the cup to the sink and went to wake Meg.

After he'd fed her breakfast, the two of them headed to Dr. Pratt's place. The physician was Verity Cooper's uncle and Ward felt certain he would know how to contact her and her husband, which he did. The physician also insisted on tending to the cut on Ward's forehead while he was there.

Armed with the information from Verity's uncle, Ward next went to the telegraph office and sent word to Nate Cooper about the break-in.

Walking down the sidewalks of town, he was very conscious of the looks he and Meg were getting from some of the townsfolk they passed along the way. Was it his imagination or was the judgment and speculation he saw reflected in those looks sharper today?

When he reached the dress shop, he saw that Hazel had ignored his suggestion to sleep late and had her shop open already. Was it because she'd had as much trouble sleeping as he had?

Since Hazel was obviously up and about, he left Meg

with her, pausing only long enough for the briefest of conversations and a promise to Meg that he would bring Pugs over later.

His next stop was the land office, where Mayor Sanders could normally be found when he wasn't taking care of town business. After he'd reported on the incident of the night before, Mayor Sanders leaned back in his chair.

"So you didn't get a good look at them?"

"No. In fact, I only saw one of them, though I did overhear some talk that leads me to believe there were at least two."

"Do we know if they took anything?"

Ward shook his head. "I won't know for sure until Nate gets back and does an inventory, but judging from how quickly they were moving when they hightailed it out of there, I doubt they were carrying much with them."

"Well, there's that at least."

Ward resisted the urge to rake his hands through his hair, wanting to maintain an in-control demeanor. "I've sent a telegram to Nate to let him know what happened." He hoped it wouldn't lead him to cut his family's travels short. Not only would it be a shame to ruin the last half of their vacation, but Ward certainly didn't want the Coopers to come home early if it meant hastening Hazel's departure.

Though he refused to examine his motives for that thought too closely.

The mayor's expression would have been called grumpy on a less dignified person. "It certainly would have helped settle the frustrations in town if you'd caught the culprit last night."

Mine included. "I agree. But whoever these scoundrels are, they're starting to get careless and make mistakes. Letting Miss Andrews hear their break-in was a major error on their part. My gut tells me it won't be much longer until I'm able to capture them."

"Let's hope your gut is right. Folks around here are beginning to lose patience with the amount of time it's taking you to resolve this matter."

Ward stood. "So am I." He had to get control of this situation somehow. "Now, if you'll excuse me, I want to look around at the Coopers' place to see if I missed anything last night."

But Mayor Sanders held up a hand. "There's one other thing I wanted to talk to you about before you leave."

Ward reluctantly settled back in his seat. He was pretty sure he knew what was coming and it wasn't going to be pleasant.

"Word of what Tim Hill witnessed this morning is circulating around town."

That hadn't taken long. But before he could respond, the mayor gave a quick disclaimer. "Of course, I believe there's an innocent explanation for what Tim saw, but perceptions can be every bit as damaging to a person's reputation as the truth."

Sometimes more so. "Nothing inappropriate happened." He kept any note of defensiveness from his voice. "Miss Andrews acted above reproach at all times. She was merely watching Meg for me while I investigated the break-in taking place next door to her home."

One of the mayor's brows went up. "So Tim was mistaken when he said the two of you seemed to be exchanging more than a polite goodbye?"

At the moment Ward could have happily sentenced

all gossips to the deepest, darkest, smelliest dungeon he could find.

But again he managed to keep his voice even as he responded. "I believe what Tim witnessed was Miss Andrews expressing her concern over my injury and trying to staunch the bleeding." He touched the bandage Dr. Pratt had applied to his forehead. "It's unfortunate if he interpreted our actions as anything more than that."

But the guilt gnawing at his gut reminded him it could have—and almost had—turned into so much more. And that it was his fault it had gone as far as it had.

"Unfortunate or not, there are those who find the mere idea of her having been in your home, especially at that hour, to be highly indiscreet at best. And as sheriff, you have a responsibility to remain above reproach." The mayor spread his hands. "I'm only telling you this as your friend, you understand, so you can be aware of what is being said."

"Then, as my friend," Ward said stiffly as he stood, "I would appreciate it if you would set the record straight whenever you overhear someone trying to spread such damaging untruths."

With that, Ward left, his jaw set and his steps firm. He didn't look either left or right, not trusting what others might see in his eyes if they stopped to greet him.

Ten minutes later, he was standing in the middle of Cooper's Saddle, Tack & Supply, taking a deep breath and trying to let his personal problems go while he concentrated on his job.

Surveying the disarray, it was hard to tell if anything was actually missing, but the intruders had certainly done a lot of damage.

The glass front on the counter was smashed, everything that had hung from pegs on the wall was now scattered on the floor, a number of boxes of brads, rivets and miscellaneous hardware had been emptied and the contents flung about. This was damage for damage's sake, pure and simple. The Coopers would have quite a mess waiting for them when they returned.

"Oh my."

Ward turned at the softly uttered exclamation to see Hazel and Meg had entered the shop behind him.

"What are you doing here?" The question came out sharper than he'd intended but she seemed not to notice.

"I wanted to see the damage for myself." She shook he head, her expression stunned. "Nate and Verity don't deserve this."

"No, they don't. But as far as I can tell, neither did any of the others who were victims of our malicious intruder."

She seemed to pull herself together and met his gaze with her usual spirit. "Once you're done with whatever official sheriff business you have in here, I'd like to do some cleaning up."

Hazel never ceased to surprise him with her big heart and optimistic outlook. "That's kind of you."

Hazel waved away his compliment. "Verity would do the same for me. And I don't want them to come home to—" she motioned with her hands "—this."

"Well, I see no reason to keep you from it." Then he gave her a stern look. "I just don't want to find you here after dark." He rubbed his chin. "If you come across something that you think doesn't belong or discover something missing that you think should be here, let me know."

Hazel glanced toward the door that hid the stairs. "Do you know if they intruded on the living quarters?"

Ward shook his head. "That door is still locked and doesn't look like it's been tampered with."

"Well, that's a relief at least." Hazel smiled down at her companion. "Meg, sweetheart, would you like to help me clean up this place for my friend?"

Meg looked around, her eyes wide. Then she gave Hazel a game half-smile. "I'll try."

Hazel embraced her in a quick hug. "Thank you. Do you know that the people who live here have a little girl not much older than you?"

"They do?"

"Uh-huh. Her name is Joy. And they also have a little dog, not much bigger than Pugs, whose name is Beans."

Meg giggled. "Beans. That's a funny name."

Ward watched the interaction between the two of them, feeling almost like an outsider looking in. And he realized he very much wanted to be on the inside, to be a part of their self-made family. But he needed to quit entertaining such thoughts.

Should he tell Hazel about the gossip spreading around town? Or let her enjoy this untainted moment while she could?

Much as he'd prefer to wait, Ward knew it would be better if she heard about it from him first so she wouldn't be caught off guard hearing it from someone else.

He picked up a large can and handed it to Meg. "Half-pint, why don't you gather up those buckles over there and put them in this container." It would keep her busy away from the broken glass while he talked to Hazel.

He drew Hazel a little distance away. "I wanted to

make you aware that there is a bit of talk circulating around town today. Talk regarding me and you."

"Oh." Her gaze searched his expression, her demeanor turning sober. "I suppose you mean gossip of some sort."

He nodded grimly. "It appears Tim exaggerated a bit when recounting what he saw in front of my place this morning."

The pink rose up her throat and into her cheeks, and her smile took on a forced quality. He hated that he was the one responsible for her discomfort.

"I see," she said, tilting her chin up. Then she flashed a not-quite-believable smile. "Well, if we ignore it and go about our business as usual, I'm certain the talk will die down soon enough."

He certainly hoped she was right. "I just wanted to make sure you're prepared for the unwanted attention that's likely to come our way over this."

"Thank you." She placed a hand against his chest. "It's why you were trying to rush me off this morning, wasn't it? I'm sorry I put you in this spot."

The warmth seeping from her palm through the thin barrier of his shirt was almost painfully sweet. He took her hand in his and gave it a gentle squeeze. "You've nothing to apologize for."

She met his gaze for a long second, her eyes wide and searching. Did she feel that same sense of connection, of wanting more, that he did?

Then Meg dropped something and shattered the tenuous link.

Hazel broke eye contact and spun around. "If that's all, Meg and I have some cleaning to attend to."

"Hazel." He waited until she met his gaze again. "I

want you to know that, if this becomes an issue, I'm prepared to do the right thing."

He saw the blood drain from her face. And then suddenly there was a flash of fire in her eyes.

"The right thing," she said, enunciating each word clearly, "would be to go on with our lives as usual. Now, I'm sure you have some business to attend to while Meg and I get to work in here."

And with that she again turned from him and went to work picking up the shards of broken glass.

Knowing he'd been dismissed, Ward took a minute to give Meg a quick goodbye hug, then headed for the door. He hadn't been surprised by her reaction, had actually expected it.

She wanted to pretend this would all go away if she just ignored it, wanted to believe that her innocence would protect her. But that wasn't how gossip and speculation worked. Which she would likely discover before the day was over.

Which only left them with one option.

Marriage.

Whether Hazel liked it or not.

Chapter Fourteen

Hazel heard Ward make his exit and was finally able to take a deep breath. Surely Ward was overreacting. After all, they hadn't actually done anything wrong or even questionable. Folks could think what they will, but if she and Ward held their heads up and didn't flinch, folks would lose interest eventually and move on to some other bit of news. Especially if the culprit who was responsible for this mess struck again.

Not that she wanted that to happen, she told herself quickly. Just some other really attention-getting something for people to focus on.

Maybe Tensy would announce her engagement soon.

She scratched her finger on a piece of broken glass and quickly lifted the digit to her mouth, fighting an unaccountable urge to cry. There had been a moment, when he'd taken her hand, when she thought he was going to say something sweet and tender. Then he'd spoiled it all with his noble assertions to do right by her.

This was all just too unbearable. She was being tested, that had to be it. Yes, she'd long dreamed of a life married to Ward. Yes, she'd most assuredly find joy in helping him raise Meg to be the wonderful person she could become.

But she'd put aside those dreams, was trying to focus on a new vision of her future. And now this—Ward's offer to *do the right thing*. Even if she wasn't leaving Turnabout, that wasn't the kind of marriage she'd envisioned. Nor was it one she wanted anything to do with.

If that was all he had to offer her, it was just as well she wouldn't be here much longer.

Dearest Lord, I know I've come to You many times in the past, asking for some kind of miracle that would make Ward want to marry me, but I never meant for it to happen like this. So if those are my choices, then I'll take New York and whatever awaits me there.

But, as always, Your will be done. Amen.

Hazel had been on edge ever since that disastrous conversation with Ward at the saddlery shop. When he'd come by to escort her and Meg to lunch, he hadn't brought the subject up again as she'd expected. It wasn't so much that she wanted to discuss it again, it was more that she felt Ward had more to say on the subject and she just wanted to get it over and done with.

The walk to and from the restaurant had been uncomfortable—she imagined every person they passed or came in contact with was staring and passing judgment. Ward seemed outwardly composed and kept up a running conversation with Meg. But Hazel knew him well enough to know that he felt the censure as well. He'd also given her a see-what-I-mean look at one point.

If only Verity were here. She sorely missed having her best friend and confidant only a few steps from her front door whenever she needed to talk.

Shortly after she placed Meg down for her nap, on

a pallet set up expressly for that purpose in the workroom, Eunice Ortolon and Eula Fay Sanders walked into the dress shop. The two women were the self-appointed town conscience. Both wore identical thin-lipped, self-righteous expressions, which was never a good sign for whomever they were focused on.

Unfortunately, it looked as if she was that lucky person today.

Putting on her best shopkeeper smile and positioning herself behind the counter, Hazel greeted them. "Good afternoon, ladies. Is there something I can do for you today?"

"We've come to speak to you." Eunice was apparently going to be the spokesperson today. "We feel it is our Christian duty to discuss a matter of extreme importance with you."

"Oh?" Thank goodness Meg was sleeping. She wasn't certain the child's presence would have deterred them.

"There has been some rather upsetting talk circulating about town this morning," Eunice continued. "Talk of a rather indelicate nature, if you know what we mean?"

"No, I'm afraid I don't know what you mean." She refused to make this easy for them.

"I never thought of you as obtuse." Apparently Mrs. Sanders was ready to chime in. "We are speaking of your being seen leaving Sheriff Gleason's home in the wee hours this morning. Do you deny you were there?"

"No, I was there. But there was nothing of an *indelicate nature* about it. I was merely watching over Meg while the sheriff did his job."

"A commendable motive but a poorly thought-out

plan, I'm afraid. And from what I hear, there was more than a quick goodbye exchanged when he returned."

Hazel tried to command her cheeks to remain cool. "One should not give credence to gossip. I would think you ladies would be above such things."

Both women drew themselves up at that.

"Of course," Eunice said. "But one should also conduct oneself in a manner so as not to invite gossip."

Hazel was ready to get this over with. "Just what do you expect from me?"

"There are ways to diffuse the situation."

Were they suggesting the same solution as Ward had? Before she could comment, Mrs. Sanders spoke up.

"Everyone knows how you feel about the sheriff. You of all people should know the most obvious solution."

Having to stand here and be lectured to in such a manner was insufferable! Right now, the move to New York didn't seem like such a bad thing after all. "And everyone also knows he doesn't return those feelings," she stated firmly.

"Regardless, one must needs think about the little girl."

Hazel's heart seemed to skip a beat. "This doesn't have anything to do with Meg."

"On the contrary, I'm sure you'll agree that protecting the innocence of a child is of utmost importance. To expose that little girl to unseemly conduct, even if it is only perceived as such, is unacceptable. And it's not as if she is either your or the sheriff's blood kin."

How dare they! Hazel was ready to deliver a strong lecture of her own, when the door opened. She wasn't sure if it was relief or irritation she felt when she saw Ward march in, a ready-for-battle look to him.

"Good afternoon, ladies."

"Sheriff." Both women gave him cool looks and only slight nods of acknowledgment.

He crossed his arms, looking as firmly planted where he stood as a fencepost in concrete. "Please don't let me interrupt your discussion. My business with Miss Andrews can wait."

"I believe we are done here," Eunice said. She gave Hazel a pointed look. "Please give some thought to what we discussed."

"Believe me, I will give it all the thought it deserves."

She could tell from their expressions that they understood her meaning. Both ladies left in something of a snit.

When they were gone, she turned to Ward. "What?"

He raised his hands in a gesture of surrender, a response to her tone, no doubt. "Where's Meg?"

"Napping."

"Good. We need to talk."

She crossed her arms, mimicking his earlier gesture. "Yes, we do. But you go first."

He raised a brow at that. Then nodded. "All right. I have two things, actually. First, we need to rethink Meg's sleeping arrangements. I don't want to risk a repeat of what happened last night."

Some of Hazel's ire cooled. "I know." She leaned her elbows on the counter. "But it'll break her heart if you try to hand her off to someone else. Even if that someone is me."

He seemed surprised by her quick agreement. Had he expected her to argue? "I've thought about that. We can keep just about everything the way it is now—we'll take meals together and she can still come to my place after work in the evenings for a couple of hours. I'll spend time with her—taking Pugs for walks, read to her, perhaps teach her to play checkers. But then at bed time, I bring her back here to sleep at your place."

So he was still thinking in terms of her being available to help. "What happens after I move to New York?"

He dismissed her question with a wave of his hand. "I hope to have Meg squared away in her new home by then. If not, perhaps I can convince the Coopers to help out."

Hazel nodded. Why hadn't she thought of that? Verity would be wonderful with Meg, and her daughter, Joy, would be the perfect playmate for the little girl. "We'll have to be careful to present this to Meg the right way but I think we can make that work."

She braced herself. "And the second thing you wanted to discuss?"

He raised a brow. "I think you know. Surely you haven't been oblivious to the talk about town. In fact, if I'm not mistaken, that was the topic of the discussion I just interrupted."

Had he come in because he saw who her visitors were? Or had the timing been mere coincidence? "Foolish talk coming from foolish people. I still think it will die down soon enough." Should she let him know they'd brought Meg into the discussion?

"I don't think so. Such talk tends to have a life of its own. It may recede but it will never completely fade."

"Then so be it. I think both of us are strong enough to survive."

"There is another way to handle this. The best solution, of course, would be to announce our engagement." His tone was matter-of-fact, as if discussing the price of coffee at Daisy's.

She couldn't imagine a more unenthusiastic marriage

proposal. "I told you before, I don't think we need go to that extreme."

His jaw worked for a moment, irritation coloring his expression. "Weren't you listening to a word I said?"

"Yes, and it's noble of you to offer such a *sacrifice*." The words tasted bitter on her tongue. "But you forget one thing. I'll be leaving for New York soon, and when I do, I'll be able to put all of this behind me." She gave him a direct look. "I'm sorry if that puts you in a bad light with the folks here. But it makes no sense for us to tie ourselves together if we are going to live our lives half a country apart."

Ward braced himself for the upcoming discussion. It was imperative that he change her mind. A part of him had hoped she would rethink her plan to move to New York by this time. But he could see now that it had been just foolish wishful thinking on his part.

Time to be practical and move past that. "And what if the gossip follows you there?"

She didn't register any concern on that score. "There's no reason to think it will. New York City is a big, bustling place with lots of other things to occupy people's thoughts and imagination besides a bit of small town gossip. But if it does follow me there, I think I'm strong enough to face it down."

He didn't doubt that for a heartbeat. But he didn't like to think of her dealing with such a trial alone. Especially when he'd played such a big part in placing her in that situation.

But he pressed on, playing what he figured was his trump card. "There's a part of this rumormongering that affects more than just you and me."

Hazel's expression softened into concern and she nodded. "Meg."

"Yes. There are apparently some people around here who feel she should be placed with more *suitable* folks until her situation is resolved."

"Eunice and Eula Fay hinted as much just before you walked in." Her expression took on a worried quality for the first time. "Oh, but taking her away from you would break that child's heart."

She nervously swiped at some hair that had fallen on her forehead. "I mean, I know you don't plan to keep her with you permanently, but to continue to move her about from family to family is just cruel."

"I agree. That's why I think we need to silence this talk as soon as possible. If the two of us were to bow to conventions, then there would be no reason for anyone to try to take Meg away."

She dropped her gaze and traced a circle on the counter. "But getting married just to appease the gossips seems to be going a bit too far."

"Not if we don't actually get married." He'd just thought of a way out of this, one that was a bit unorthodox. Would she go for it?

Her gaze shot back up to meet his and her brow arched in question.

"Announcing our engagement should be enough to settle things down for now," he explained. "I'm sure we can find believable reasons to postpone the actual wedding itself."

Her brows drew down in thought. "Postpone for how long?"

"Long enough to keep Meg with us until her situation is resolved."

She eyed him quizzically. "If the idea is to draw this

out, there are definitely ways to do that. For instance, as the town's seamstress with a professional reputation to uphold, I certainly wouldn't want to get married until I have the most glorious wedding gown ever constructed."

He smiled. "And just how long can you draw that out?"

She waved a hand airily. "As a demanding bride-to-be, I can find all kinds of little details to fuss over and all sorts of special materials to order from my aunt back east." She nodded. "I dare say it could take several weeks."

His smile broadened. "Perfect."

"Perfect? I don't understand. What are you suggesting?"

"First, I want you to understand that I am absolutely ready and willing to step up and give you the protection of my name if that is what you wish. In fact, given our situation, that would be my preference."

He held up his hand to stop the protest he saw forming on her lips. "But I have no desire to force you to do so if you feel you can make a better life for yourself in New York as a single woman."

She stared at him for a long moment, her expression remaining inscrutable. Then she gave a short nod. "I do."

"Then the next best thing will be for us to get engaged, temporarily."

"Temporarily engaged?"

"That's right. Once Meg's situation is safely resolved we can break it off."

"So, you don't really expect me to marry you?"

He tried to read her mood but her expression gave nothing away. "Not if you don't want to."

She hesitated a moment, then nodded. "Very well."

"So you agree to become engaged?"

"I just said so, didn't I? For Meg's sake."

Why did she sound so grumpy? Was the idea of an engagement to him so distasteful to her? Or was it just being forced into it by external forces that she objected to?

Then her expression shifted. "This feels wrong, deceitful."

"Would you prefer that we make it real? As I said, that's actually my preference." How much clearer could he be? Though he wasn't certain what answer he wanted her to give.

She fiddled with her collar, her expression troubled. "Going into a marriage for the wrong reasons feels like a lie too." She seemed to be gathering her courage. "Because you don't truly love me, not in that way, do you?"

How did one answer such a loaded question?

Truthfully.

"Hazel, I care for you a great deal. I suppose, in my own way, I do love you. But you need to understand something—"

She held up a hand, interrupting him. "There's no need to go on. Tagging a *but* of any sort onto a declaration like that says everything that needs to be said."

There was no way he was going to leave it at that. "For once, let me have my say, because you need to hear this."

Her gaze bore into his stubbornly for a moment and then she waved a hand, indicating he should go on.

"Thank you. What you need to know is about me and who I am. Being sheriff of this town is important to me. It's more than a job to me, it's a calling. It's the one way I can make a difference in this world, have a positive impact in a real way. And I know from experience that when I have divided loyalties I end up failing one or both. Because of that, I'm just not prepared to put having a wife above being sheriff."

He placed his hand over hers on the counter. "And you deserve someone who will always put you first."

Her expression had softened and she slowly nodded. "For what it's worth, I believe your thinking is wrong, that your heart and spirit are big enough to allow you to have both. But that's neither here nor there if *you* don't believe it. The question right now is how do we go forward without lying to all our friends?"

"I suppose, if it makes it more palatable for you, we could merely tell people that we are engaged, which is true. We don't mention a wedding or a wedding date." The warm softness of her hand beneath his, so small and delicate, was quite distracting. It took him a moment to notice that his words hadn't erased any of the worry lines in her face.

"That's just splitting hairs," she said.

He removed his hand and reined in his thoughts. "So, do you have a better suggestion?"

She grimaced, as if surprised he'd thrown it back in her lap. "Perhaps we should use this engagement period as a time to really and truly pray about it," she said slowly, "to try to discern God's plan for our future, whether it be together in name only as you suggested, or separate as I'm leaning toward. That leaves open the possibility at least that, in the end, we will marry after all."

He studied her carefully, his traitorous heart latching on to her implication. "Does that mean you really are open to the idea of marriage?"

"If we go through with this, that has to be how we

approach it. It's the only way to be true to ourselves and to our faith."

So why didn't she just outright agree to marry him? But he would take this small commitment since it was all she was willing to give right now.

Hazel gave him a half-smile. "Now that that's decided, how do we go about letting folks know?"

He allowed himself a wry smile. "I think that by telling just a few key people the word will get out quickly enough."

Hazel grinned. "I believe a visit to the mercantile may be on my agenda this afternoon. I can place an order for some special thread that I'll need for my wedding gown."

"And I should probably give the mayor an update on my latest findings."

Her expression shifted to one of eager interest. "Do you actually have some findings?"

His smile faded. "Nothing much. One of the varmints who broke into the Coopers' place last night stepped in a bit of spilled oil on his way out. I managed to find some tracks and followed them along Oak Street into the woods. But I lost the trail at the stream."

This time she squeezed his hand. "I have faith in you. You'll catch him soon."

"Thank you." He wasn't sure which affected him more, her obvious sincerity or the touch of her hand. Both made him want to succeed if only to keep from disappointing her.

Then he pulled his hand back to scratch his chin, wanting to distance himself from those feelings. He gave her a mock grimace. "I just wish the rest of the town felt the same way."

Before either of them could say more, Meg stepped

from the workroom, clutching her doll with one hand and rubbing her eyes with the knuckles of her other. She smiled when she saw Ward standing there. "Hello. Is it time for me to go to your house now?"

"Not yet, Half-pint. But I do need to talk to you."

He lifted her up and seated her on the counter. "We need to change things up a little bit."

She squeezed her doll closer to her chest. "Change what up?"

"Starting tonight, you're going to be sleeping here at Miss Hazel's place rather than at my place."

"Is it because you want your bed back?" Her words were rushed and had a desperate edge to them. "Because I can sleep on the sofa again."

"No, no, it's nothing like that. It's because I sometimes get called out in the middle of the night and you are so important to me that I want to keep you safe."

"I'm important?"

"Absolutely! So important that I want to make sure we still spend lots of time together."

"But you just said you want me to move here."

"At bedtime, yes. But that's the only thing that will change. You'll still come with me to my place after work, and we'll still take our meals together and walk Pugs and do everything else we did before."

"You promise?"

He gave her a quick hug, then stepped back. "I promise."

"Okay." Then she glanced Hazel's way. "Maybe Sheriff Gleason could sleep here, too, so we could all be together."

Ward coughed to cover his reaction to her innocent suggestion.

After a quick, reproving glance his way, Hazel smiled

down at the child. "That would be nice. But I'm afraid it isn't proper for a grown man and woman who aren't kinfolk and aren't married to live together."

"Oh." She appeared crestfallen but, to Ward's relief, didn't ask any additional questions.

He cleared his throat, then lifted Meg off the counter and set her on the floor. "Now, I need to get back to work, but I'll return around five thirty to take you gals to supper."

Hazel walked him to the door. "You don't have to keep buying my meals, you know. My financial situation isn't quite that dire."

Did she think that was the only reason he was inviting her? Perhaps he was doing a better job of hiding his feelings than he'd thought. Best to keep up the act.

He shrugged. "We're engaged now, remember? It'll be expected that we spend more time together, not less. Besides, I no longer have to concern myself with paying for Bethany's care so I have the funds to cover it."

Hazel tried to process what Ward had confided to her. How could he feel that he needed to fully dedicate himself to his job and sacrifice every other part of his life in order to make a difference? Didn't he realize it was the man he was inside that was important, not the job he held? But that way of thinking, as wrong as it was, explained so much about Ward. This was what had gotten twisted inside him when Bethany had her accident.

How could she help him to see how wrong he was? How much more he was and could be?

By the time Ward came by the emporium to escort her and Meg to supper, word of their engagement had spread through town. As they strolled down the sidewalk, they were stopped at least a dozen times by folks who wanted to offer congratulations.

Hazel smiled and accepted the well-wishes with what grace she could, but it felt wrong.

Then, as Ward seated Meg, the child looked at him with a puzzled expression. "What does being engaged mean?"

Hazel cut Ward a quick look, then realized he was leaving it to her to answer.

She turned to Meg, touching the child's knee to claim her attention. "When two people are engaged, it means they are thinking about getting married."

Meg immediately started bouncing in her seat. "You're getting married! Now we can be a real family."

Hazel looked at Ward, not quite certain how to respond to that.

But before either of them could say anything, Meg continued. "And that means after you're married we can all live in the same house together." She turned to Ward. "We should live in Miss Hazel's house 'cause it's got more room."

Ward finally spoke up. "We won't be getting married right away, Half-pint, so for now things need to stay the way they are."

"How long do we have to wait?"

"We're not sure yet."

Meg squirmed happily in her chair. "That's okay. I can wait." She lifted Chessie up until the doll was at eye level. "Did you hear that, Chessie? We're going to be a real family someday."

Hazel's gaze locked with Ward's and she saw the same concern she felt mirrored there. She closed her eyes and offered up a silent prayer that, whatever happened with her and Ward, they didn't break that little girl's heart. Or her trust.

And right now, she only saw one way to ensure that.

Was her and Ward's mutual reluctance to hurt Meg a strong enough foundation to base a marriage on?

Chapter Fifteen

It had been three days since she and Ward agreed to
announce they were engaged. The announcement had
even been printed in *The Turnabout Gazette*. And Hazel
still felt decidedly uncomfortable about the whole thing.
It wasn't just that she and Ward weren't sure they would
go through with the wedding—she'd come to terms
with that. Or at least as much as she could ever come
to terms with such a thing. It was more that everyone
in town knew, or at least suspected, that Ward had only
proposed to her because his hand had been forced.

Even when she received gushing congratulations, she
was left wondering what the well-wisher *really* thought
of the whole thing. The last thing she wanted was to be
an object of pity.

And adding to her general lack of peace over the
whole situation was that she couldn't stop thinking
about the explanation Ward had given her. Did he really view himself that way, as a man who had to remain
set apart, a man whose entire belief about who he was
as a person was tied to his role as sheriff? How heart-
breaking. Didn't he realize he could be so much more,
that he *was* so much more?

Her prayers had taken on a new intensity, a new focus. Regardless of what kind of future she and Ward had—or didn't have—together, she wanted to help him discover the man he was meant to be.

He'd believed in himself once, in how much more he could be. She remembered the boy, teasing his little sister and her friend, watching out for them, teaching them to fish and find the best skipping stones and how to tell when the wild persimmons were ripe enough to eat without puckering your mouth. That boy had been responsible and honorable, yes, but he'd had dreams too.

There had to be a way to get through to that part of him again.

Tensy showed up at the dress shop bright and early on Saturday morning but this time Hazel was ready for her. "Hello, Tensy. Your timing is impeccable. I have enough of your gown basted together to do an initial fitting."

As the two stepped into the fitting room, Hazel eagerly awaited her client's reaction. She'd added a few extra touches in an effort to cater to Tensy's desire for something princess-like. After all, she'd just paid the last invoice on her stock and she wouldn't be ordering any additional inventory. Except for the show she was putting on over her own wedding dress of course. She might as well get some use from what was already on hand. It would save her having to ship so much of it to New York.

She smiled at Tensy as she approached the dress form. "I'm really pleased with the way this turned out, I can't wait to see it on you."

Tensy nodded, studying the dress from several angles. "Oh, I really like the touch of beading on the bodice."

"I thought it would add some sparkle and flair to the dress."

Tensy nodded, then gave Hazel a sly smile. "Pa's been under the weather the past few days and I've had to take care of him so I'm just now hearing your good news. It looks like you may beat me to the altar."

Everything in Hazel froze as she tried to figure out how to respond to that. If only it were true.

But she kept a smile on her face and replied in as offhand a manner as she could. "Not necessarily. Sheriff Gleason and I don't plan to rush into this. I have to make my own gown, which will take some time. And of course I wouldn't dream of having a wedding without Verity here."

Tensy nodded as Hazel helped her ease the nearly complete dress over her head.

"I must say, I was surprised when I heard." The woman's voice was muffled beneath the fabric. "I thought you had your heart set on going to New York and pursuing a career there as a dress designer."

It had been more her mind than her heart that was set on it. "Plans change."

Tensy's head and arms finally came through the appropriate openings and she shook her head to settle her hair in place. Rather than looking at herself in the mirror, however, she studied Hazel. "Pardon me for saying so, but you don't have the joyful glow of a woman in love. I know it's not my place to be so personal, but as someone who knows what love is, I would hate for you to settle for something less."

If only Tensy knew just how much she agreed with her. But there wasn't much she could reveal about this mess she'd found herself in. "I appreciate your concern, but I assure you, I know what I'm doing." She prayed that was true.

Tensy continued to study her, a troubled expression on her face. Apparently Hazel hadn't been very convincing.

It was time to change the subject. She gestured toward the large cheval glass. "Look at how beautiful you are. Your groom won't be able to take his eyes off of you."

Tensy turned to the mirror and a delighted smile blossomed on her face. "Oh, Hazel, thank you. It's so beautiful."

Hazel gave her a hug. "It's you who are beautiful, the dress just helps you shine. Now, let me get some pins so we can see what adjustments need to be made."

Had Tensy been able to see through her happy-bride pretense because she hadn't seen a reflection of her own joy when she looked at her? Or was her own lack of belief that this wedding would ever take place seeping through for everyone to see?

She would have to be really careful how she conducted herself going forward.

"Are you making any progress in identifying who's responsible for all these senseless crimes?"

"Not yet." Ward faced the mayor across his desk, listening to yet another discussion of what a poor job he was doing.

"I've been getting complaints about the way you're handling this situation. Or rather *not* handling it."

He couldn't say as he was surprised. He'd heard the rumblings himself. "What kind of complaints?"

"Some think you're more concerned about that little girl and Miss Andrews than you are about doing your job."

Ward stiffened. "Since when is my personal life up for discussion? I've done a good job these past nine years. And I'll take care of business this time too. I'm getting closer to identifying the culprit."

"Identifying the culprit? Everyone knows it's the Lytle boys behind this. Frankly, I'm not sure why you haven't arrested them yet."

Ward swallowed a sarcastic retort. "I won't arrest them without proof. Besides, I don't think there's anyone in this town who believes all four of them would work together. Elmer's boys and Orson's boys would be more likely to go at each other than to join forces to commit these acts."

The mayor waved his words away with an irritable gesture. "I'm telling you, you need to figure this out, and quickly too."

"I'm working on it." Then he met the mayor's gaze and held it. "What are you not telling me?"

The man tugged on his vest in an officious gesture. "If you must know, there's some as say this is your first real test in all the years you've worn the badge. That you appear to have done a good job up till now because you've never been *challenged* until now." He leaned back in his chair. "For instance, when that Walker girl got kidnapped last year, you didn't have much of a hand in getting her back."

Ward's jaw tightened at this reminder of his past failure. The fact that it had happened quickly and then moved to another town was no excuse. "You keep repeating what 'some say.' What do *you* think?"

Mayor Sanders cleared his throat, his gaze shifting away from Ward's. "Look, you know I stand behind you. But I have a duty to this town to represent them to the best of my ability."

"And I have a duty to protect them to the best of *my* ability. And I take that job very seriously." Ward stood, ready to take his departure.

But the mayor wasn't quite done with him. "Of course you do. Just see that you don't let other—" he paused long enough to emphasize his point "—*distractions* keep you from tackling your job with the focus it requires."

Ward jammed his hat back on his head and spun on his heel without saying a word.

Mainly because he didn't trust himself to say anything.

The thing he'd feared all along about getting seriously involved with a woman was coming to pass. Truth be told, having Meg and Hazel in his life these past two weeks had felt really good, had made him feel like he was part of a real family again. But it *had* taken his focus away from his job. He enjoyed being in their company, perhaps a bit too much. The time he spent with them, however, was time he wasn't spending doing his job.

He needed to get Meg's situation resolved soon because, to be honest, he'd been dragging his feet a bit on that lately. And perhaps it would be best, for his ability to do his job, if not his personal happiness, if Hazel did go through with her plan to go to New York.

Strange how reaching those decisions brought him no joy whatsoever.

Chapter Sixteen

Monday morning started off slow in the Fashion Emporium. Most of the town had satisfied their curiosity about Meg and about Hazel and Ward's engagement, so the only folks with any reason to come by were legitimate customers. Which meant she had lots of time to work with Meg on her sewing skills.

In fact, the bell over the door didn't sound until about an hour before lunchtime. Hazel stepped out of the workroom and froze in place for a heartbeat. Then she squealed. "Verity!" she called out, rushing forward to embrace her friend. "Oh, I've missed you so much."

Verity laughed as she returned Hazel's embrace. "I missed you too."

Hazel released her friend with a puzzled frown. "But what are you doing back already? You were supposed to be gone for at least another week and a half."

Verity fiddled with a locket at her throat. "When Nate got word about the break-in, we decided to cut the trip short and come back right away."

"Oh, I'm so sorry. I know you two had been planning this trip for some time."

Verity waved a hand airily. "If you must know, I was

actually glad. I was ready to come home." Then she gave Hazel a sly smile. "But what's this I hear about you and Ward? Did the man finally come to his senses? I knew this would happen when he heard you were thinking about leaving town."

"How in the world did you hear about our engagement already? The train pulled into town less than an hour ago."

Verity grinned. "You know how quickly news travels around here. It was actually Lionel over at the depot who mentioned it." She placed her hands on her hips in mock-accusation. "I must say, I was insulted to have to hear the news from him instead of you. You could have sent me a telegram at the very least."

Had Lionel also mentioned the circumstances that forced Ward's hand? "About that…"

Verity's smile changed to uncertainty. "What's the matter? I—"

Hazel cleared her throat, cutting her friend off in mid-sentence as she realized Meg had stepped out of the workroom as well. "Meg, honey, come here a minute. I'd like you to meet a friend of mine."

The little girl came as far as Hazel's side and studied Verity shyly. "Hello."

To give Verity credit, other than throwing a quick, startled look Hazel's way, she gave no other sign that she was anything but delighted at the introduction. "Why, hello there," she said with a smile. "That's a very nice doll you have there."

Meg held the cloth creation up. "Her name is Chessie. Miss Hazel made her this dress." She held out one side of her skirt. "She made my dress too."

"Miss Hazel is a very good seamstress." Verity put a finger to her chin. "If I'd known there was a little girl visiting over here I would have brought Joy with me to meet you."

"Oh, I'm not visiting," Meg said. "I live here now. And one day Sheriff Gleason will live here, too, and we'll be a family."

This time Verity couldn't quite keep the surprise from her expression but she covered it quickly. "That sounds lovely."

"I know." There was a very self-satisfied note to Meg's voice.

"Well, then, perhaps I could bring Joy by later to meet you. Would you like that?"

Meg nodded, her pigtails bobbing enthusiastically.

Hazel gave Meg a bit of ribbon to entertain Buttons with, then drew Verity a short distance away.

"It seems you've been *very* busy while I was gone." Verity's expression was full of questions. "Who is she and are you and Ward truly adopting her?"

It seemed Lionel hadn't given Verity *all* of the gossip. Hazel quickly explained how Meg had come to be part of her and Ward's lives.

Verity seemed every bit as affected by Meg's story as she herself had been. "That's awful. How could her sister have done such a thing?"

"Reprehensible, I agree."

Then Verity's eyes narrowed in speculation. "Does Meg have something to do with your upcoming nuptials?"

Hazel moved to straighten a display of ribbons. "I'm pretty sure there won't be any nuptials. At least not between Ward and me."

"I don't understand."

"There was a…misunderstanding of sorts. The night someone broke into your place, I heard the intruder and ran to fetch Ward. Meg was staying with him at the time, and since he couldn't leave her alone, I volunteered to stay with her while he went out to investigate."

"Oh."

Hazel heard the note of understanding in her friend's voice and nodded. "Mr. Hill saw me leaving Ward's home just before dawn and drew the wrong conclusions."

Verity touched her arm, her expression one of soft sympathy. "Oh, Hazel, I'm so sorry."

Hazel shrugged, hating that she couldn't keep the heat from climbing into her cheeks. "Ward, naturally, felt the need to do *the honorable thing.* Which I told him was ridiculous, especially since I plan to leave Turnabout soon anyway."

"But, don't you think, even if you wed for the wrong reasons, love would eventually—"

She couldn't let Verity finish that thought. "Ward has made it very clear that it's not what he wants."

"But, I thought, I mean—"

"There was some talk of finding a more appropriate, less scandal-ridden home for Meg, even if that meant a children's asylum. Ward and I couldn't stand by and let that happen. So we got engaged but put off the wedding itself, using the creation of a proper wedding gown as an excuse." She waved toward the back of the shop. "Thus that extravagant monstrosity of a gown I have in the workroom. I figure I can keep working on it until it's time for me to leave for New York." Which, she supposed, would be soon since Verity was now home.

That thought left her feeling empty and sad.

"So you do still plan to leave?"

Hazel sighed. "It's not definite. Ward and I agreed to give a marriage, albeit a platonic one, serious consideration. But unless something changes, then yes, I will probably go ahead with my plans to move."

Verity glanced across the room. "Is Meg aware of your plans?"

"No. In fact, Ward is still operating under the belief that he will find another home for her."

Verity's brows drew down. "What do you mean *operating under the belief*?"

"He's holding out hope that there is some relative other than her sister who can take her in."

"And you?"

"I think it's very likely no such relative exists. And even if this person does exist, if Ward looks at what's best for Meg, he'll think twice about handing her off."

"Because?"

"Ward isn't ready to admit it yet, not even to himself, but he needs that little girl in his life. And she needs him."

"And you?"

She needed them both with a longing that was almost a physical ache. But some things just weren't meant to be. "For me, nothing has really changed since you left for your trip. Here in Turnabout, my business is still in decline and, engagement notwithstanding, Ward still has no inclination to be anything more than friends. On the other hand, I have my boisterous family in New York full of aunts, uncles and cousins too numerous to count, all of whom are more than ready to welcome me into their midst. And Aunt Opal has grand plans that will keep me fabulously busy learning new skills and doing a job I love. I'll be fine."

Verity jabbed one fist on her hip. "How can you say nothing has changed when *everything* has changed?

The man you love has proposed to you and the two of you are sharing the care of that little girl."

"He only proposed to me because he felt obligated."

"That may be what drove him to do it, but I doubt that is the only thing Ward Gleason feels toward you. I've seen the way he looks at you when he thinks no one is watching."

If only that were true. "At any rate, I don't have to decide anything right this minute." But soon. Much too soon.

Verity straightened. "I want to see this extraordinary wedding gown that is going to take you multiple weeks to create." She marched into the workroom and studied the work in progress draped on the dress form. "So how much longer do you think you can legitimately draw this out?"

"At least two weeks." She placed the fingertips of her right hand delicately over her heart. "There's not nearly enough beading and embroidery work on it for a finicky bride such as myself. And I absolutely must have some of the exquisite ribbon embellished with metallic threads I saw last time I was in New York."

Verity grinned. "And of course, now that I'm here, I must create a veil equal to the magnificence of the dress."

"Absolutely." Hazel gave her friend another hug. "It is so good to have you back home again."

Verity gave Hazel an arch look. "You know, I was serious when I said I was ready to return home."

Something about Verity's tone and expression told Hazel her friend had more to say. "Were you not enjoying the trip?"

"Oh, we were having a fine time. Although I did begin to feel a bit under the weather the past few days."

Hazel eyed her friend closely, searching for signs of poor health. "Are you okay?"

"Very much so." She grinned and patted her stomach. "Though it'll probably be about eight more months until I'm completely back to normal."

It took a heartbeat for Hazel to understand her meaning and then she squealed in delight. She embraced her friend in an enthusiastic hug. "A baby. Oh, Verity, this is wonderful news."

"Thank you. Nate and I are quite happy about it."

"And Joy?"

"We haven't told her yet. We want to wait a few more weeks—eight months is such a long time for a little girl to wait."

"It's a pretty long time for a grown-up girl to wait as well."

Verity grimaced. "I know. And Nate is already getting overly solicitous."

Hazel tried to ignore the little stab of envy. "There are worse problems to face."

Verity touched her friend's arm in a gesture of sympathy, then changed the subject. "I must say, I was surprised when we arrived to find that Nate's shop was not nearly as chaotic and messy as I'd feared. Something tells me I have you to thank for that."

Hazel waved a hand dismissively. "I just straightened a few things here and there. Ward wanted to know if anything was missing but I'm afraid I wasn't familiar enough with the shop to be able to say."

"Nate's going through the merchandise now. It doesn't appear that whoever it was made it upstairs to our living quarters, thank goodness." She gave Hazel a troubled look. "And the sheriff has no idea who's been doing this?"

"If he does, he's not saying." She clasped her hands together as the two of them moved back into the main shop area. "Oh, Verity, people are saying the most awful things about Ward. It's as if they don't think he's good enough to be the sheriff anymore."

"I'm sure they don't mean any such thing. Folks are likely just upset that the culprit is still on the loose."

"Even so, I'll be glad when this whole thing is resolved. I don't think I can leave Turnabout until it is."

Verity gave her a crooked grin. "That almost makes me wish the culprit would never be caught."

Before Hazel could do more than smile, Eunice Ortolon and Mrs. Sanders stepped into the emporium.

Hazel swallowed her groan and pasted a welcoming smile on her face. "What can we do for you ladies?"

Eunice looked to Verity as she responded. "We were passing by and saw the Coopers were back in town. We just wanted to welcome you home."

Verity smiled, apparently ready to take the greeting at face value. "Thank you, Eunice, Eula Fay. It's nice to be back."

From the corner of her eyes, Hazel saw Tensy pausing on the threshold. Her eyes had widened like a startled deer's and she looked ready to bolt. Hazel remembered she had a fitting today, something she probably wouldn't want anyone, most especially these two women, to know about.

Before the future bride could retreat, however, Mrs. Sanders turned and caught sight of her. "Well, hello, Tensy. Are you in the market for a new dress or hat?"

"I, uh—"

Hazel quickly spoke up. "Tensy, you must be here to look at those ribbons I talked to you about. They're in that blue bin over there on the far wall if you want to look them over and decide which ones you like best. I can be with you in just a few minutes."

The woman gave her a grateful nod and scurried toward the other end of the room.

Eunice turned back to Verity, continuing as if they hadn't been interrupted. "You're home early, are you not? Is it because of the break-in? We were all so shocked when we heard about it."

Verity's expression gave nothing away. "It was unpleasant news to hear, of course, but I was ready to come home anyway."

Hazel smiled at this reminder of her friend's good news.

"Well, I know just how horribly devastated you must feel." Eunice dramatically placed a hand over her heart. "I, too, was a victim of this criminal's actions."

Verity's expression turned suitably sympathetic. "I'm so sorry to hear that, Eunice. Was the boardinghouse broken into as well?"

The woman's face reddened. "Not exactly. The shameful hooligan had the temerity to invade my yard in broad daylight and scatter my clean laundry all about the grounds."

Hazel noticed she refrained from mentioning the specifics of the culprit's actions.

"I for one think this has been going on for much too long." Mrs. Sanders declared. "There are a number of us who think it's time to talk about whether Ward Gleason is still the right man for the job of sheriff."

Hazel stiffened, prepared to defend Ward's reputation. After what he'd told her, she knew how devastating it would be for him if the town lost faith in him.

But Verity placed a hand on her arm and spoke first. "Sheriff Gleason is a good man who is doing a very good job of enforcing the law in Turnabout. Neither I nor Nate hold him in any way accountable for what happened at our place."

"No one is saying he's not a good man. Just that perhaps he is no longer a good sheriff." Eunice probably intended for her expression to be pleasant. She failed.

Hazel stiffened. "You can't mean that."

"I'm sorry, Hazel, I know this must be unpleasant to hear. As his fiancée, you would naturally want to believe the best of him." Eunice gave her a condescending smile. "Then again, it's not as if yours is a love match."

Eunice's pitying tone set Hazel's teeth on edge.

Again Verity stepped in before Hazel could trust herself to speak. "I think it's rather presumptuous to think we truly know another's heart, don't you?" Her expression remained pleasant but her tone was firm.

Eunice's expression shifted uncertainly, as if she wasn't quite certain if she'd been insulted or not.

Even as angry as Hazel was at the moment, she couldn't help but admire Verity's ability to deliver a pointed set-down with grace and a charming demeanor.

"Be that as it may, this is not a matter for us ladies to decide," Eula Fay said primly. Then she turned a concerned look Hazel's way, one Hazel didn't find at all convincing. "My husband was just saying that it's time we took a closer look at Sheriff Gleason's handling of this situation. The council is contemplating calling a special town meeting to hear what folks have to say on the matter."

"And if they do," Hazel responded with a kind of angry confidence, "they will no doubt learn that most folks around here support Sheriff Gleason and would be appalled to hear anyone doubts his abilities to do his job."

Her words earned her another round of pitying looks that set her fingernails stabbing into her palms.

"That's very loyal of you, dear. One would expect nothing less from the sheriff's fiancée."

"Well, thank you for stopping by and for the welcome home," Verity said as she ushered them toward the door with a sweet, innocent smile on her face. "As soon as I've had a chance to unpack and settle back in, you'll have to let me tell you all about the trip."

"Why, yes, of course. Good day to you." And with slightly dazed looks on their faces, the two ladies made their exit.

Once the door closed behind them, Verity returned to Hazel's side and touched her arm in a sympathetic gesture. "I wouldn't pay them much mind. You know how they're always making mountains out of molehills and trying to stir things up."

"It just makes me so angry—" A movement across the room reminded Hazel that they weren't alone.

Taking a deep breath, she turned and smiled at her customer. "Sorry, Tensy, I didn't mean to ignore you."

Verity straightened. "I need to get back to help Nate go through the inventory. We'll talk again soon." And with that, she too was gone.

"For what it's worth," Tensy said as she approached, "Pa and I agree with you. Even though these trespassers worked their mischief at our place three different times, we don't blame Sheriff Gleason for it. He's a good man and I know he'll eventually arrest someone for this."

Hazel was glad to hear those words of support for Ward after what those other two had said. "Let's hope you are in the majority. The sheriff could use a nice strong show of support right now."

Realizing Ward wouldn't want her discussing him

this way, she changed the subject. "Now, let's see which ribbons you selected."

As she discussed the pros and cons of the different selections Tensy had made, Hazel couldn't get Eunice and Eula Fay's comments out of her mind. How widespread was this discontent they'd mentioned? Would the town council seriously consider asking him to step down?

She couldn't let that happen. When and if that town meeting was called, she'd make certain she was there and that her voice was heard, even if she was a woman. If the people of Turnabout needed to be reminded of all the good Ward Gleason had done for this town, then she was more than willing to do so.

Later that evening, while Meg studied the books in Abigail's library, Ward carefully studied the menu. "I suppose you know the Coopers are back," he said without looking up.

She nodded. "Verity stopped by the emporium to let me know."

"Of course she did."

He paused but she could tell he had something on his mind so she held her peace.

"How does this affect your departure date?" he finally asked. "If you're still planning to leave, that is."

"I have not yet decided one way or the other," she said carefully. Which wasn't entirely a lie. She still held onto a smidgen of hope that Ward would find a place in his heart for her. "But even if I do decide to leave, I don't think I can go until I know that Meg will be well cared for."

His mood seemed to lighten after that and she was almost sorry to have to darken it again. But it needed to be said. "Eunice and Mrs. Sanders came by the emporium again today."

Ward raised a brow. "Twice in one week. Lucky you. Are they looking for some fancy new frocks?"

She rolled her eyes at his frivolous question. "They came in ostensibly to welcome Verity back to town."

"Ostensibly?"

"They also wanted to commiserate with her about the break-in at her place. Which gave them the opportunity to say what a poor job they think you're doing about finding the culprit."

Except for the fact that a muscle near his mouth jumped, his expression remained impassive. "Everyone's entitled to their own opinion."

The man could be so maddening. "Will you stop pretending this doesn't bother you? This is me you're talking to and I'm on your side."

He spread his hands. "And what do you suggest I do? My getting all riled up about folks' attitudes is not going to change anyone's mind."

"You need to stand up for yourself. Let folks know you believe in yourself."

He gave her a disgruntled look. "Don't you go telling me how to act now. I've had enough—"

"Are you two fighting?" Meg's eyes were big, her expression troubled as she looked from one to the other of them.

Hazel mentally kicked herself for not realizing Meg had returned. The child didn't need any other disruptions in her life. "Oh no, sweetheart. We're just having a disagreement. It's nothing for you to be concerned about."

"Is that why you're leaving and going way far away?"

How had she heard about that? "Of course not. And I still haven't decided for sure if I'm going."

"So you might stay here with us?" She took Ward's hand as she asked her question.

The hopeful note in her voice shot straight to Hazel's heart. But she couldn't make a promise she wasn't certain she could keep. "Like I said, I haven't decided yet." She gave Meg a hug, then helped her into her chair. "Now, let's have a look at the new book you picked out, shall we?"

Ward was concerned about Meg. She'd only picked at her supper and when they'd walked Hazel home afterward, she'd been uncharacteristically quiet despite Hazel's attempts to draw her out. She'd also seemed subdued when they took Pugs for his evening walk.

He found Half-pint's continued quiet and unhappy expression disquieting. Over the past few days he'd not only gotten used to her bubbly disposition but had grown to enjoy it. This quiet, listless child was foreign to him.

Was she still worried about what she'd perceived as an argument between him and Hazel? Or was it because she feared Hazel was leaving? Should he try to discuss either or both situations with her or let her work things out for herself?

He was still pondering that question as they returned from their walk. "Would you like to play a game of checkers?" he asked. He'd been teaching her how to play the past few evenings and she seemed to enjoy the challenge of it. He was discovering she had a delightful competitive streak.

But she hugged Chessie and looked at him with tired eyes. "Can we just read a story now?"

"Sure." He'd thought he'd figured this parenting duty out but he was back to feeling entirely inadequate again. "Get your book and let's sit on the sofa."

She fetched the book from the bench where they'd placed it when they came in, then handed it to him before climbing up on the sofa. Pugs jumped up beside her, inserting himself between Ward and the girl.

Ward wasn't sure what to do. How could he give the little girl the reassurances she obviously wanted and still tell the truth? He cleared his throat. "You know, Half-pint, Miss Hazel and I both care for you very much."

She nodded. "And me and Chessie care for both of you very much too."

"And even if, for some reason, we don't get married, that doesn't mean either of us will love you any less."

Her lower lip trembled slightly. "But if you don't get married then we won't all be a family."

He wasn't sure what he'd do if she started crying. "That's not true. People don't have to live in the same house to be a family."

Her lip stopped trembling and she wrinkled her nose. "They don't?"

"Of course not. Why, Miss Hazel has a lot of family that lives all the way over in New York, but they are still her family. And she still loves them and they love her."

"Oh."

She didn't seem entirely convinced so he tried again. "I promise, we will both love you, no matter what." He brushed the hair from her forehead and then frowned. The girl was burning up. His perception of her listlessness shifted and his pulse kicked up in alarm. No wonder she'd been so lethargic—she was ill, not unhappy. How could he have missed the signs?

He scooped up the girl and stood. "How are you feeling, Half-pint?" he asked as he headed for the door.

"Don't be mad. I'm okay."

"You're not okay. And I'll only be mad if you lie to me."

She swallowed and hugged her doll tighter. "My head hurts and my tummy does too. And I'm hot." She looked up at him with watery eyes. "But I'll be good, I promise."

Had someone made her feel bad about getting sick before? "I know you will. But next time you feel bad I want you to tell me, okay?" He kissed her feverish forehead as he reached for the doorknob.

"Are you taking me to Miss Hazel's now?"

"No, I'm taking you to see Dr. Pratt. He's going to make you feel better." Ward prayed that was true.

He wouldn't delay getting Meg to the doctor by detouring to Hazel's place but he did need to let her know what was going on. If for no other reason than that she would be worried if he didn't show up with Meg at the appointed time. He could drop Meg off with the doctor and then run by Hazel's to let her know what was going on. But that didn't—

As he approached Dr. Pratt's place, he spotted Riley Walker, who lived in the house next door.

The man leaned forward on his porch rail. "Hey, Sheriff, is something wrong?"

"Meg here isn't feeling well. Would you mind going down to Miss Andrews's place and asking her to meet me at Doc's?"

Riley straightened and started down his steps. "Of course."

That problem taken care of, Ward hurried to the clinic, praying it was nothing serious.

Chapter Seventeen

Hazel practically ran all the way to Dr. Pratt's clinic. As soon as she entered, she rushed up to Ward and placed a hand on his arm, trying to catch her breath. "Mr. Walker told me Meg was sick. How is she?"

Ward closed his hand over hers. "I don't know, Doc hasn't finished examining her yet."

"What was wrong with her?"

"She's got a fever and a stomachache." He gave her a haunted look. "Do you know she was afraid to tell me she was sick because she thought I'd get angry?"

"Oh, that poor lamb."

Before they could say more, Dr. Pratt came out of the examining room.

They both turned to face him and Hazel braced herself for whatever he had to say. Then she felt Ward's hand snake around her shoulder and give her a squeeze and she suddenly felt like whatever the news was, the two of them would handle it together.

"Where's Meg?" Hazel asked.

"What's wrong with her?" Ward asked at the same time.

"Meg is with my wife, who is giving her a draught

to make her more comfortable. As for what's wrong with her—" he shrugged "—children get fevers from time to time for seemingly no reason at all. It's part of growing up."

"But you don't think it's serious?"

"No. In fact she'll probably be her old self by morning."

Hazel inhaled her first calm breath since Mr. Walker had delivered the news. "What do we do now?"

"Well, since I take it neither of you are familiar with taking care of children who are ill, it might be best to let her stay here overnight, just so we can keep an eye on her. Betty can sit with her."

Feeling more reassured the longer he spoke, Hazel smiled. "Thank you, that's a very kind offer. And I think we'll take you up on it."

She cut a quick glance Ward's way to make certain he had no objection. At his nod she turned back to the doctor. "But I don't want to put your wife to any extra trouble. Besides, Meg would be happier if she had someone she knows sit with her. Would it be all right if I stay?" She was pretty sure she wouldn't get much sleep at home anyway.

Dr. Pratt nodded with an understanding smile. "Of course." He spread his hands. "Meg is the only patient here tonight so there are extra beds in the clinic and a couple of comfortable chairs for visitors. Feel free to make use of them."

Ward gave her shoulder another squeeze, then let his arm drop. "I'll stay too."

"If you like." Dr. Pratt looked from one to the other of them, his expression indulgent, as if they were Meg's actual parents.

Hazel turned back to Ward. "There's no point in both of us staying with her."

But he shook his head. "She's my responsibility too." He rubbed his chin. "I tell you what, though, why don't we take shifts? I'll escort you home and come back to sit with Half-pint for a few hours. Then, when it's time for me to make my rounds, you can take over."

"I don't know…"

Dr. Pratt cleared his throat. "If you don't want to go back home, we have a spare bedroom you can use until your shift."

Hazel thought that over. The doctor's home was attached to the clinic so she would be only steps away if something happened with Meg. And it made sense that they take shifts. She met Ward's gaze, giving him her best attempt at sternness. "I want your word that you'll fetch me if Meg gets worse. And that you'll let me take my shift."

He raised his hands palms out in a sign of surrender. "I promise."

Hazel turned to the doctor. "Then, if you're sure Mrs. Pratt won't mind, I'll take you up on your very kind offer. Right after I go in and say good night to Meg."

Ward left the clinic to do some late-night patrolling. He'd got in the habit of making extra rounds the past several nights in an effort to catch, or at least deter, the town's habitual lawbreaker.

He rubbed the back of his neck wearily. At least it appeared Dr. Pratt had been right, Half-pint was going to be fine. She was already sleeping more comfortably and hadn't even stirred when Hazel had come in to take her shift.

But tonight's scare had revealed something to him in a very powerful way.

Half-pint had come to mean a great deal to him, had actually begun to feel a part of him. Discovering she was sick and that he hadn't even realized it had, for just a moment, put him right back into the skin of that scared youth who'd found his sister twisted and crumpled on the barn floor all those years ago.

Seeing Half-pint in pain had stabbed him with a keen sense of helplessness, knowing he couldn't take any of it on himself for her. It was a feeling he didn't like, not one bit.

The other thing he'd discovered tonight, if he was being entirely honest with himself, was that Hazel was becoming important to his world as well. Standing side by side with her while waiting to learn if there was something seriously wrong with Meg, watching his own worry mirrored in her expression, had given him a taste of what it would be like to share his responsibilities and burdens with her. It had touched something deep inside him, something warm and vulnerable and yearning.

Something he hadn't let himself feel in a very long time.

Something he wasn't sure he wanted to let himself feel even now.

Ward resisted the urge to growl out loud. The lack of sleep was starting to wear on him. He needed to focus on his job, stay alert for any signs that the culprit was skulking about.

It frustrated him that he still wasn't any closer to capturing the perpetrator than he'd been before. There was something about this whole situation he was missing, some reason whoever was doing this was, well, doing this. At least there hadn't been any further incidents since the one at the Coopers' nearly a week ago. Maybe the culprit had finally tired of the whole thing. Or accomplished whatever it was he'd wanted to accomplish.

An out-of-place sound caught his attention, a disruption he couldn't quite place. Whatever it was, it had stirred up several of the dogs in the area as well. It appeared to be coming from the vicinity of Main Street.

Ward headed off at a run, praying it was nothing more than someone out for a late-night stroll or a tomcat on the prowl.

But his gut told him it was something more.

He slipped behind the town hall and stopped in his tracks. Someone had pried open the back door, which now hung open. Whoever was doing all this had just taken his crime spree to a whole new level. It took a train-car-load of audacity to break into the governing seat of the town this way.

Ward slipped inside but knew he wouldn't find the culprit there—the dogs had no doubt marked the progress of the invader's getaway flight. He lit a lamp, bracing himself for whatever damage he'd see inside.

The large room used for trials and town meetings was in disarray, with chairs tipped over and pictures on the wall tilted crazily, but nothing more than nuisance activity. When he stuck his head in the mayor's office, however, he found an entirely different story. Books had been pulled off of shelves, papers scattered and torn, an inkwell spilled on a rug in front of the desk and the town map that normally hung on the wall behind the mayor's desk was down on the worktable and the glass that had covered it was cracked.

If Mayor Sanders wanted another reason to fire Ward, he'd certainly have it now.

Taking a deep breath, Ward moved on to check the rest of the building.

It was nearly dawn by the time he returned to the clinic. He'd spent some time at Town Hall looking for any clues that the intruder might have left behind but they were scant.

Then he'd had the pleasure of waking the mayor and informing him of what had happened. That meeting had not gone well. Ward was definitely ready for some more pleasant company.

He stepped into the clinic to see Hazel sitting in the outer office, sipping on a cup of coffee.

"How's Meg this morning?"

"A little quieter than normal but otherwise fine. Dr. Pratt is checking on her now." She gave him a crooked smile. "I never realized all the little worries that go into parenting."

Is that how she saw herself, as Meg's mother? He was pretty sure that's how Meg viewed her as well.

That boded well for the plan that had been forming in the back of his mind. It was looking more and more like no one was going to come forward to take responsibility for Half-pint. And even if some long-lost relative were found, he didn't think anyone would do a better job of raising, or loving, the little girl than Hazel would. He thought it would be best all the way around if he asked Hazel to take Meg in even if she and he didn't marry. That would give Half-pint the opportunity to grow up in a good home with a mother who loved her.

Even if that home was in New York.

Ward shoved that thought away as he scrubbed a hand over his face. He needed a shave.

"Dr. Pratt says I can take her home just as soon as he's done checking her."

"That's a relief. If you don't mind, I need to get back to my place and get cleaned up before I start the day."

Hazel frowned. Had Ward been up all night? Studying him more closely, she saw beyond the weariness in his eyes to the tightness of his jaw. "What's wrong? Did something happen after you left here last night?"

He gave a short nod. "Someone broke into Town Hall and made a mess of the meeting room. They also did significant damage to the mayor's office itself."

"Oh, Ward, I'm so sorry." Of all places to attack, the criminal couldn't have struck a sharper blow to Ward other than striking his own place. She saw the frustration and self-recrimination on his face.

"I was too late, again. Maybe everyone is right."

"No." She reached out for him instinctively, placing a hand on his chest. She couldn't bear to hear that self-doubt in his voice. "Don't even think that. You're a *good* sheriff but you're just one man. You can't be everywhere at once and no one should expect that of you."

He placed his hands over hers, pressing it more firmly against his chest. The beat of his heart under her hand was strong and steady and his gaze bore into hers as if seeking some answer there. For an eternity of seconds they stood that way, gazes and hands locked together.

Then his expression closed, he gave her hand a squeeze and he stepped back.

But her spirits fell when she realized her words and his tender gesture hadn't made any difference, the self-recrimination was still there in his eyes.

"Tell Half-pint I'll be by to check on her later this morning." And with a tip of his hat, he turned and made his exit.

Hazel watched him leave, raising her hand to her cheek. She could still feel the beat of his heart, the warmth of his hand capturing hers. Hadn't he felt that connection between them the way she had?

If he had, he was doing a poor job of showing it.

But she was being selfish, thinking about her own feelings. He'd been dealt a blow tonight and it had obviously hit him hard. The fact that he'd left without looking in on Meg was evidence enough he was not himself.

She wanted to help him but didn't quite know how.

Why was this person plaguing the town this way? Did he consider it a lark of some sort, a prank to boast of? Was it really a boy or could it be a grown man? Whoever it was, did he have any idea how his actions were affecting good, decent folks even beyond the direct victims?

He should be ashamed of himself no matter how old he was.

Hazel paced across the room and back again.

What would the mayor do? Surely they wouldn't seriously consider firing Ward? That would—

Dr. Pratt walked in, then paused and gave her a searching look. "Is everything all right?"

She forced a smile. "Yes, of course. I'm just anxious to get Meg back home."

"Of course. You can go on back to see her. You can take her home as soon as you're ready."

With a nod, Hazel headed back to the patient area of the clinic. She pasted a smile on her face, imbuing it with as much warmth as she could muster.

No point in giving Meg something to worry about.

She was doing enough worrying for the both of them.

Chapter Eighteen

By midmorning, one would never be able to tell by looking at Meg that she had been sick the night before. She and Verity's daughter, Joy, were sitting on the floor in a pool of sunlight by the display window, playing with their dolls while being watched over by an indolent Buttons.

"Does it ever get any easier?" Hazel asked Verity. "Being responsible for a little one, I mean."

Verity glanced fondly at the little girls. "I'm afraid not. But never doubt for a moment that it isn't worth every bit of worry. A child is an incredible gift from God, and one that brings such abiding joy." The milliner touched her stomach in a protective gesture.

Hazel had no trouble relating to what Verity had just said. She might not be Meg's blood kin, but she loved the child every bit as much as a real mother could.

"I heard about the break-in at Town Hall last night." Verity's tone was full of sympathy and understanding.

Hazel grimaced. "You and everyone else in town."

"I hear the mayor has called a special meeting to discuss this whole vandalism matter with the town."

"I'm not surprised. He hasn't been secretive about

how unhappy he is that Ward hasn't made an arrest yet. It's almost as if folks are blaming Ward for these incidents."

Verity touched her arm lightly. "Don't worry. I think the mayor will be surprised at just how many friends Ward has in this town."

"But how many of those people will be willing to speak up in his support?"

"He can definitely count on Nate and me."

"I'm sure he'll appreciate that."

Ready to change the subject, Hazel waved to the dress form that was situated near the large mirror on the back wall. "What do you think of the progress I've made on my wedding gown?"

Verity grinned. "I noticed when I came in that you have it on display. That was deliberate, I take it."

Hazel nodded with a demure grin. It was strategically placed, putting it in easy view from just about every portion of the shop. "I'm so proud of it that I wanted everyone to see."

"To see that it's not yet ready, you mean."

"That too."

Eve Dawson came in just then, wanting to speak to Verity about a new hat. Hazel left them to it while she headed for the wedding gown in progress. Grabbing her pincushion, she went to work pinning a row of lace across the bodice, taking great pains to ensure the row was perfectly straight. There would be two dozen such fussy, overlapping rows before she was done.

As Hazel worked, she imagined what her real wedding dress might look like, the one she would make if she truly were to get married. It would be a smoky blue-gray color, the exact shade of Ward's eyes, she decided, not this prim ivory.

Rather than a full skirt that would need a large number of stiff petticoats to support it, hers would be narrower, trumpet-shaped.

And no lace. Instead there would be satin cording creating subtle yet elegant patterns and perhaps a richly dressed satin underskirt that would peek out near the hem. The bodice would have some seed pearls or perhaps some soft floral appliqués.

The silhouette would be feminine yet strong.

She could imagine herself in such a dress, walking down the aisle to join her waiting groom, who would look at her with admiration and love.

But of course, imagining it was as close as she was likely to come.

The prick of the pin against her finger brought her focus back to the task at hand. She certainly didn't want to get blood on the dress she was making. Because if she did go through with this sham of a marriage, she would be stuck wearing this dress.

Which, like the ceremony it would be part of, was superficial and without heart.

Ward's day hadn't gotten any better as the morning progressed. At the mayor's insistence, he'd hauled in all four of the younger Lytle boys and questioned them individually about the incidents. By the end he'd been more convinced than ever that it couldn't have been one of them. They were hotheads and were quite capable of destroying things in the heat of the moment. But none of them seemed conniving or patient enough to have planned and carried out these incidents.

Of course that wasn't the answer the mayor wanted and it still didn't lead him to any answers. By noon Ward was in a foul mood and sent word to Hazel that she and Meg should go on to lunch without him. Not only did he not want his mood to keep from souring their day, but ever since last night he'd wondered if it wouldn't be a good idea for him to start pulling back from Half-pint a bit. It would help prepare the little girl for the not-too-distant day when he might have to send her away with Hazel.

Because he was pretty sure Hazel was going to follow through with her plans to leave Turnabout.

And to leave him.

Ward slammed his fist on his desk. This self-pity was getting him nowhere. Time to focus back on his job.

If he couldn't do anything about the things happening in Turnabout, perhaps he should try following up on some of his leads where Meg was concerned.

He grabbed his hat and headed out the door, turning toward the telegraph office.

Fifteen minutes later, when he returned to his office, he found it was no longer unoccupied.

"Hi, Sheriff Gleason!" Meg came running up to him, arms outstretched for a hug. "Are you surprised?"

"I certainly am, Half-pint." He reached down and picked her up. "But what's all this?"

His desk had been cleared of its normal clutter and was now spread with a small cloth topped with a feast. Hazel stood nearby smiling expectantly.

"Miss Hazel said since you were too busy to get your own lunch, we should bring it to you. She called it an office picnic surprise." Meg giggled. "Isn't that funny?"

He tapped the little girl's nose and set her down, meeting the clever dressmaker's gaze. "Miss Hazel says lots of funny things."

She had a very smug, pleased-with-herself grin on her face. Did she suspect his reason for cancelling?

Shaking his head at Hazel's ability to get around his attempts to keep his distance, Ward turned back to Meg. "It looks like you're feeling better today than you were last night."

She nodded. "I'm all better. Dr. Pratt is a nice man." Then she tugged on his hand. "Come see what all we brought."

Ward allowed her to lead him across the room and studied the food arranged picnic-style on his desk. There were thick slices of roast liberally topped with a rich-looking gravy, butter beans cooked with bacon and some smothered potatoes. And the picnic was staged for three.

He raised a brow as he turned back to Hazel. "You prepared all of this?"

She grinned. "You are not the only person in this town, Ward Gleason, who knows how to purchase food from Daisy Fulton." She waved him to a chair. "Now, if you will say grace, Meg and I are ready to eat even if you aren't."

And for the first time today, the smile that curved his lips felt genuine and unstrained.

Once he'd done as he was told and they dug into the meal, Meg started chattering away about her morning.

"I made a new friend today," she told Ward proudly.

"You did? That sounds like fun."

"Oh yes. Her name is Joy. And she has a doll named Rosie so Chessie has a new friend too." She squirmed happily in her seat. "We had a tea party today and Miss Hazel gave us pretty cups and a teapot to use. And we borrowed one of her music boxes so we would have music for our tea party."

"That sounds like it must have been a very fine party." Yep, Hazel was going to make a good mother for Half-pint. Too bad that couldn't happen right here in Turnabout so he could be a part of it.

Then again, it was probably best he wasn't. But it was getting harder by the day to remember that being sheriff and having a family didn't mix.

"I heard about the town meeting that's been called."

Hazel's quiet statement and concerned look reinforced what he'd been thinking.

"There's no need to discuss that now." He tilted his head meaningfully Meg's way.

But she didn't take the hint. "I just wanted to let you know I plan to be there and so are a lot of other folks who support you."

"It's not necessary for you to be there. I'm sure some would find it a little too heated." Again he indicated Meg.

Hazel got that stubborn, mulish expression on her face that indicated she was about to dig in her heels on something. "I wouldn't dream of missing it. And by the way, Verity's aunt will be watching over Joy and Meg this evening so the Coopers can go as well."

At least she'd thought that far ahead. "There's still no need for you to go out of your way. But if you must go, there's certainly no need for you to get too deeply involved in the discussion." There was no telling what she would say if push came to shove. Hazel was good at giving impassioned speeches when she felt strongly about something, but that was not what he needed right now.

She gave him a haughty look as she stabbed a few hapless beans with her fork. "As a citizen of this town, I have every right to speak my mind on the issues that affect it and that's what I intend to do."

That's just what he was afraid of.

* * *

Hazel's stomach was churning nervously as she walked to the town hall meeting with Verity and Nate. She hadn't gotten a clear sense of what Ward was feeling at lunch today and she hadn't seen or spoken to him since. The man held too much of his feelings inside, took too much blame and responsibility onto his broad shoulders.

What would the mood of those in attendance be— supportive, blaming, undecided? She knew with absolute certainty that Ward would not want her speaking up in his defense if things turned ugly—he'd all but said as much. But she wasn't sure she could go along with that.

When they walked into the meeting room, it was already crowded. Hazel studied the room itself for a moment. Everything looked as it should—any traces of whatever had happened in here last night were gone.

The people here, however, were another matter. Folks were abuzz with talk. The room was packed and everyone was obviously feeling passionate about the upcoming discussion.

Her gaze immediately sought out Ward.

He sat at the front of the room with the town council but held himself slightly apart.

His gaze latched on to hers as soon as she looked his way and the connection was both immediate and intense. The fierce emtional link between them almost stole her breath. She'd already taken a half-step in his direction when his expression closed off and he deliberately looked away. The message was clear; she was to keep her distance.

Still feeling somewhat unsettled from what had just passed between them, Hazel returned to her assessment of the room. People were gathered in small groups and both voices and gestures were animated. How many of these folks were here to support Ward? And how many were ready to turn their backs on him?

One thing was for certain—no matter what Ward's feelings were on the matter, she would not hold her tongue if insults started flying.

She made her way across the room and noted that several of those she assumed were Ward's detractors wouldn't quite make eye contact with her. Being Ward's fiancée put her into this discussion, whether Ward wanted to admit that or not.

She caught snatches of conversations from various groups.

"The hooligans have no shame! And no one's doing anything…"

"He didn't have trouble handling the job until recently. If he'd just put aside these distractions, he…"

"Everyone knows who did it. Why won't he just…"

Verity touched her arm. "Why don't we take a seat? It's almost time."

With a nod, Hazel walked down the center aisle, head high. She took a seat in the very front row, eyeing Ward defiantly.

Almost immediately, the mayor pounded his gavel and the talk slowed as folks began to take their seats.

Once things settled down, Mayor Sanders called the assembly to order. "This special town meeting has been called today to discuss the crisis that has hit our town."

Hazel shifted irritably in her seat. The man was being unnecessarily dramatic.

"First, we'll let Sheriff Gleason give us a report of what progress he's made in handling these criminal activities. Then we'll give anyone else who wants to speak on the matter the opportunity to do so."

The mayor then swiveled his chair slightly to face Ward and leaned back. "Sheriff Gleason, would you please give us a report of what your investigation into this rash of crimes has unearthed to date?"

As if he'd been merely asked to discuss the weather, Ward nodded and got unhurriedly to his feet. "Over the past three and a half weeks, there have been eight incidents involving six different locations. On two occasions, a culprit was spotted but in both cases it was just a split-second glimpse, not enough to make an identification. I've investigated each scene and talked to anyone who might have information, but so far I have uncovered very few clues to point to the identity of the perpetrator."

Glen Bastrop, the town councilman who sat to the mayor's right, leaned forward. "In other words, you've made no progress." His tone, at least, had been matter-of-fact and not accusatory.

"I didn't say that. I've learned a lot about how this person works and thinks." Ward shrugged. "Unfortunately, it's not enough to identify the individual, at least not yet."

"Seems to me the only identifying that needs to be done is which set of Lytle boys are guilty." The comment had come from somewhere behind Hazel.

She turned to see Saul Carson, the rancher whose horses had been released, standing, feet braced and arms crossed.

Elmer Lytle sprang to his feet across the aisle. "It ain't my boys!"

Orson Lytle stood as well, his posture even more combative. "It certainly ain't mine!"

Mayor Sanders's gavel came down in several hard raps. "Enough! If Sheriff Gleason says he isn't ready to make an arrest yet, then that's the way it is. We're here to discuss, not accuse." He leaned back again. "Now, does anyone have anything productive to say?"

Tim Hill stood. "This has dragged out way too long. We all want to know, when *are* you going to be ready to make an arrest?" His question was followed by a swell of supportive murmurings.

"As soon as I have proof of who did this, I'll make the arrest."

Did anyone else see how tightly Ward's jaw was clenched, despite his seemingly impassive demeanor?

Nate Cooper stood. "I for one applaud Sheriff Gleason's desire to not act until there's solid proof. It won't do any of us any good to act in haste and put the wrong person behind bars."

"I agree." This time it was Adam Barr who stood. "Sheriff Gleason is a man of integrity and dedication. I think we should trust him to do his job."

Hazel glanced around the room and was pleased to see a number of heads nodding. Did Ward see it as well?

"That's all well and good," Gilbert Drummond, the town's undertaker, said. "But our town has been growing and changing quite a bit lately. And Sheriff Gleason's situation has changed as well. He's acquired new responsibilities, responsibilities that can be distracting for a lawman. While we can all agree that Sheriff Gleason was the right man for the job in the past, perhaps it's time for him to step down if he can't do the job we pay him for any longer."

Arnold Davis stood almost as soon as the undertaker stopped speaking. "This has been building for a long time. Look at how he handled the kidnapping of that little Walker girl last year. Didn't lift a finger to stop it, didn't play a part in rescuing her."

Riley Walker jumped in at that. "Now see here, there's nothing wrong with the way the sheriff conducted himself. I knew Guy better than anyone and I never saw that kidnapping coming—there's no way the sheriff could have prevented it. And Guy was captured two towns over, completely out of Sheriff Gleason's jurisdiction. To want to replace the sheriff over that is—"

Mayor Sanders held up his hand. "Now, now, no one is saying Sheriff Gleason should be replaced. The town council merely wants to gather the input from the town on this very volatile situation."

Volatile? Hazel had heard enough. She stood, ignoring the warning look Ward shot her way. "I think you're looking at this in the wrong light."

"It figures that she'd speak up for him," someone behind her muttered. Hazel stiffened but didn't waste time trying to identify the speaker.

"As Mr. Drummond mentioned, the town *is* growing. And because of that, it's unfair of you to expect the sheriff to continue to do this job alone. One man cannot be available twenty-four hours a day, seven days a week. I think it's time Turnabout hired a deputy."

Councilman Jed Carpenter leaned forward. "So you agree Sheriff Gleason can no longer handle the job."

"That's not what I said." Had the man deliberately twisted her words? "I said that no *one* man should be expected to do it."

Someone else stood to speak and so it went for the next forty-five minutes. Some of the speakers were supportive of the job Ward was doing, some were detractors.

It frustrated Hazel that Ward wasn't defending himself against some of the more egregious statements. The only time he spoke up at all was to answer questions directed specifically at him.

The meeting finally ended with the mayor thanking everyone for their open and honest comments and declaring that he and the council would take everything they'd heard this evening under consideration going forward, but for now Ward Gleason was still sheriff.

Hazel asked Verity and Nate to go on without her and to let Meg know she'd be along to get her soon.

"Ward will walk me home," she assured Verity. She didn't intend to give him a choice.

Most of the folks had left the meeting room by the time Ward finished speaking to the mayor. When he turned and saw her still there, he checked for a moment, then approached her. "Where are the Coopers?"

"They headed home to check on the girls. I told them you would escort me back."

"Did you now?"

She raised a brow. "I wasn't mistaken, was I?"

Rolling his eyes, he extended his elbow.

With a smile she placed her hand there and the two of them moved to the door, like the happily engaged couple they were pretending to be.

Once they were out on the sidewalk, she gave his arm a sympathetic squeeze. "I'm sorry you had to sit through that."

He kept his gaze focused straight ahead. "It's part of the job."

"I just got so angry at some of the things that were said."

Ward rubbed the back of his neck and gave her a sideways glance. "Look, I appreciate your show of support tonight, but perhaps it would be best if you stayed out of this in the future."

"Why should I? I have just as much right as anyone else in this town to express my opinion."

"I know you mean well but I don't need you to make excuses for me or defend me."

His words stung and Hazel wasn't quite sure how to respond.

But he wasn't done yet. "You're leaving soon, remember. The business of this town will soon no longer be of any concern to you."

Had he already given up on their promise to pray for direction before making a final decision? Or had he already received his answer?

This time she knew exactly how to respond. "What a mean thing to say, Ward Gleason. Even if I leave here, that doesn't mean I'll no longer care what becomes of any of you."

He grimaced and nodded. "You're right, I'm sorry. I'm just tired."

She was immediately contrite. Of course he was. He probably hadn't slept at all last night. And if she knew him, he probably wouldn't get any real sleep tonight. "I meant what I said about Turnabout needing a deputy. The folks in this town are going to work you into an early grave if you let them."

"It's only because everyone is on edge about when and where this culprit will strike next. And I can't blame them. If I can catch him, things will settle back down again."

"When, not if."

He gave her hand a squeeze. "You're right, *when* I catch this guy, then things will go back to normal."

Hazel wasn't sure what normal was anymore. So much had changed that had nothing to do with the criminal incidents—their engagement, her plans to move, Meg's appearance in their lives.

Did he realize that things would never go back to exactly what they were before?

And that maybe, just maybe, that was a good thing.

Ward didn't tarry when he escorted Hazel home. He made sure she and a sleepy Meg made it inside her home okay and then headed to his place. He'd try to get a few hours' shut-eye and then head out to patrol again.

That meeting tonight was still eating at his gut. It had been hard to hear people criticize the job he'd been doing. Something that had been made even more difficult because they were right. He hadn't caught the criminal yet. And he had been distracted by Meg and Hazel's intrusion into his well-ordered world.

Even Hazel, his self-proclaimed biggest supporter, didn't seem to think he could handle the job on his own anymore.

And he didn't see any kind of end to his split focus in sight, at least not until Hazel moved away and took Meg with her.

He reached over and rubbed the forearm where she'd rested her hand as they walked down the sidewalk. It had felt good to have her on his arm, to feel the soft warmth of her touch, the sense of her nearness and comfort in his presence.

No, he just couldn't make himself wish for the day she boarded that train bound for New York to come any sooner.

Was that wrong of him?

Dear Father, I don't know what to pray for anymore, so I'll just pray for this: Thy will be done.

Chapter Nineteen

❧

"What a beautiful dress."

It was the morning after the town hall meeting and also Tensy's final fitting. But it was Hazel's not-yet-completed wedding dress that Tensy was admiring, not her own. And she was studying it with what Hazel could only describe as a look of pure covetousness.

Hazel couldn't very well disagree since she herself had created this ostentatious gown as her supposed ideal wedding dress. So she swallowed her true opinion and pasted on a smile. "Thank you."

Tensy gave her an accusatory look. "I thought you didn't approve of such showiness."

Oh dear. Was the girl comparing this one unfavorably to her own? She gave her customer a self-recriminating smile. "I'm afraid I may have gotten a bit carried away when I started working on this one. It is a bit overmuch, isn't it?"

"Oh no, it's lovely. And you'll look beautiful in it. Just like a princess."

Hazel winced at the bitter edge to the girl's tone.

Then Tensy gave her a disappointed look. "I suppose this means you really have decided to marry the sheriff. Somehow I figured you would snap your fingers at folks' expectations and pursue your adventure in New York as you'd planned."

Had she fallen off of the pedestal Tensy had set her on? How was she supposed to respond to such a statement?

Fortunately, Tensy changed the subject. "It was wonderful the way you stood up for the sheriff last night."

"I meant every word I said."

"I'm afraid I'm not quite brave enough to speak up in public like that. Pa says it's not a woman's place."

Hazel had no patience for such sentiments. "And why not? We women live in this town too. We should have some say in how it operates." She saw how taken aback Tensy was at her passionate response and decided it was time to change the subject.

"Were you planning to wear a hat or a veil with your gown?" she asked. "Because now that Verity is back in town I'm sure she would be able to make you a beautiful hat to match your dress."

"I'd planned on a veil." Her tone was tentative, uncertain. "What do you think?"

"I think a veil would be lovely. Would you like to look over the selection of lace and netting I have? In fact, I'd be honored to provide the materials as my wedding gift to you."

As Hazel ushered her to the area of the shop where the bolts of netting and lace were located, her thoughts drifted back to her own engagement.

It appeared Ward had given up all pretense, at least with her, of thinking they would go through with a wedding or even that she would remain in Turnabout. What would he say if she told him she'd decided she wanted to stay here with him and Meg, that she wanted the engagement to be real?

He would go through with it, of course, that wasn't even a question in her mind. But would he be happy or merely resigned?

And could she ever be truly happy with anything less than his love?

"I've heard from a Jonathan Eversby, the pastor of the church in Daltonville." Ward reported at lunch. "He was able to help with the final pieces to Meg's story."

"Oh, I'm so glad." Hazel glanced across the restaurant where Meg was happily showing a picture book to Chessie. "So tell me everything."

"Her name is Megan Leigh Johnson, daughter of Luther and Sally Johnson, sister of Frieda Johnson. As Meg told us, her mother died in childbirth and her father and sister resented her for it for most of her life."

How had the little girl grown up around such people and retained her sweet, sunny disposition? "The pastor knew this?"

"According to the letter he sent, he tried to counsel Meg's father to show the child some love but to no avail. Luckily she had a very motherly Sunday school teacher who gave Half-pint what extra attention she could."

"Well, that's a blessing at least."

"The pastor also knew that Frieda had taken up with a young man named Rory Dunkin, a relationship her father frowned on. Then Luther died about two months ago. Frieda sold the home place and then, as far as the pastor knew, she, Meg and Rory seemed to disappear off the face of the earth. He had no idea the pair had so unceremoniously abandoned Meg."

"Are there any other relatives?"

"Not as far as the pastor knows."

"So what does this mean for Meg? Surely you won't put her in an orphanage? I couldn't bear even the thought of it."

"Of course not." Ward looked insulted that she'd even brought it up. "She needs a loving home."

Hazel gave him a pointed look. "Like yours."

"I can't be Meg's father. Surely you of all people understand why."

"But I don't. In fact, I believe just the opposite. You've done very well with Meg so far."

His posture was rigid, his jaw muscles stretched taut. "After what happened with Bethany, I—"

That again. Would he never let go of his sense of guilt? "What happened with Bethany was *not* your fault. Just like you can't be everywhere at once now, you couldn't then either. A board broke, it was an accident."

"What you don't know is that I knew all about that rotten board. I'd been meaning to fix it for days, I just hadn't gotten around to it yet. If I'd done my job, Bethany would never have fallen."

Had he been carrying this guilt around with him all these years? She placed a hand on his arm. "Ward, you were sixteen years old and you were trying to carry the weight of the world on your shoulders. Both your parents were gone, you had the family farm and a younger sister to take care of. You were doing the best that you could."

"I'm not sure Bethany would feel the same way."

"I am." She squeezed his arm. "Look at me. I mean it. I knew Bethany like she was my twin. Bethany *loved* you. She also worried that you were working too hard, trying to do too much."

She saw the stubborn refusal to believe her or forgive himself in his expression and decided it was time for a confession of her own. Taking a deep breath, she looked him square in the eyes. "Besides, if anyone is to blame for her accident, it's me."

That got his attention. "Why do you say that?"

"Because I'm the reason we were up in the loft to start with. I had something important to tell her, something that just couldn't wait even though she had chores to do, and I insisted we find somewhere private. And our favorite place to have those chats was up in the loft."

"You two were just thirteen years old."

"Exactly. And you were just sixteen. We both loved Bethany and we both feel we let her down. But she wouldn't want us to wallow in that for the rest of our lives."

She saw the emotions playing out in Ward's face and thought for a moment that he would give in.

Then his expression closed off again and he changed the subject. "This is getting us nowhere. We still need to figure out what the best thing is for Meg going forward."

Hazel let go of his arm and leaned back in her seat, disappointed.

Ward kept his tone even. "She's grown quite fond of you."

"And I've grown fond of her as well. But it's you she feels most connected to."

"Is there no room in your life for her now that you plan to move to New York?"

She stiffened. "That's not fair. The question is not whether I want her in my life, the question is what is best for Meg."

"Hazel, everything else aside, I'm a bachelor with a job that demands a great deal of my time. There's no way I can give Meg the kind of attention she needs, the kind of attention she deserves. And you and I both know, a little girl needs a mother."

But Hazel wasn't going to back down. "She needs a father just as much."

"No, not just as much. I'm right and you know it. You're just too stubborn to admit it."

Feeling she was losing the battle, Hazel changed her approach. "This would break her heart."

"I know. But it will heal, in time." His expression closed off even more. "And with that in mind, I think it best I start spending less time with her. Sort of ease myself out of her life so it won't be as big a change when it comes time for the two of you to leave."

"Absolutely not. I won't allow it." She was not going to budge on this point. "This is the time for her to be building memories, memories she can carry to New York with her and help carry her through the loneliness she's going to experience."

He gave her a crooked smile. "You're not going to make this easy on me, are you?"

"Not in the least."

Even though it was barely dawn, Ward was already downstairs pulling on his boots and wishing for a cup of strong coffee. He hadn't seen much during his midnight patrol last night but he hadn't been able to shake the feeling ever since he'd returned home that something wasn't right. It wasn't anything he could put his finger on, but he'd learned a long time ago that it didn't pay to ignore his gut. So he'd finally given up on getting any shut-eye and decided to make another round before he started his day.

The conversation he'd had with Hazel at lunch yesterday still bothered him. She could be so stubborn. But she was also usually right nine times out of ten. Should he continue with Meg as usual?

The sound of someone pounding on his door pulled his thoughts back to the present. That was never a good sign—folks didn't come by here to report good news.

He crossed the room and jerked open the door to find Tim Hill, hand raised to knock again.

The man blinked, obviously not expecting Ward to respond quite so fast. But he recovered quickly. "Sorry to bother you, Sheriff, but I thought you ought to know. Them boys been at it again."

Not at all happy that his instincts had been proved right, Ward was already reaching for his gun belt and hat. "Whose place did they hit this time?"

The lamplighter gave him a you're-not-going-to-like-this look.

"It was Hazel Andrews's dress shop."

Chapter Twenty

Ward stood in front of Hazel's shop, studying the large, splotchy splatters of red paint that had been liberally applied to her display window. It was a mess, but thank goodness that seemed to be as far as it went—there were no signs that the place itself had been broken into.

Seeing a light already on upstairs, he rang the door chime on the shop door. Truth be told, he would have done the same even if the light *hadn't* been on upstairs. He wouldn't breathe easy until he assured himself Hazel and Meg were okay.

It took several minutes but finally Hazel opened the door. The overwhelming sense of relief at seeing her there, obviously calm and unaware that anything was amiss, was telling in its intensity.

"Good morning. You're here mighty early. Is everything okay?"

"I'm afraid not. Where's Meg?"

"She's still in bed. I was just about to get her up." Then she gave him a sharp look "Something's happened, hasn't it? What?"

"Step out here for a moment, please."

Her expression apprehensive, she nonetheless did as he asked without question. When she saw the vandalism on the front of her shop, her eyes widened and she inhaled sharply.

Ward put an arm around her shoulder, not caring that there were already others gathered on the sidewalks, watching. She was his fiancée so he had every right to comfort her. But even beyond that, he cared about her, deeply.

A moment later she took a deep breath and gave him a smile that was an odd mix of vulnerability and humor and that touched something deep inside him.

"At least they picked a bright, cheery color."

He squeezed her shoulder and returned her smile. He'd like to do more, to brush the hair from her face, take her in his arms, kiss away her worries, but not here in public view.

So he stepped back. "Go on and tend to Meg. I want to look around back and downstairs in your shop, just to make sure nothing else was done."

Her eyes widened again, as if she hadn't considered that invasion until now. Then she nodded and headed back inside.

Ward painstakingly checked Hazel's shop, both inside and out, but found no signs that anything had been done besides the splattered paint. When he stepped back on the front sidewalk he found Nate Cooper scrubbing the paint off of the window.

Ward tipped his hat back. "This is mighty neighborly of you. I'm sure Miss Andrews will be grateful."

Nate shrugged without pausing in his task. "She straightened up our place after the break-in. I figure this is the least I can do to repay her. Besides, my wife works here too."

By the time Hazel and Meg came downstairs, the window looked as good as new. Fortunately, there would be no need to try to explain the incident to Half-pint.

But there were still splatters of paint on the woodwork below the window and sidewalk in front. Those wouldn't be as easy to remove as the smears on the glass had been. Perhaps he would get some paint and paint over it for her.

While Ward stood in front of the dress shop speaking to Nate about any suspicious sounds he might have heard, Eunice Ortolon and Mayor Sanders's wife walked by. "I suppose," Eunice said to her companion in a voice pitched to carry, "now that the dress shop has been affected, something will finally get done about all this criminal activity."

Ward just couldn't win. If it took much longer to find the culprit, they would fire him for not doing his job. If he managed to catch the culprit soon, folks would say he'd finally taken action because of his concern for Hazel and Meg.

Ah, well, he hadn't taken this job to become popular. It was to help people and make a difference. He'd just keep doing the best he could and hope that was enough.

Ward checked in on Hazel several times that morning, just long enough to stick his head in the door and assure himself that she and Meg were doing okay.

He couldn't help feeling that this attack on her shop had somehow been aimed at him, that he was in some way responsible for what had happened.

But Hazel refused to dwell on the act of vandalism. When he tried to bring the subject up at their noon meal, she waved his concerns away and changed the subject.

"Tomorrow is Joy's birthday and Verity and Nate are

going to take her on a picnic to celebrate. She's invited us to join them."

Ward rubbed his jaw. "I don't know. It's probably not a good idea for me to be away from town right now."

She frowned indignantly. "Surely you're allowed to take a few hours off to relax and enjoy yourself. Besides, other than when they attacked the laundry on Tensy's and Eunice's clotheslines, the culprit seems to only strike at night."

"I'll compromise with you. I won't stay for the whole afternoon, but I will come by for a little while to have lunch with y'all."

He wasn't exactly sure why he'd given in to her. After all, wasn't he supposed to be putting some distance between himself and Meg?

But he kept seeing that vulnerable, brave smile Hazel had given him this morning, kept feeling the slight tremble of her shoulders under his arms as she surveyed the vandalism to her shop, and he couldn't hand her another disappointment.

Hazel was disappointed Ward wouldn't spend the entire afternoon with them but she understood his reasons. He wouldn't be Ward Gleason, the man she admired and, yes, loved, if he hadn't felt his responsibilities so strongly. So she would be happy with what she could get.

When he walked her and Meg back to the dress shop, she tried to ignore the blotches of paint still staining the sidewalk in front of her display window.

Why would someone have done this, or any of the other incidents for that matter? Didn't they realize how it made their victims feel? Or didn't they care?

But she was doing everything in her power not to

let Ward see how it affected her. She didn't want to add any additional worries, or reasons to feel guilty, to his already full plate. Maybe the picnic tomorrow would help lighten his spirit, even if only a little.

Later that afternoon, as much to distract herself as anything else, she took Meg shopping to find a birthday present for Joy. Meg really threw herself into the occasion and studied the offerings at the mercantile long and hard before declaring that none of the things there were right for her new friend.

Then Hazel remembered the wooden toys Chance Dawson created over at The Blue Bottle and brought Meg there. The little girl immediately latched onto a wooden box with some intricate carvings that had a floral theme.

"It's a treasure box," Meg declared. "She can put all her special things inside it."

"That's perfect," Hazel agreed. "And you know what? I think if we ask Mr. Dawson to paint Joy's name on it, he'd do that for us. Would you like to do that?"

Meg nodded eagerly and in no time it was done. Once their purchase was complete, Meg insisted on carrying the gift herself, proudly chattering on about how much she knew her friend would love the box.

When Hazel handed Meg off to Ward for the evening and locked her shop door, she felt uneasy in her home for the first time. Which was silly, of course. Once the hooligans had moved on from the Lawrence place, they hadn't attacked any one place twice. They were likely done with her, and as incidents go, the one against her had been relatively mild.

But had it really and truly been against her? Somehow, this incident and the one at the town hall seemed more aimed at Ward than anyone else.

Because whether that was the intention or not, it had certainly hit him harder than the other incidents had.

The picnic the next day went a long way toward getting everyone's spirits back up. The two little girls had a great time together. And even Pugs and Beans contributed to the merriment.

Joy seemed genuinely pleased with the gift Meg gave her and the two girls had already found a blue jay feather and a curiously shaped rock to store inside it.

Hazel watched the interactions between Nate and Verity with a wistfulness she couldn't control. The looks they exchanged, the easy touches and solicitous mannerisms, the way they seemed to communicate without saying a word—it all spoke of the kind of love Hazel longed to have in her own life.

True to his word, Ward showed up in time to join them for lunch and stayed for about an hour. Hazel could tell, though, that beneath his easy manner, he was distracted and ready to return to town.

Shortly after he left, they packed up the hamper and followed suit. Joy invited Meg to come over to her place to play and with Verity's permission, Hazel gave the little girl the go-ahead. She wanted some quiet time to think anyway. Now that the Coopers were back in town and Meg's situation was more or less decided, it was time for her to make some decisions of her own.

Hazel stepped into the shop and opened the blinds, letting the sunlight pour in like water from a fall. She would just step upstairs for a moment and then—

Hazel stopped in her tracks, not quite absorbing what she was seeing.

It was her wedding dress.

Or what was left of it.

Chapter Twenty-One

Hazel all but ran to Ward's office. She wasn't aware of her surroundings, of whether the streets and sidewalks were teeming or deserted. All she could think about was getting to Ward, of drawing on the comfort she knew he would offer.

She prayed all the way there, the same prayer, over and over.

Please, God, let him be in his office.

It seemed to take an eternity to cross the block and a half between her shop and the sheriff's office. When she finally arrived, she shoved open the door and all but stumbled inside.

He was here! She paused, unable to speak for a heartbeat. But Ward was already up and crossing the room, a look of concerned alarm on his face.

"Hazel, what's wrong? What happened?" He took hold of her shoulders, his grip warm, protective, comforting.

For the first time since she'd found that ugly surprise in her shop, she took a deep breath and placed her palms against his chest, feeling the strong pounding of his heart through the fabric of his shirt. She stared into his eyes, drawing on his strength to steady herself. "Everything's going to be all right now."

Something was very wrong. Hazel wasn't making a lot of sense and she appeared to be in some kind of shock. She was trembling and there was something wounded and vulnerable shadowing her expression. Every protective instinct inside him had roared to life and was thrashing inside him, ready to act. He was torn between wanting to storm off and slay whatever dragons she'd had to face down and the ache to pull her to him, to stroke her hair and comfort her. But first he needed to find out what had happened. If anyone had tried to hurt her—

He did his best to rein in his growing alarm, to keep calm so he could get through to her. "Hazel, honey, you need to tell me what's happened."

She seemed to finally snap out of the haze she'd been engulfed in since she'd burst into his office. The color slowly returned to her cheeks and she lowered her hands, denying his chest the warmth of her touch. "Someone broke into my shop while we were at the picnic."

It was as if someone had slammed a fist to his gut and he felt his hands reflexively tighten their hold on her shoulders. No wonder she seemed so rattled. "Are you all right? And where's Meg?"

"We're both fine. Meg went straight to the Coopers' when we returned from the picnic so she doesn't even know about this yet. Nobody does. I came straight here as soon as I realized."

He released his grip on her shoulders and led her to a chair. "That was the right thing to do." He held her arm as she settled into the chair, then straightened. "Wait here just a minute."

He moved to the back room where he had a pot of coffee he'd just brewed up shortly before she arrived. He poured her up a cup while he took a moment to compose himself. It had happened again. Right under his nose.

And to Hazel.

He grabbed the back of a nearby chair and bowed his head. What if she'd walked in on them? What could have happened made his knees weak.

He couldn't let this continue.

Pulling himself together, he straightened and added the sugar he knew she liked with her coffee, then carried the cup back to his office.

"Here, drink this," he said, handing it to her.

With a soft thank-you, she accepted the cup with hands that were almost steady.

She took a sip and then smiled up at him. "I'm sorry to act like a frightened schoolgirl over this. I know I'm not in any physical danger, I just—"

Ward touched her shoulder, halting her apology. "You've nothing to apologize for." He found maintaining physical contact was something he needed right now as much as she did. "I assume you didn't see anyone."

She shook her head. "Whoever did this was long gone when I got there. I'm sorry."

"I'm not." He figured that was the one thing that had gone right. "So tell me what you did see."

"It was my wedding dress—someone destroyed it beyond repair."

Ward clinched his jaw in an effort to keep from growling. No wonder she'd been so upset. Attacking her wedding dress gave this incident a particularly personal, targeted feel.

He gave her shoulder one more squeeze. "You stay here and finish your coffee. I'm going to go down to your shop and look around." He'd check things out and then get rid of the dress so she didn't have to look at it again.

But Hazel, predictably, had other ideas. She stood and set the cup on his desk. "I'm going with you."

One look at the set of her mouth and he knew it was useless to argue. With a nod, he offered her his arm.

They didn't speak on the walk to her shop. The closer they got, the more tense Hazel became. He should have insisted she stay in his office, but it was too late for that now.

When they stepped inside, his eyes went immediately to the vandalized dress and again he had to smother a growl. No wonder she'd been shaken.

The skirt was shredded so thoroughly it now seemed more a ragged fringe than fabric. The vandal had also taken a bottle of ink from her desk and splashed it in ugly splotches across the bodice and sleeves. The rows of lace that she had applied to the collar, cuffs and bodice had been ripped away and now hung like limp bunting.

Ward slid an arm around her shoulder. "I'm sorry all your work was ruined. I know you put a lot of time and effort into it."

She shrugged. "It's not as if I was going to really use it as a wedding dress."

But he could tell Hazel wasn't as calm as she pretended. To find her place the object of this criminal's attacks two days in a row had taken its toll on even *her* ability to bounce back.

"Whoever's doing this, he's getting bolder." Ward stared assessingly at the dress. "This destruction took time. I'm beginning to believe the mayor and townsfolk are right. I'm not the right person for this job."

That seemed to restore some of Hazel's spirit. "Don't be ridiculous." She pulled away to better face him. "Of course you're the right person. I defy anyone else here in town to do a better job."

He ignored her comment and glanced around the shop. "I see they left all the hats alone as well as your bolts of fabric. Do you have any other garments you're working on?"

"Tensy's dress!" Hazel's hand flew to her mouth as she raced for the workroom. "Please let it be untouched," she said as she threw open the door.

Then he heard her quick sigh of relief as he stepped up behind her. Sure enough, the gown she had stored there looked untouched. "So either they didn't see this dress or they only wanted to wreak havoc on the other one," Ward said.

"If they had to pick one, I'm glad they chose mine. It represented a lie anyway."

He let her comment go, changing the subject slightly. "Was anything else besides your dress damaged or taken?"

Hazel looked around. "Not anything obvious. But I haven't really looked closely yet."

She gave him a smile that didn't quite reach her eyes. "And looking on the bright side, having to start over on the dress gives us an excuse to push the wedding date back even further. If we need one."

He didn't return her smile. "I refuse to let you make light of this. Whether you intended to wear it or not, you put a lot of time and effort, and probably expense as well, into that dress. And someone just destroyed it."

Her expression softened and she touched his arm. "Thank you."

The tremble of her lip and vulnerable moistness of her eyes was too much for him. "Come here." He wrapped his arms around her and felt a sense of triumph when she leaned her head against his chest. He stroked her hair, whispering soothing nothings while thinking how very good, how very *right* this felt.

Yet also knowing that it was very wrong. Because he could never be the man she needed and it wasn't right to let her think he could.

On that thought, he finally released his hold and straightened.

Her gaze sought his and he saw the question there. Best to leave it unanswered.

"Better?" he asked.

She nodded and stepped back.

"Good." He fisted his hands at his sides to keep them from reaching for her again. "I'm going to look around outside. If you're up to it, why don't you take a quick look around inside and make sure nothing is missing?"

"Of course."

With a smile and a nod, he forced himself to turn and walk away.

As Hazel watched Ward walk away, she hugged herself, trying to hold captive that warmth and comfort she'd enjoyed in his arms. It had felt so achingly sweet to be held by him that way, to feel wanted and cherished and safe. As if nothing, or no one, could harm her as long as she had him by her side.

He'd broken that heartwarming contact much too soon. And it was obvious something about it had shaken him up. But could it be the first step to something deeper, more lasting?

She moved from the workroom to the shop floor and cringed again at the sight of the maliciously destroyed dress. But somehow it wasn't so frightening now. Now that she'd had time to absorb the shock and draw comfort from Ward, she was more angry than sick over what had happened. It was just a dress, after all, and she hadn't even liked it. She could always make another one. And this time she'd make one she would be proud to wear.

Tilting her chin at a determined angle, Hazel rolled up her sleeves and went to work cleaning up the shredded fabric that seemed to be everywhere. She didn't want there to be any sign of this ugliness when Meg returned. With any luck, the little girl wouldn't even notice the dress was missing.

Ward returned from the back of the shop just as she was finishing up.

"It looks as if the intruder came in through the window near your back entrance," he said. "It was wide open."

Hazel frowned. "But that window is always latched."

"Are you sure you didn't leave it unlocked today by mistake?"

Hazel started second-guessing herself. Perhaps the latch hadn't been closed properly—it did stick sometimes.

"Maybe I should hire someone to keep an eye on your place."

She waved a hand dismissively. "Don't be ridiculous. I know I overreacted earlier but it's obvious that, whoever is doing this, he doesn't intend to harm anyone."

"At least not yet."

She raised a brow at the implication. Then crossed her arms. "You haven't set guards at anyone else's place."

"This isn't anyone else's place."

Before she could explore that interesting declaration in more depth, he continued. "I intend to discourage whoever is doing this from paying you a third visit."

Sometimes she could almost believe he really did have warm feelings for her.

He cleared his throat. "After all, Meg is still my responsibility, even if she's staying with you."

Almost.

Ward was shaken by the attack on Hazel's dress shop more than he cared to admit. And it wasn't just because of his personal relationship with the occupants. Lately the perpetrator had gone from being mischievous and impudent to outright vindictive and destructive. First with the mayor's office, and now this. The destruction of Hazel's wedding gown had not only been calculatedly deliberate but particularly thorough and vicious.

Why the change? Was this a sign that the perpetrator was getting bolder? Or was it specifically targeted against Hazel? And if it was targeted at Hazel, was it actually someone trying to get to him through his apparent bride-to-be?

Whatever the case, and whatever Hazel's feelings on that score, he planned to keep an extra-close eye on her place in the coming days.

And he'd have a word with Nate as well. Not only was the man next door, but he was sharp and knew how to handle himself if it came to that.

And Eunice was right. Now that it was personal,

he'd be redoubling his efforts to find this man and put an end to this havoc he was causing.

Deciding not to give the criminal the satisfaction of knowing he'd upset her, Hazel decided not to say anything to anyone about what had happened to her dress. Except for Verity, of course. And while her friend was outraged on her behalf, she honored Hazel's request not to discuss it, especially not in front of Meg.

By the next day, Hazel was tired of being reminded of the attacks on her shop every time she stepped outside and saw those paint smears on the sidewalk. Something had to be done.

Making up her mind, she turned to Meg. "Come on, we're going to the mercantile."

An hour later, she had the sidewalk in front of her place cordoned off and four large cans of paint and several paintbrushes arranged in a row in front of her shop window. Letting Verity know what she had in mind, she tied large aprons around Meg and Joy, then handed each of them a paintbrush. "All right, girls, your job this morning is to make this sidewalk beautiful. Paint whatever you like."

Verity stood beside her. "Are you sure about this?"

"Absolutely."

The activity drew lots of curious glances but for the most part folks looked on with indulgent smiles. In no time at all the sidewalk was covered with childish but colorful images of flowers, suns, rainbows, stick figures and rather indistinguishable animals.

"Do you like it?" Meg asked.

"I love it. It makes me feel happy."

"Can we do this in front of our place, Momma?" Joy asked.

Verity rolled her eyes Hazel's way. "Look what you started." Then she turned to her daughter. "Not today, darling."

Hazel smiled, then something past Verity's shoulder caught her attention. The woman striding their way, with her fiery red hair, command-the-room presence and unique style looked very much like—

"Aunt Opal!"

Chapter Twenty-Two

Hazel rushed across the half block that separated them and embraced her aunt. "How wonderful to see you."

"And you as well, my dear." Her aunt dropped the valise she was carrying and gave Hazel a quick peck on her cheek as she returned the hug.

Hazel released her aunt and took her hands instead. "I have to ask, what brings you all this way? Is everything all right?"

"Everything back home is just fine. As for what brings me here, it was an announcement in your delightful newspaper about upcoming nuptials."

Hazel's stomach did a guilty flip as she reached down to retrieve her aunt's bag. "You got hold of a copy of *The Turnabout Gazette*?"

"Of course." Her aunt gave an imperious wave. "I'm a subscriber. How else am I to keep up with the things affecting my favorite niece?" She tapped Hazel's arm as if she were a recalcitrant schoolgirl. "Now, about this engagement? Why did I have to find out about it by reading a newspaper? Surely you intended to invite me?"

Hazel's mind scrambled frantically for a response.

What could she say to that? There was no way she would lie to her aunt but she couldn't reveal the whole story standing out here where anyone might overhear.

Fortunately, they had reached her shop by then and she bought time by introducing her aunt to Verity.

Then Aunt Opal examined the two little girls and their artwork. She clasped her hands in obvious approval. "What's this? A pair of talented budding artists having their first art exhibition, I presume."

"We're making pretty pictures to decorate for Miss Hazel," Meg explained.

"So I see."

"Would you like to help?" Joy asked.

Aunt Opal held up a hand. "Thank you, but I think you two girls have it well in hand."

"Aunt Opal, allow me to introduce the two artists to you. The one currently dipping her brush in the blue paint is Joy, Verity's daughter. And the other little painter is Meg, who is currently living with me."

Her aunt cut her a surprised look at that, then turned back to the girls. "I'm very pleased to meet you young ladies. You may call me Aunt Opal."

Verity gave Hazel a smile. "I'm sure your aunt would like a place to freshen up and perhaps a nice cup of tea after her long trip. Why don't you take her upstairs where she can be more comfortable? I'll take Meg and Joy over to my place after we close up these paint cans and get them cleaned up."

With a grateful nod, Hazel turned and ushered her aunt inside her shop.

"It appears I have new questions to add to my list. Who is Meg and why is she living with you?"

Then she paused and looked around. "What a delightful little shop. I must come down and explore a bit once I've had that cup of tea."

While her aunt freshened up, Hazel brewed the tea. She braced herself for the upcoming conversation. She would tell her the truth of course, all of it. But she wasn't looking forward to the disappointment her explanation about the sham engagement would bring to her aunt's face.

Fifteen minutes later, Opal picked up her teacup and raised it to her lips. She studied Hazel silently over the rim, then set it down firmly. "I take it from your reaction to my question earlier that there is something going on here besides a simple engagement." She patted Hazel's hand. "However, it is not my intention to pry into matters you're not ready to discuss. If you prefer not to speak of your upcoming nuptials, we can speak of other things. Just first tell me if this man makes you happy."

Hazel chose her words carefully. "I love him, with all my heart. But you're right, there is more going on here. It's a long, rather complicated story, I'm afraid."

"As I've traveled all this way specifically to find out what's going on, I think I have the time to hear this story. If you want to share it with me, that is."

Hazel hesitated. Aunt Opal had given her an out and she knew the woman would never bring the subject up again if she asked her not to. But not only did she love and respect her aunt, but she was moving to New York specifically to work with her. She deserved to hear the truth.

"To start with, there very likely won't be a wedding."

"Oh?" Opal took another sip, her expression nonjudgmental.

Hazel quickly relayed the entire story, starting with Meg being left in Ward's care and ending with the misunderstanding surrounding her being at Ward's place in the wee hours.

"So you and Sheriff Gleason announced your engagement to quiet the gossips."

There was no trace of censure in her aunt's voice but Hazel still squirmed. "Not at first. I mean, I was willing to face down the talk and go on as we were."

"Until?"

"Until there was talk of Ward and I not being proper guardians for Meg. I just couldn't take the chance someone would try to take that little girl from him."

"I see."

Hazel got the impression that perhaps her aunt saw a little more than she had intended.

"You said earlier that there *very likely* wouldn't be a wedding."

"We decided that we would stay engaged at least until Meg's situation is resolved. Beyond that we would pray for God's direction."

"But you don't sound as if you think it will work out as you'd like."

"If you're worried I won't move to New York as I promised—"

Opal waved a hand in dismissal. "That shouldn't play into such an important decision. Of course I would love to have my favorite niece close by, but I am much more interested in making sure you are happy, my dear."

Oh, she did love this dear woman. "The truth is, I don't really know how this will turn out."

"But you do know how you *want* it to end up."

Hazel nodded. "I love Meg. It would give me great joy to be her mother."

"And you love *him*."

Hazel nodded, without meeting her aunt's gaze. Instead she studied the rim of her cup.

"So why are you so unhappy?"

"When I was younger I thought I loved him. But I'd come to realize lately that what I thought of as love was merely infatuation. And since it was clear he had no feelings for me, I decided I needed a fresh start somewhere else."

"And how did you arrive at the realization it was mere infatuation?"

"When I began to seriously consider your invitation and found I *could* bear to move away from him."

"But something has changed?"

She nodded. "When Meg was dropped into our lives, that created a need for us to spend a lot more time in each other's company than we ever had before, at least not since we were children. Seeing him with Meg, how he cared for her and took responsibility for her, showed me a different side of him, showed me his heart. And that's the man I fell in love with."

"Then you must fight for him."

"I've tried. He's just too stubborn, too much of a loner to want to have anyone else in his life."

"So tell me about this little girl. What's going to happen to her now?"

"That's still not decided. But I think she might end up with me in New York." She looked at her aunt. "If you think that will be a problem—"

Her aunt waved a hand. "Pish posh. We will make it work if that is what ends up happening." Then she gave Hazel a thoughtful look. "If you had the power to resolve this any way you wanted, what would you like to see happen?"

"Other than having Ward suddenly realize he loves

me after all?" Hazel took a sip of her tea while she pondered that question. "I truly believe the Good Lord put Meg in Ward's life for a reason. Whether he will admit it or not, Meg has become an important part of his life. It's forced him to see himself as a father, as a protector of an individual rather than a town."

Then she set her cup down and gave her aunt an apologetic smile. "I'm so sorry you came all this way for nothing. If I'd realized you'd seen the announcement, I would have contacted—"

"No need for apologies. After all these years of you traveling to New York, it's high time I came here and visited you in your hometown. And now that I'm here, I'd like to stay a while, if that's all right with you? I will, of course, take a room at the hotel."

"Nonsense. I mean yes, I would love to have you stay but there is no need for you to take a room at the hotel. I insist you stay here with me. Meg and I can double up in my room."

"Well, if you're sure it wouldn't be an imposition?"

"No imposition at all. Where are your bags?"

"At the train depot."

She stood. "I'll have them sent on here while you rest."

Perhaps this would be a good thing. If Meg traveled to New York with her, there would be at least one person she'd already know when they arrived. And Aunt Opal and the little girl would take to each other, she was sure of it.

As soon as Hazel shifted Meg's things from the guest room to her room, Aunt Opal declared she would take a nap. Hazel used the time to make arrangements to have the luggage delivered, then fetched Meg from Verity's place.

"Is Aunt Opal from New York?" Meg asked.

"She is."

"Did she come to take you away from us?"

"Oh no, sweetheart, she just came for a visit."

Reassured, the little girl gave a little hop-skip. "She seems nice."

"She is. Very nice. And lots of fun too."

Ward turned the corner just then and Hazel waited for him to catch up. "I hear you have a visitor," he said by way of greeting.

"It appears my aunt Opal, the one who has a dress design business, subscribes to *The Turnabout Gazette*."

"Oh?"

"Yes. You know, the newspaper that our engagement announcement appeared in."

Light dawned. "Oh. I see."

"We just had a nice long talk where I explained the entire situation to her." She gave him a pointed look. "Aunt Opal's quite eager to meet you."

He grimaced. "I imagine she is."

"I'd introduce you now but she's taking a nap at the moment."

He held up a hand. "Quite right, no need to disturb her. We'll meet soon enough."

Hazel was rather enjoying watching him squirm uncomfortably. He could do with something so trivial to worry about. "Shall I invite her to join us for supper this evening?"

"Of course. I can't wait to meet her."

"She let me call her Aunt Opal too," Meg said, claiming Ward's attention.

"Well, that was mighty nice of her."

Meg bobbed her head, making her pigtails dance. "So now I have an aunt just like Joy. And don't worry,

Aunt Opal is just here to visit, not take Miss Hazel back to New York with her."

He glanced up and met Hazel's gaze, his gaze almost a caress. "Good to know."

Now it was Hazel's turn to squirm just a bit. Was she reading more into his look than was actually there? She wished she was better at reading Ward's expression than she was.

"Aunt Opal, this is Sheriff Ward Gleason. Sheriff Gleason, this is my aunt, Opal Eldridge."

Ward executed a short bow as he took her hand. "Mrs. Eldridge, it's a pleasure to meet you." He'd been worried about this meeting all afternoon.

This woman was important to Hazel. It was obvious from the way she spoke of her that she loved and respected her a great deal. He wanted to make a good impression on the older woman, but after Hazel had divulged the story behind how they got engaged, he wasn't sure that was even possible.

Hazel's aunt nodded her head regally, studying him like a rancher examining a herd to decide which animals to cull and which keep. "Likewise, Sheriff."

As they strolled down the sidewalk toward the restaurant, Ward somehow found himself walking beside Mrs. Eldridge while Hazel and Half-pint walked behind them.

"Tell me, young man, isn't being a lawman a rather dangerous profession?"

"It can be. But Turnabout isn't like New York or other big cities. It's peaceful for the most part."

"If that's true, then why do they need a sheriff?"

"Someone has to make sure it stays that way. And

by peaceful, I meant that we rarely have violent crimes, not that we have no crime."

"I see." Then she changed the subject. "My niece told me about Meg's unfortunate situation. It's an honorable thing you're doing, giving her some stability in her life."

"Haz—Miss Andrews has been a big help in that department."

"Yes, I imagine she has. I can see she's developed a fondness for the child."

"As Meg has for her."

"Yes. I assume it will be difficult for both of them to adjust when Hazel moves to New York."

"Not if Meg goes with her."

The woman raised her brows. "You think that's possible?"

"We need to do whatever is best for Meg."

"I agree. But don't you think what would be best for Meg would be to have a home with *two* parents?"

Ward almost missed a step, but he recovered quickly. "True, but I'm afraid not every child is quite that lucky."

Mrs. Eldridge sighed. "So true. But I will have to see what I can do to rectify the situation as soon as I get Hazel to New York. I can't fathom what's wrong with the men in Turnabout but I know quite a number of eligible bachelors who would find a girl like Hazel quite irresistible."

All through the meal, Ward found himself replaying Mrs. Eldridge's words in his mind. How long would it be before Hazel became a married woman, before Meg would have a new man to look up to and call Father? It was what he'd told Hazel she needed to do, after all.

So why did the idea of it tie his stomach in knots?

If only he had the right to ask her to stay. Or was it the courage that he lacked?

Either way, he knew she deserved so much more than he had to offer. The trouble was going to be letting her go without giving in to the urge to tell her how he felt.

An urge that was growing stronger by the day.

Chapter Twenty-Three

After church the next morning, they all four had lunch together. To Ward's relief, there'd been no more matchmaking talk from Hazel's aunt, though he didn't doubt the woman intended to follow through on her plan.

After they finished their meal, Hazel asked her aunt to watch over Meg while the girl took her nap. "There's something I'd like to discuss with the sheriff," she explained.

That was news to him. What did she have on her mind now?

Her aunt waved a hand of dismissal. "Of course, dear, take all the time you need. I am quite capable of amusing myself."

When they stepped out on the sidewalk together Ward looked at her somewhat warily. "What did you want to talk to me about?"

"I was thinking last night… I always find, when I have a problem I'm trying to work through, that talking it over with Verity helps. Sometimes all she does is listen without saying much of anything. But just the simple act of trying to explain my problem helps me see it in a new light."

Where was she going with this? Did she want his help with a problem? "And?"

"And I was thinking perhaps that would work for you as well."

"You want me to talk over my problems with Verity Cooper?"

"No, I meant—" She stopped when she realized he was teasing.

"So are you volunteering to listen to me try to talk this problem with the town hooligan through?"

She gave him a saucy grin. "What could it hurt? And I'm a very good listener."

"At this point I'm ready to try just about anything." He rubbed the back of his neck. And spending time with her while they talked this over was a not-unpleasant way to spend the afternoon. "So, how does this work? Do I just start talking?"

"With a problem this big, it might be best to try to write it all down as we talk. Sort of get a look at how things might connect to each other."

"That would take a mighty big piece of paper." Then he raised a brow as an idea struck. "Or a mighty big chalkboard."

Hazel grinned. "Perfect. I doubt Mr. Parker would mind if we borrowed his classroom, especially since school is out for the summer."

"Let's go."

"By the way," Hazel said as they made their way to the schoolhouse, "I told Aunt Opal about the problems we've been having here in town. I thought she ought to know, just in case something were to happen again."

Ward planned to do everything in his power to make sure *nothing* happened again, especially where Hazel's place was concerned. "How did she take it?"

"Quite well, actually. She's a strong woman, it takes a lot to frighten her. Besides, since she subscribes to *The Gazette*, she was already aware of some of it."

It only took them a few minutes to reach the schoolhouse. When they stepped inside and reached the front of the classroom, Hazel grabbed a piece of chalk and handed it to him. "Since you're the one with the puzzle, it'd be best if you do the writing." She leaned back against the teacher's desk, grasping the edges with her hands.

"So let's start by listing all the incidents with the dates beside them." She wrinkled her nose a moment. "And leave spaces so we can add other things that pertain to each one."

"Now you sound like a schoolteacher." But he took the chalk and turned to the board. Once he'd finished, he stood back and looked the list over thoughtfully.

Hazel turned her attention to the board as well. "So, the three incidents at Enoch and Tensy's place happened on three consecutive days, then whoever the culprit was waited a day before moving to Saul Carson's place."

Ward nodded. "The incident at Saul's place happened on a Friday. Then they bided their time until the following Wednesday, when they broke into the mercantile." He added another note. "I happened to be out of town for that one."

"Which happened the evening after the Lytle boys were thrown out."

"Are you changing your mind about giving them the benefit of the doubt?"

"Not at all, but I think we should list everything that could be relevant. For instance, what if one of their fathers got upset about his boys being thrown out?"

With a nod, Ward made a note beside the mercantile break-in.

"Any other notable circumstances around any of these incidents? Or is there anything about any of them that stands out to you?"

"There was something a little different about the incident at Eunice's from the ones that happened before it. The perpetrator took the time to throw those undergarments up in the tree, as if just causing mischief wasn't enough, he wanted to publicly embarrass Eunice." He added the words *publicly embarrass* next to Eunice's incident.

"What about the instances after that?"

"I didn't see any sign of that at the Coopers' place. Of course, it might just be because I interrupted them. But yes, there was an element of that at the mayor's office." His jaw tightened. "And then there was what happened at your place."

"While I appreciate your concern for me, we need to take the personal out of this while we talk through it. So let's go back to the beginning. This started on a Monday four weeks ago at the Lawrences' place. What happened in the days leading up to that? Do you recall anything at all that was a little out of the ordinary?"

Ward rubbed his chin. "Out of the ordinary? Let's see, Mrs. Carlton left town to visit her sister in Jefferson. Dave Hobson broke his arm falling off his roof. A tree over on Saul's place got struck by lightning." He shook his head. "But I don't see where any of this gets us anywhere."

"We're just trying to get a big picture, not focus on anything right now. Write them up there." She tapped her chin. "And, if I remember correctly, school let out the Friday before that first incident."

"That's right." Her words triggered a memory. "In fact, I had to rescue Tensy Lawrence from a stampede of boys running through town after that final dismissal."

Hazel raised a brow. "Were the Lytle boys among their number by any chance?"

"As a matter of fact they were."

"And did you or Tensy say anything to them?"

"I warned them to pay closer attention to where they were going otherwise they'd spend the summer having to answer to me." He rubbed his jaw. "Things seem to keep coming back to the Lytle boys, don't they?" How had he missed that?

"It could be nothing, but it's worth noting. Not everything that happened is relevant. For instance, that Saturday was when I got the letter from Aunt Opal saying she wanted to groom me to take over her business."

That might not have anything to do with the criminal activity but it had certainly complicated his life.

But Hazel was still focused on the board. "As for the incidents themselves, do you think there's any significance to *what* was done at each place, either separately or together?"

Ward looked at the list again. "A trampled flower garden, a paint-spattered chicken coop, stealing a few pieces of old clothes from the line—these are all nuisances rather than major crimes. Not that I intend to minimize what happened at Enoch's place, but nothing about these incidents caused harm or major damage."

He stepped back to better see the board as a whole. "In fact, I'd begun to wonder why in the world anyone would target Enoch. It didn't make sense to me—the man's no saint, but he's fair in his dealings with folks and is one of the most inoffensive people I know. But if the Lytle boys were out to get even with Tensy for the scolding I gave them on her behalf, that makes a little more sense."

"So if that was what triggered the incidents at the Lawrence place, what made him move on and why pick on Mr. Carson next?"

"That last time at Enoch's, Tensy almost caught them. Maybe they figured they couldn't risk going there again. And by that time they'd got a taste for causing mischief." Before she could prompt him, he turned and made note of that.

"They skipped a day, then opened the horse pen at Saul Carson's place and ran his livestock off." She scrunched her face in thought. "Why his place?"

"You're asking all the same questions I've been asking for days now." He nearly growled in frustration.

She gave him an understanding smile, no doubt picking up on his frustration. "But now we're working on it together." She turned back to the board. "So they might have gotten spooked when Tensy caught a glimpse of them. What are some other reasons?"

"They might have tired of revisiting the same place."

She nodded. "Good. Anything else?"

"If we're just reaching for ideas, it could be that someone else caught their attention."

"So why target Mr. Carson?"

"It's adjacent to Enoch's place—maybe location is important. Or maybe the horse pen was an easy target."

He was doing a lot of writing but he wasn't sure it was getting them anywhere.

"Anything about the mercantile break-in besides the fact that the Lytle cousins were thrown out that morning?"

"Several things come to mind. It's the only incident that happened while I was away. It was the first time they focused on a business rather than a residence. And it was the first time they carried out their crime inside of town."

Hazel nodded. "So let's talk about what happened between the mercantile break-in and what happened at the boardinghouse."

"Let's see, I returned with Meg. My sister's funeral took place. You announced you were leaving Turnabout."

She fluttered a hand toward the board. "Write it all down."

They went through a similar exercise with the last four incidents until Ward was afraid there wasn't space enough left to fit one more word.

Ward set the chalk down and stepped back, dusting his hands against each other. "Now what?"

"Now we try to see any links or patterns."

They both studied the board for a few minutes, though Ward still wasn't quite sure what he was looking for.

"You know," he mused, "it's almost as if I called this trouble down on myself."

"What do you mean?"

"Nothing really. It's just that, several weeks ago, there was an article Everett posted in *The Gazette* about a big bank robbery that happened in St. Louis and the robbers got away clean. Then the lead detective on the case followed the clues the robbers left behind and captured them."

He cut her a guilty look. "When I stepped in the mercantile later that day, I saw Doug Blakely reading the article and I told him that I sometimes wished for a bit of excitement of that sort around here to test my mettle." He grimaced. "It was just an idle comment, I certainly didn't mean it."

Hazel rolled her eyes at him. "Of course you didn't. As Aunt Opal would say, pish posh. Even if you meant it, saying it wouldn't make it so." She waved to the board. "Now, focus!"

A moment later, Hazel stiffened. "Oh my goodness!"

"What is it?"

"There's one thing that many of these do have in common."

He stared at the board, trying to see whatever connections she'd made. "What's that?"

"You."

Ward frowned. "Explain."

"You confronted the Lytles before the first incident. Eunice was grousing about the job you were doing before her place became a target. The incident in the mayor's office spurred them to call the town meeting about you. And the attack on my dress was obviously aimed at our wedding."

"Hold on, that doesn't make a lot of sense. If my confrontation with the Lytles is what sparked the first incident, why go after the Lawrences? Why not just go after me?"

"Because, as the sheriff, making you the direct target might be too intimidating. All of these could be indirect attacks on you. In the case of the incidents at the Lawrences', your defense of Tensy might have been interpreted as a sign of personal affection for her. Which would be the same reason for going after my wedding gown."

It was fascinating to try to follow the way her mind worked. "What about the rest of these?"

"I'm not sure about the Carson place and the mercantile. But everyone knows how vocal Eunice is when she's unhappy. If they wanted to stir things up against you, then stirring her up was a good way to do it. And the mess they made in the mayor's office tipped the balance on having him call that town meeting."

"You think the Lytle boys would think things through that way?"

"I'm still not convinced it *is* the Lytle boys."

He wasn't either. "But you can't have it both ways. If it's not the Lytle boys, doesn't that make your whole argument for what started up this spree invalid?"

She frowned, then sat back appearing deflated. "I suppose so." Her finger tapped against the desk. "I suppose it could have been one of the other boys that was with them when you scolded them."

She studied the board again and hopped up to sit on top of the desk. "There's got to be a connection of some sort. I refuse to believe this was all completely random."

Ward looked at the notes again. What she said made sense, if only the finger was pointing to someone other than the Lytles. Could it be the elder Lytle cousins? Except this didn't feel like the way they would act either. But if wasn't them, then who else would have a reason?

"Maybe it didn't start with the run in between Tensy and the boys," he said. "Maybe there was some other trigger."

She turned to him, her expression hopeful. "You have something in mind?"

"Not yet."

"Oh." She went back to studying the board, but he could tell she had something on her mind. Finally she spoke up again. "There *was* something Tensy shared with me…"

She seemed reluctant to continue. He resisted the

urge to press her, waiting instead for her to work through whatever was worrying her.

"The thing is," she finally said, "it's her secret to tell and I promised not to share it."

"But you think it could have some bearing on this?"

"I'm not sure, but as I said, we shouldn't rule anything out."

Ward studied her for a moment. "I hadn't realized the two of you were close enough friends to be sharing confidences," he said thoughtfully.

She shifted uncomfortably, then waved a hand airily. "It's a small town and Tensy doesn't have many close friends. I think she just wanted someone to confide in."

"And as you were quick to tell me earlier, you're a good listener." Come to think on it, Tensy had been spending an unusual amount of time in the dress shop lately. Why? If he'd given it any thought at all, he'd just assumed she was having a dress made.

Dress! He suddenly remembered the image of that other gown that had been in Hazel's shop, untouched by the vandal who'd destroyed Hazel's gown. Hadn't Hazel said something about it being Tensy's dress when she'd thought it might have been vandalized as well?

Why would Tensy need such a fancy dress? Did she have a beau?

He needed to look at this from another angle. Could all of this possibly be the work of a jealous suitor? Had this mystery man mistaken Ward's rescue of Tensy as a play for her hand?

But no, that didn't make sense either. Such a motive wouldn't lead the man to start with the Lawrences, especially not multiple times. That would only force him, his supposed rival, to visit Tensy and her father more often, not push him away.

Maybe he'd guessed wrong and Tensy didn't have a suitor—it didn't make sense that she was keeping her suitor secret if she was already having a wedding gown made. The fancy dress must be for some other occasion.

Still, his gut told him he was right on the edge of figuring this out.

"Maybe this wasn't such a great idea after all," Hazel said resignedly. "We don't seem to be any closer to solving this than when we started."

"I disagree. If nothing else, you've helped me think through some options I hadn't considered before." He straightened. "But we've probably left your aunt and Half-pint alone for long enough. I'd best be getting you back to your place."

He waved to the board. "I'll leave our notes here until I have a chance to copy them. With school no longer in session, they should be okay."

"I agree." Hazel started to hop down from her perch on the desk when she hit a snag—literally.

"Oh bother. I think the back of my dress is caught on something."

"Here, let me look."

The edge of her dress had inadvertently caught on a small spindle. He had her freed in no time. Then he put his hands at her waist. "Here, let me help you down."

But something happened between the time he touched her and her feet touched the floor. It was as if his hands had developed a will of their own and didn't want to let go. And her hands, resting on his shoulders, seemed to be similarly afflicted. In fact, if anything, she tightened her hold.

His gaze locked with hers and he couldn't have looked away if he'd tried. He wanted this—this closeness, this warmth, this kiss that he knew was coming.

Had wanted it since she burst into his office appearing frightened and looking to him for comfort.

Yes, she would soon be moving away and yes, her matchmaking aunt would probably have her married off to another man before the year was out. But right now, this was their moment, their chance to, as she called it, build memories to draw out like treasures in the future.

He brushed the hair from her forehead, waiting for her to pull back, praying that she didn't. Instead she lifted her face to him and her eyes fluttered closed.

Chapter Twenty-Four

Her upturned face was all the invitation Ward needed. A heartbeat later he was kissing her, gently at first, wanting to let her know how very special she was, how much he cherished her. Then her hands moved from his shoulders to encircle his neck and he deepened the kiss.

When they finally parted he pulled her head against his chest with not-quite-steady hands and all the old doubts came flooding back. Kissing her like this, when he knew he couldn't give her the kind of love and commitment she wanted, she *deserved*, had been wrong.

But it hadn't felt wrong and Ward couldn't find it in himself to be sorry.

He moved back and put his hands on either side of her face, looking for any signs of contrition or regret. He saw none.

He smiled down at her. "I've been wanting to do that for quite some time. I must say, it was worth the wait."

Her face turned a becoming shade of pink. "I agree."

Then he tapped her nose, stepped back and folded his arms across his chest. Primarily to keep himself from reaching for her again. "Let's get you home."

He saw a look of confusion cross her face. She'd expected more from him, sweet words perhaps, hugs, declarations of love? Those were things he couldn't give her.

Much as he might want to.

On the short walk back to her place, Hazel didn't know whether to be angry or sad. She did know that if she'd had a bucket of water right now she'd gladly have chucked it at him.

That spontaneous kiss they'd shared had been so wonderful. Feeling the warmth of his touch, the gentleness combined with that tightly leashed strength—it was everything she'd ever dreamed a kiss from him would be and more.

It had given her real hope that they could have a future together, one built on love and trust.

Then he'd gone and ruined it all. He'd pulled away again in that maddening way he had, returned to the closed-off Ward he'd been before. She wasn't sure she could bear much more of the ups and downs she'd endured these past few weeks. Perhaps it was time to pack up and head for New York, sooner rather than later.

Ward spent most of the evening and night trying not to think about that kiss.

Instead he focused his thoughts on the work the two of them had done before he'd lost his head.

He went back to the schoolhouse after he returned Meg to Hazel's that evening and studied the board again. He couldn't shake the feeling that the answer to this puzzle rested with Tensy's secret that Hazel had alluded to.

And there was only one way to figure it out.

As soon as breakfast was over the next morning, Ward headed out to the Lawrence farm.

He found Tensy in the garden, a sunbonnet on her head and a hoe in her hand.

She paused when she saw him and leaned on the handle of her hoe. "Good morning, Sheriff. Isn't it a fine day?"

"It certainly is. Miss Lawrence, I—"

She waved a hand. "Call me Tensy, please. And if you're looking for Pa, he's out in the barn."

"Actually, I wanted to speak to you."

She smiled in obvious pleasure and waved toward the house. "Of course. Let's get out of the sun and sit on the porch. I can fetch you some lemonade if you like."

"Thank you, but that's not necessary." He waited until she'd sat on the bench, then doffed his hat and leaned a hip against the porch rail. "I wanted to speak to you one more time about those three incidents that happened here."

"Of course. But I'm not sure what else I can add to what I've already told you."

"I don't want to ask about what you saw. Right now I'm more interested in figuring out *why* these things are happening instead of who's doing them." Though he was pretty sure the *who* would follow close on the heels of the *why*.

But Tensy was frowning and shaking her head. "I'm sorry, but I don't think I can be much help there either."

"Your father has already told me that there's no one he could think of who might have reason to do mischief against him, but I was wondering if you can think of anyone who might want to do mischief against you?"

Her hand flew to her heart. "Me? You think someone might be trying to get back at me for something?"

"I'm not trying to alarm you but I need to be thorough and check every possibility."

"I truly appreciate your concern, Sheriff, but I honestly can't think of anyone."

Ward tried to curb his impatience. What had Hazel been alluding to in regard to this woman? But he couldn't betray her confidence by asking Tensy outright what secret she might be hiding.

"Are you sure there haven't been any changes in your life lately, any new friends or changed relationships?"

Her face reddened and she gave him what could almost be called a coy smile. "Why, Sheriff, you know what's changed. You—"

"Hello there."

Ward turned to see Enoch approaching from the barn. Hiding his irritation at the untimely interruption, Ward returned the man's greeting.

"What can we do for you this morning, Sheriff?" Enoch asked as he reached the porch.

"I was just talking to your daughter to see if she had any insights about the trouble that happened out here a few weeks ago." He turned back to Tensy but she'd already closed off.

She stood, wringing her hands nervously. "I'm afraid I don't have any more to add to what I've already said. If you'll excuse me, I need to get the stew on the stove for lunch." And without another word, she all but bolted for the door and disappeared inside the house.

Ward spent another few minutes chatting with Enoch, then took his leave.

Something about the way Tensy had looked at him just before Enoch showed up, something about the words she'd almost said. Could it possibly be...

Ward mulled it over, went back to the schoolhouse

to study the board. The theory that was trying to take root in his mind was too outlandish, too incredible to believe. Yet the more he studied the board, the less outlandish it seemed.

Looking through the filter of his new theory, he could find a way to tie his suspect to every incident except the one at the mercantile. With that one exception, it all appeared to fit together snugly, the why, the who, the when.

Hazel had been right after all, she just hadn't taken it far enough.

In fact, it was time to share his theory with her. It would be good to talk this through with her, to get her unique insights, to let her share in what he hoped was the solution to the puzzle.

And perhaps even help him figure out how to prove it.

Ward headed straight for the dress shop.

For the second day in a row, Hazel found herself leaning against the teacher's desk and staring at the note-filled blackboard.

Ward stood nearby and she wondered if he was remembering how their session had ended yesterday. In fact, thoughts of that kiss hadn't been far from her mind ever since it had happened.

He cleared his throat. "Thank you for coming."

So it was going to be all business. "Of course. I have to admit I'm intrigued." And flattered that he'd want to get her input on his theory. "So what have you discovered?"

"Not discovered so much as figured out." Hazel listened as Ward explained about his visit to the Lawrence place this morning and everything he'd worked out since. She was impressed with the connections he'd made, the motives he'd deduced, the leaps of logic he'd made.

Impressed, but not surprised. Ward was one of the smartest men she knew, not necessarily in book learning but in the things that really mattered.

"So, what do you think?" he asked as he wrapped up his explanation.

"I think it makes perfect sense. So much so that I can't believe I didn't see it before now."

"Don't feel bad. It took me this long as well and this is my job."

"But I had a piece of the puzzle you didn't, remember?" She braced herself to hop up on the desk, then changed her mind. "So what now?" she asked, trying to cover her aborted action.

"Now I try to prove it." He raised a brow at her in mock challenge. "Any ideas?"

Hazel grinned. "As a matter of fact…"

Later that afternoon, Hazel looked up as the shop door opened. She was alone in the emporium at the moment. Verity was at home minding the saddlery shop for Nate and Meg was upstairs with Aunt Opal.

"Oh, Tensy, I'm so glad you could make time to come." She stepped out from behind the counter to greet her customer.

"I got word you wanted to see me." The woman looked nervous, as if she might bolt from the shop at any moment.

"I wanted to show you something that I think will really add that special touch you wanted for your dress."

Tensy's whole expression brightened and she stepped forward. "What's that?"

Hazel reached into a box on the counter and pulled out a roll of ivory ribbon that was decorated with iridescent sequins in shades of gold and bronze. She held it up so that it shimmered in the sunlight. "I'd ordered this for my own gown but since that was destroyed, I thought you'd like to have it for yours."

"It's so beautiful." Tensy touched it reverently. Then she reluctantly dropped her hand. "But it's probably much too expensive for me to purchase."

Hazel smiled. "Consider it my wedding gift to you. What do you think, we can stitch it along the neckline and at the waist?"

"Oh, thank you, that's so generous."

"You're welcome. And I *am* feeling generous today. The sheriff and I decided last night to set the wedding ceremony for tomorrow."

Tensy gave her a startled frown. "Tomorrow? Isn't that rather sudden?"

"I know. But we want to get married before my aunt Opal leaves on Friday."

"But your dress is ruined. Surely you don't have time to create another one by Friday."

Hazel waved a hand, dismissing Tensy's concerns. "I know. But I have other very nice dresses. And the important thing is the ceremony itself and what it signifies, don't you think? And that you have loved ones with you to help celebrate, like my aunt Opal." Then she gave a happy sigh. "Besides, I do have something very special to wear."

"Oh?"

"Verity is making a headpiece for me using some of the lace from my mother's wedding dress. I'm so glad it wasn't down here when those cads destroyed my gown.

Wearing it will be like having my mother's blessing on our marriage."

She gave a delicate little shudder. "If something happened to that piece, after everything else that's gone wrong, I think I'd take it as a sign that this wedding was really not meant to be." She turned to Tensy. "Would you like to see it?"

Tensy nodded and Hazel led the girl to the workroom. "Here it is. Isn't it lovely?"

Tensy touched the delicate lace and seed pearl creation with near awe. Then Hazel ushered her back out. "I'm sorry to rush you but Aunt Opal is having a small engagement party for us tonight so I've got lots to do before the ceremony tomorrow."

"I understand. I need to get back and finish my chores myself. But if there is anything I can do to help, just let me know."

"Thank you, but I think we have everything under control."

As Hazel watched Tensy leave, her smile faded as she gave into a thoughtful, almost melancholy feeling. A part of her hoped Ward was wrong about who was behind the vandalism the town had been experiencing.

But the logical part of her knew he wasn't.

Ward sat in the dark in the dress shop. If he was right, the town troublemaker's string of crimes would come to an end tonight. Nate Cooper was with him. He didn't figure he really needed the help but the man had stubbornly insisted when he learned the plan.

Once Ward had determined that Nate was not merely after retribution for what had been done to his place, and had the man's word that he would hang back unless needed, he had agreed to let him sit watch with him.

The dinner party at the hotel was currently in full swing and should last for another hour. That was the window of time their quarry had to break in here so Ward figured they wouldn't have much longer to wait.

And he was right. The sound of a window opening brought both men alert. Ward signaled for Nate to remain where he was while he moved quietly to the workroom.

When he heard the sound of someone dropping to the floor, he stepped inside. "Hello, Tensy."

Chapter Twenty-Five

Behind him, Nate struck a match and lit the lamp they had brought for just that purpose. But true to his word, the man made no move to interject himself into the confrontation.

Tensy looked at Ward and actually smiled. "You figured it out. I knew you would."

"You've been a busy woman." He was feeling his way right now, like a wrangler with an agitated stallion, not really sure what tone to take with her.

"I know. And the surprising thing is, I discovered I'm quite good at this sort of thing."

"That you are." Almost too good.

"I did it all for us, but surely you already know that."

"Tensy, there is no us." He decided not to leave any gray area as far as that part of her delusion.

She shook her head, her expression one of indulgent exasperation. "Don't tease me. I know Hazel forced your hand by putting you in a compromising position, but all I have to do is destroy this veil and she'll realize that she was never meant to marry you."

Then Tensy paused, a tiny frown marring her serene expression. "Where's the veil? I could swear it was right here earlier."

"It's been put away somewhere safe."

Her expression took on a desperate quality. "No! You've got to get it for me. Once I destroy it, Hazel will go away and you will be free to marry me."

"Tensy, for the last time, there is no us. I'm truly sorry if anything I did led you to believe we were anything more than friends but we're not." He could see the madness in her eyes now. Had it always been there?

"No!" She screamed the word. "You love me, I know you do. Why else would you have stood up for me? It's why you kept making excuses to come back to the farm to speak to me. You belong with *me*, not her."

This was so much worse than dealing with a thug or hardened criminal. "No, Tensy, you misinterpreted my actions. I was doing my job as sheriff, that was all there was to it."

The woman let out a bloodcurdling scream and lunged for him, her hands curled into claws.

She was surprisingly strong and Ward was handicapped by his desire not to hurt her, but with Nate's help, they quickly subdued her.

Almost immediately Tensy reverted to the coquettish bride-to-be. It was chilling to watch.

She gave Ward a teasing smile. "You shouldn't be in here where my gown is. The groom shouldn't see the bride's dress before the wedding."

Ward and Nate exchanged glances over her head, then Ward took her arm. "Come along, I'm going to take you someplace where you'll be safe."

"Of course. I'll follow you anywhere you want to go. Can we talk about a wedding date now or should we wait until Hazel leaves for New York? It won't be much longer now, I'm sure."

He turned to Nate. "Would you mind riding out to get her father? She needs someone familiar to be with her tonight."

And he needed to see Hazel. Needed her to wash away this sad, pitiable glimpse of madness he'd just had to deal with.

It was a long night. Nate stayed with him until Tensy was safely behind bars, but the woman was surprisingly docile now and there was no repeat of the manic attack she'd attempted earlier.

Mrs. Pratt was called in to sit with Tensy while Nate rode out to fetch Enoch and while Ward made the notifications.

He first stopped at the hotel to let Hazel and Verity know they'd resolved the matter without anyone getting hurt. He knew both women had been concerned.

Then he headed over to the mayor's office where he had to lay everything out for the disbelieving official. It took quite some time to convince the mayor that it was a woman who'd caused so much angst in the town. In fact, he had to go through the whole litany of motives.

"A few weeks ago I took some boys to task who nearly ran her down and she apparently got it in her head that I was sweet on her. She orchestrated those incidents at her father's place as an excuse to have me stop by. Then, when I started to question why it was all happening at her place, she moved to Saul's place to throw suspicion off of her. The incidents at Eunice's place and your office occurred after she overheard slights made about me. She considered Hazel a rival so she hit the Coopers' place because Hazel had said she planned to leave town once Verity returned and she wanted to hasten that date. And she hit Hazel's place in an attempt to scare her off."

"And the mercantile?"

"I haven't figured that one out for sure, and we may never know. But if I was guessing, I'd say she was taking advantage of the incident that happened earlier that day to throw suspicion on the Lytle boys. Remember, they were the ones who set this whole chain of events in motion."

Though Ward suspected if it hadn't been that, it would have been something else. Tensy had obviously been "not quite right" for a long time.

The mayor shook his head, obviously having trouble taking it all in. "I must say, this is one for the books. Who could have imagined that all this fuss would be caused by a lovesick woman?" He stood and extended his hand. "Congratulations, Sheriff, well done. I had faith all along that you'd get this matter resolved."

By the time Ward got back to his office, a distraught and confused Enoch had arrived. He accepted Ward's story of what had happened but seemed a broken man.

Ward set a chair inside Tensy's cell and let Enoch in to see her.

He left the two of them alone to talk while he handled some of the paperwork required by the arrest. Finally he stood and moved to the cells. Tensy was asleep on her cot and Enoch sat on the chair with his head in his hand.

Ward opened the cell to let the man out.

"If you don't mind, I'd like to spend the night in the cell next to hers, just so I'll be close by if she awakens."

"Of course." Ward had a feeling this situation was going to be every bit as difficult for Enoch in the days to come as it was going to be for Tensy.

As Enoch sat on the cot in his cell, he looked up at Ward. "What's going to happen to her? I know she done bad things, but she's still my little girl."

For a moment Ward tried to imagine what he'd be feeling if it was Meg in that cell and his sympathy for the man deepened. "I honestly don't know. But I promise you I'll do everything in my power, such as it is, to make this as easy on her and you as I can."

Enoch nodded. "You're a good man." Then he turned and lay down on the cot, staring up at the ceiling.

Ward watched him a moment, then rubbed the back of his neck as he turned to the storeroom where he brewed the coffee. Other than that quick notification in the hotel restaurant, he still hadn't spoken to Hazel, and he felt it was long past time he do so. But it was well past midnight now so he'd have to wait a little longer.

Was this what love felt like?

This yearning to discuss the important matters in your life with that special someone?

This urgent need to just lay eyes on that person to help refresh your spirit when it's taken a blow?

This feeling like there's a hole in your heart that only she can heal?

How could he let her go to New York knowing he might never see her again?

Chapter Twenty-Six

"What's going to happen to her now?" Hazel had waited all night to hear something from Ward. It was just past dawn now and he'd finally shown up at her shop door. She'd all but pulled him inside and made him take a seat on one of the upholstered benches that were scattered around her shop. He should have looked out of place in this setting but somehow he didn't.

What he *did* look like was tired and weary of spirit.

"She's no longer in her right mind." Ward raked a hand through his hair, weariness and something more seeming to weigh him down. "It's as if she's living in a world of her own, sort of the way Bethany did these past twelve years. It would be wrong to keep her in jail."

Hazel agreed, and yet… "But you can't just send her back home with her father as if nothing happened."

"I know." He rubbed the back of his neck. "I've been giving that a lot of thought and I'm going to recommend that Enoch look into sending her to the same facility that Bethany was at. I think that's the best thing for everyone involved. They have some very fine doctors and nurses there who will see that she's comfortable and that she doesn't hurt herself or anyone else. And Enoch can find a place to stay nearby if he's a mind to."

"You're a good man, Ward Gleason."

She fiddled with her collar. "Do you think folks around here will be okay with that arrangement? After all, some of the people she caused problems for might not be quite so forgiving."

"Tensy didn't really hurt anyone. And Enoch is well respected around here. Given the chance, most folks are willing to do the right thing. I think if the recommendation is couched properly, and folks know she'll be sent away to a place like that, then they'll be willing to forgo pressing charges against her."

"I should have seen this sooner." How could she have been so blind? All the signs had been there—the secret beau, the frequent trips into the dress shop where she was able to keep tabs on things being said about Ward, her constant insistence that Hazel "follow her dreams" to New York.

"It's not the sort of thing one looks for. And we all thought it was a boy or man doing this. Even now Mayor Sanders is having trouble believing a woman could have been behind everything. It's hard to see past those in-grained perceptions."

She studied him closely, worried by the dark circles under his eyes. "Did you get any sleep at all last night?"

He shrugged. "I dozed in my chair a bit."

"That's what I thought. You and I need to talk, but I prefer to do it when you're in full control of your faculties."

He nodded and stood. It was telling that he didn't ask what she wanted to discuss. "Enoch is staying with Tensy for now and Nate has promised to look in on them from time to time this morning so I can get some shut-eye. How about I meet you for lunch, just the two of us, so we can talk? If your aunt or Verity won't mind taking care of Meg for a spell."

Hazel nodded. "I'll pack us a lunch and we can take it down to the cemetery."

He raised a brow at that.

"I happen to like it there," she said in response to his unasked question. "It's very peaceful and beautiful. And that bench under the big oak is the perfect spot to sit and talk."

He gave her a short bow. "The cemetery it is. I'll stop by here around noon and escort you there myself."

Hazel watched him walk away, an unsettled feeling in her gut. She hadn't been able to read anything in his expression so she didn't know what he was thinking. But by this afternoon, she would know if she was leaving for New York with her aunt or staying in Turnabout to marry Ward.

It was probably one of the biggest turning points of her life. And it would all be over in just a few short hours.

The afternoon was hot but beautiful. And here under the shade of the oak, even the heat was made bearable.

Hazel handed Ward one of the sandwiches she'd made, then folded her hands primly in her lap.

"Aren't you going to eat with me?" Ward asked.

Hazel shook her head. "I'm not really hungry." Truth to tell, her stomach was too unsettled for her to eat anything. She was both anxious and reluctant to have this conversation with him.

He set his sandwich back in the hamper. "All right, let's have it. What did you want to discuss?"

"You know good and well what I want to discuss. Us, our future."

"Hazel, we've been through this before. I care for you a great deal, but I believe, all things considered, you and Meg would be better off if you get on that train with your aunt when she leaves the day after tomorrow."

The look he gave her was intense. "However, if you decide to stay, you need to know two things. One, I insist on giving you the protection of my name so that both you and Half-pint are shielded from gossip. And two, it will be a marriage in name only. I'll continue to live in my house and you in yours."

This was even worse that she could have imagined. "That makes absolutely no sense."

"I care for you, Hazel, more than I realized perhaps. But if I moved in with you and Meg, if we tried to make a real marriage of it, I could never be the sheriff I want to be. Being sheriff requires that my job come first, and that's just the way it has to be."

"Does it? Have to be that way, I mean?" Why couldn't he see he was so much more?

"Being sheriff is who I am. If I wasn't sheriff, then I don't know who or what I'd be."

"You'd be the man I love," she said softly. "Wouldn't that be enough?"

His expression shifted, softened, and she thought for a moment she'd won him over. But then he stood and turned away.

She had her answer. Apparently that *wasn't* enough for him.

She stood and lifted the hamper with the uneaten food, trying to hold on to her composure at least until she could reach the privacy of her bedroom.

"I'll break the news to Meg when she wakes from her nap. She's going to take it hard."

"She'll get over it, in time."

Hazel wasn't so sure of that. Without another word she turned and walked away, leaving Ward standing under the oak, alone.

Just the way he wanted it.

Chapter Twenty-Seven

Hazel sat between her aunt and Meg as the train pulled out of the Turnabout station. Meg kept her nose glued to the window as the train chugged down the tracks. Farther away from Ward with each passing *clickety-clack* of the wheels.

Finally Meg turned away from the window and huddled in her seat, burying her tear-stained cheeks in her doll. Separating the little girl from Ward had been every bit as painful as Hazel had feared it would be.

Though there had been promises of letter writing and return visits, the little girl hadn't understood why she couldn't stay and now was obviously feeling confused and betrayed.

Ward had wanted to send Pugs along with them but Meg wouldn't hear of it. Even though she was hurt and scared by all the decisions the grown-ups were making for her, she insisted Ward needed to keep Pugs so he wouldn't be all alone after they left.

Hazel had seen the stoic sheriff almost break down at that point. It served him right as far as she was concerned.

Hazel tried to push away thoughts of all she was

leaving behind by focusing on her surroundings inside the train. There was a harried-looking woman with two children in the row in front of them and a snoring gentleman in the row behind. The conductor stood in the aisle several rows ahead, listening to an officious-looking gentleman with a ridiculously long mustache level complaints about the lack of comfort provided by the seats.

Other conversations were going on around her but Hazel did her best not to listen to specifics. Instead she let all of the voices and sounds blend together, providing a buzzing backdrop for her unhappy thoughts.

"Are you paying attention, dear?"

Her aunt's question brought Hazel's mind back in focus. "I'm sorry, Aunt Opal. I guess my mind was wandering."

"Are you sure you made the right decision?"

Hazel didn't pretend to misunderstand. She was tired of pretending. She pitched her voice so Meg wouldn't hear. "He doesn't love me."

"Are you sure?"

"He told me straight-out that his job had to come first."

Her aunt shook her head sympathetically. "That poor man. Let's hope he comes to his senses before it's too late." She gave Hazel a pointed look. "Of course you won't be around to see it even if he *does* come to his senses."

What was her aunt trying to say? Did she think Hazel had made the wrong decision? Didn't she want her to move to New York to work with her?

What about this opportunity that had opened up for her, this new adventure? There had to be a reason it had come along at just this point in her life. Was she supposed to just ignore it in favor of an uncertain future in Turnabout?

"George!" The woman in front of them was sounding more and more strident, her irritation obviously rising. "I told you, do *not* open that window."

"But, Mother, I'm hot."

"I'm sorry but if you open the window it'll just let soot and dust in. Not all windows are meant to be opened."

Not all windows are meant to be opened. Those words reverberated in Hazel's mind. She said she'd prayed over this and she had. But had she really waited on God for her answer? Or had she tried to wrest control of the situation from Him and step through the first opportunity that came her way?

She'd been looking at this as an either-or situation—either she'd win Ward's love or she'd move to New York. But those weren't really her only choices.

The Good Lord had given her a great gift—the opportunity to be a mother. Perhaps she was not meant to be a wife. But she could be a good mother to Meg. And being a good mother meant doing what was best for the child. And she was beginning to think that what was best was not going to be found in New York City.

And so what if Ward had given her an ultimatum that if she chose to stay she would have to enter into an in-name-only marriage? His was not the final say on that matter. If she wanted to stay single and raise Meg, that was her business. And if she had to battle a mob of self-righteous matrons for the right to do it, then she would do that as well.

Her finances were still an issue, especially with a child to care for now. But she had an idea on how to handle that situation as well.

Suddenly feeling better than she had in quite a long time, Hazel turned to her traveling companion.

Only to discover her aunt Opal smiling knowingly at her. "You've made a decision, I see."

Hazel nodded. "Meg and I will be getting off at the next stop and heading back to Turnabout. I'm sorry if—"

"No need to explain, my dear. I'm just glad you finally came to your senses."

"But your business—"

"Will be just fine. Gracie may not be kin but she is very talented and very dedicated. She'll do a fine job running Eldridge Fashion Design."

Hazel gave her aunt a hug. Then she leaned back and gave her aunt a speculative look. "In the meantime, I have a business proposition I'd like to discuss with you."

Her aunt raised a brow, then nodded. "I'm listening."

Ward walked down the sidewalk of town. When he turned on Second Street, he tried to ignore the now-vacant dress shop. He knew Verity intended to keep it open as a hat shop, but she planned to wait a little while before reopening it.

Turnabout without Hazel in it already seemed like a duller place. And she'd been gone less than a day.

Verity stepped out of the saddlery shop and stopped him with a hail. "Good morning, Sheriff. It looks like we might be in for a little rain later today."

"Could be. The farmers will be glad to get it." And it would match his mood.

"Joy certainly does miss Meg. Nearly as much as I miss Hazel." She cut him a sideways glance, as if expecting him to spill his guts to her. Or perhaps his heart.

"New York will be good for them, both of them.

Hazel will be around her family, doing what she loves. And Meg will be able to grow up in a big city with all kinds of big-city advantages."

Verity didn't seem to share his optimism. "Hazel was doing what she loves *here*. And the only advantage Meg needs is to be raised in a good home by loving parents."

He shrugged, not liking the accusatory tone in her voice. "It was her choice to leave."

"Was it?"

"It was." But he hadn't given her much choice. With a tip of his hat, he quickly moved on.

Somehow, without quite planning it, Ward ended up at the cemetery. Removing his hat, he made his way to Bethany's grave. The grass had grown over it already. He'd have to remember to bring some flowers here next time he came.

Feeling the need to say something, Ward ran his finger along the brim of his hat. "Bethany, I never got to apologize to you properly, not because I didn't try, but because you didn't understand. I'm thinking that maybe you understand now so I'm going to say this one more time. I am more sorry than I can ever say that I didn't look out for you better, that I didn't keep you safe like I should have. I missed you so much after the accident, missed your laughter and those funny faces you were always making, missed your curiosity and your joy for life, I just missed *you*. And most of all I missed watching you grow into the amazing woman I know you could have been. I wish I could go back and do it right this time, but we don't get do-overs in this life. So I just hope you'll accept my apology and know that I will always love and miss you."

He put his hat back on and felt a small sense of peace. Then he glanced up and saw the bench and he was suddenly hearing Hazel's words again, seeing the hurt that he'd put on her face.

You would be the man I love, she'd whispered. *Wouldn't that be enough?*

Ward almost fell to his knees as those words finally sunk in and the enormity of the mistake he'd made hit him full force. She'd offered her heart to him, had made herself achingly vulnerable to let him know how she felt, and he'd stomped on her oh-so-precious offering as if it were nothing of any consequence.

How could he have thought his job more important than her love? A job was fleeting, could be taken away on a whim or by a twist of circumstance. But love, true love of the kind she'd offered him, was an incorruptible treasure, something to see him through all of life's ups and downs.

And he'd cavalierly thrown it back in her face.

He was a fool.

Worse, he was a heartless fool.

He had to find a way to fix this. Surely it couldn't be too late.

Ten minutes later, Ward was marching into Mayor Sanders's office.

The public official looked up, clearly startled by Ward's aggressive entrance. "What can I do for you today, Sheriff?"

"I've come to tell you I'm going to be out of town for several days, maybe even a couple of weeks." He would stay in New York as long as it took to convince Hazel to come back to Turnabout with him.

The mayor raised a brow at that. "When do you plan to leave?"

"Today."

The man steepled his fingers. "That doesn't give us much time to make other arrangements."

"For that I apologize. But I am leaving on this afternoon's train. And there's something else you need to know. I plan to marry Hazel, if she'll have me. And if she does, there will have to be some changes. I'll still do the job to the best of my ability, but not seven days a week, twenty-four hours a day. Which means the town will need to hire a deputy, someone who can share the responsibility with me. If that doesn't work for you, then you should probably find a new sheriff."

And without waiting for a response, Ward marched out.

Chapter Twenty-Eight

Hazel sat on the edge of her seat, staring out the train window as they rounded the final turn heading into Turnabout. She and Meg had had to spend the night at the hotel in Kittering while they waited for the west-bound train.

Even with a now-happy and excited Meg to entertain, the time had passed slowly, like watching a slug cross a garden walk. She hadn't slept well but not because she was second-guessing her decision—this felt more right than anything had in a long time.

No, it was because she couldn't wait to get back to Turnabout. She wasn't certain what kind of reception she'd get from Ward, especially when she informed him there was no way she'd agree to an in-name-only marriage, but for Meg's sake they would work it out.

And she had a new venture to keep her busy. She and Aunt Opal had had a long talk while waiting for the train to make its first stop. Hazel had discussed adding a children's clothing line to her aunt's offerings. Her aunt had already said how impressed she was with the clothing Hazel had made for Meg so it hadn't taken much to sell her on the idea. And Hazel declared herself confident that she could work on the designs and the actual creations from her home in Turnabout and ship the finished products to New York when she was done.

Aunt Opal had agreed to give it a six-month trial. It was an amazing compromise and Hazel couldn't wait to get started.

But first, there was Ward to confront.

The train began to slow and Meg started bouncing eagerly in her seat. "Won't Sheriff Gleason be surprised to see us?"

A definite understatement. "That he will." She patted Meg's knee. "And I imagine Joy will be happy to see you as well."

Her plan was to drop Meg off at Verity's while she had her initial confrontation with Ward. Ward and Meg could have their reunion afterward.

As soon as the train came to a complete stop, Hazel and Meg were ready to disembark. Making sure she had a firm hold on the little girl's hand, Hazel headed for the depot office. She'd make arrangements to have their bags delivered and then—

Hazel stopped dead in her tracks. Striding out of the depot was Ward himself.

Meg had spotted him as well. "Sheriff Gleason!" she screeched at the top of her lungs, and launched herself straight at him.

Ward whipped around, Hazel's surprise mirrored in his own expression. Then his face split in a wide grin as he swooped down and lifted Meg high in the air. "Aren't you just a sight for sore eyes?"

Meg giggled as he brought her to rest on his hip. "Are you surprised to see us?"

"Very surprised. And very happy." His eyes met Hazel's as he said that and she blinked, not quite believing what she saw reflected there.

Then he turned back to Meg. "Half-pint, what do you say we bring you over to Joy's house so you can surprise her too? Then you can stay and play with her while me and Miss Hazel have a little talk."

His high-handed manner irritated Hazel, though she wasn't quite sure why it should, since it was identical to what she herself had planned. As they set off for the Coopers' place, Ward casually tucked Hazel's hand on his arm, covering her hand possessively with his, but they allowed Meg to monopolize the conversation.

Hazel was thrown completely off balance by this Ward, who was so different from the one she'd left behind just yesterday. How would this Ward react to the stand she planned to take?

It seemed a matter of mere seconds and they were standing in front of the saddlery shop. Verity rushed out as soon as she spotted her and gave her a big hug right there on the sidewalk. Joy and Meg had a similarly happy reunion.

Then Ward cleared his throat. "Mrs. Cooper, might we impose on you to keep an eye on Meg while Miss Andrews and I go for a walk?"

Verity gave them a knowing look, then made shooing motions with her hands. "Go. Take as long as you need. We'll be fine here."

With a tip of his hat, Ward led Hazel away, still keeping her hand secured on his arm.

Not that she minded. It was actually kind of nice holding on to him this way. She was surprised, though, to find he was leading her to the churchyard and then on to the cemetery.

He handed her down to the bench. "If I recall, you find this a good place for private talks."

"I do." Was he going to insist yet again that she allow him to give her the protection of his name?

"First let me say how very happy I am that you've returned to Turnabout."

"And I'm glad to be back. But there is something I need to make very clear." She had to get this out before she lost her nerve. Because the way he was looking at her was sending little bubbles dancing around in her insides. "I don't care what your code of honor tells you that you must do, I absolutely will not take part in an in-name-only marriage. I am quite able to stand up to whatever gossip might remain from our little indiscretion that wasn't really an indiscretion at all." She was babbling a bit, but she was finding it hard to concentrate when he was looking at her with what she could only call joy in his eyes.

"You're quite right."

She blinked. "I am?"

"Absolutely. I should never have demanded such a thing from you."

Now she was thoroughly confused.

He sat and took one of her hands. "It's my turn to make something very clear. By returning, you saved me from having to undertake a long, anxious trip, though it is no less than what I deserve."

"Trip? You mean you weren't at the depot to send a telegram?"

"No." He fished something out of his pocket. "I was purchasing a ticket for the next eastbound train."

Sure enough, he was holding a train ticket. She looked up and met his gaze. "You were coming after us?"

"I was. It was my very manly plan to find you and beg your forgiveness for being such a complete and utter fool. And to ask you to do me the very great honor of marrying me."

"But I just told you—"

"I'm not asking for an in-name-only marriage. I want a real, for better, for worse, happily-ever-after, love match of a marriage. And I want it with you."

"But your job—"

"Is just a job." He squeezed her hands. "I love you, Hazel Andrews, every maddening, stubborn, brave, wonderful ounce of you. Tell me I'm not too late, that you haven't changed your mind. Tell me I can still be the man that you love."

Hazel pulled her hands away from him and then threw herself in his arms. "Ward Gleason, you will always be the man that I love. Yes, absolutely I *will* marry you."

They exchanged a very long, very satisfying kiss, right there under the oak. And when they were done, Ward stood and reached down to help her up. "Come on, let's go tell Half-pint that we're going to be a real family, at last."

Epilogue

Hazel stood at the back of the church, awaiting the signal to start her march down the aisle. She wasn't the least bit nervous though, even if she was breaking with tradition.

Rather than looking around for a stand-in father to walk her down the aisle, she had asked Aunt Opal to perform that ritual for her, and her aunt, who also enjoyed breaking from tradition occasionally, had pronounced herself delighted.

Meg was with them, proudly holding on to the handle of a basket filled with rose petals. She was so proud to be a part of the ceremony and had been practicing walking and tossing petals for days. The local meadows and roadsides had been stripped of their glory as a result.

Meg had already started calling Ward Poppa rather than Sheriff Gleason and she was now Mommy rather than Miss Hazel. And she couldn't think of a title she liked better. Except perhaps Mrs. Ward Gleason.

"I do believe you are the most beautiful bride I have ever had the honor of dressing," her aunt said. "The color and style suit you to perfection."

Aunt Opal had insisted on making the wedding

gown, but she'd made it to Hazel's specifications. The smoky blue color was a perfect match for Ward's eyes and the slim tailoring suited her figure nicely, even if she did say so herself.

Aunt Opal, on the other hand, wore a severely cut, unadorned dress in a fawn color. She'd stated that it would be wrong of her to try to upstage the bride on her wedding day.

Meg looked sweet in a white organdy concoction with a large pink satin ribbon at the waist and matching ribbons on her pigtails.

Just then the organ sounded and Hazel smiled down at Meg. "Okay, sweetheart, it's time for you to make your grand entrance."

Aunt Opal opened the door and Meg stepped forward with the supreme confidence of an almost-five-year-old who knows she is loved.

Hazel peeked through the open door, looking past Meg to the handsome gentleman waiting at the altar. He was watching Meg's progress with a great deal of love and pride shining from his eyes. And then, as if he felt her gaze, he looked up and met her gaze.

Basking in the smiling love from the man she happily planned to spend the rest of her life with, Hazel took her aunt's arm and confidently took the first step toward the real window the Good Lord had opened for her.

Ward's heart swelled with joy. His girls, both of them, walking toward him with big, beautiful smiles on their lips and love shining from their eyes. Was ever a man so blessed as him?

When Meg reached the front of the church, she set her basket down on the front pew, then stepped up and took her place beside him. He smiled down at her with a wink, then turned his attention to his beautiful bride.

He still couldn't believe how close he'd come to turning his back on all of this. How could he ever have believed that duty came before love?

It had taken him so long to understand what true love was—that it was more than infatuation or desire or distraction. True love was a precious gift, a recognizing of that person who makes you feel whole and fulfilled and equipped to face whatever life throws at you. True love accepts you just as you are, without pretense. And true love is finding that one person tailor-made to complete you and make you strive to be more than you could ever hope to be on your own.

At least, that's the kind of love he'd found with Hazel.

And God willing, he'd never let it, or her, slip through his fingers again.

He stepped forward and accepted her hand from her aunt and together they each took one of Meg's hands and turned to face Reverend Harper to speak the vows that would join them, now and forever, as a family.

* * * * *

*If you loved this story,
pick up the other books in the*
TEXAS GROOMS *series:*

HANDPICKED HUSBAND
THE BRIDE NEXT DOOR
A FAMILY FOR CHRISTMAS
LONE STAR HEIRESS
HER HOLIDAY FAMILY
SECOND CHANCE HERO
THE HOLIDAY COURTSHIP
TEXAS CINDERELLA

Available now from Love Inspired Historical!

Find more great reads at www.LoveInspired.com.

Dear Reader,

I hope you've enjoyed Hazel and Ward's story. This one was a long time in the making. Both of these characters have appeared in many of the previous *Texas Grooms* books, but it wasn't until Hazel popped up in *Second Chance Hero* as Verity's best friend that she really came to life for me. And it was only then that I realized the sheriff was the object of her long-standing affection.

Hazel and Ward's story simmered in my mind as I wrote two additional books in the series, until I was finally ready to tell their story. And what a story it turned out to be. Ward came to life for me as a hero in so many unexpected ways—I fell in love with him right along with Hazel. And I hope you will too.

For more information on this and other books set in Turnabout, please visit my website at www.winniegriggs.com or follow me on Facebook at www.facebook.com/WinnieGriggs.Author.

And as always, I love to hear from readers. Feel free to contact me at winnie@winniegriggs.com with your thoughts on this or any other of my books.

Wishing you a life abounding with love and grace,
Winnie Griggs

COMING NEXT MONTH FROM
Love Inspired® Historical

Available July 3, 2017

MONTANA COWBOY'S BABY
Big Sky Country • by Linda Ford

Cowboy Conner Marshall doesn't know the first thing about fatherhood, but he's determined to do right by the abandoned baby left on his doorstep. As the doctor's daughter, Kate Baker, helps him care for the sick baby, they forge a bond that has him wondering if Kate and baby Ellie belong on his ranch forever!

THE ENGAGEMENT CHARADE
Smoky Mountain Matches • by Karen Kirst

In order to protect his pregnant, widowed employee, Ellie Jameson, from her controlling in-laws, Alexander Copeland pretends to be her fiancé. But can this temporary engagement help them heal old wounds...and fall in love?

THE RENEGADE'S REDEMPTION
by Stacy Henrie

With nowhere else to go, injured Tex Beckett turns to his ex, Ravena Reid, who allows him to stay on her farm under one condition: he must help her with the orphans she's taking care of. But what will she do if she finds out he's an outlaw?

LONE STAR BRIDE
by Jolene Navarro

When Sofia De Zavala's father discovers she dressed as a boy to go on a cattle drive and prove she can run the ranch, he forces her to marry trail boss Jackson McCreed to save her reputation. Now she must convince Jackson their union can become a loving partnership.

———

LOOK FOR THESE AND OTHER LOVE INSPIRED BOOKS WHEREVER BOOKS ARE SOLD, INCLUDING MOST BOOKSTORES, SUPERMARKETS, DISCOUNT STORES AND DRUGSTORES.

LIHCNM0617

Get 2 Free Books,
Plus 2 Free Gifts—
just for trying the Reader Service!

Love Inspired HISTORICAL

YES! Please send me 2 FREE Love Inspired® Historical novels and my 2 FREE mystery gifts (gifts are worth about $10 retail). After receiving them, if I don't wish to receive any more books, I can return the shipping statement marked "cancel." If I don't cancel, I will receive 4 brand-new novels every month and be billed just $5.24 per book in the U.S. or $5.74 per book in Canada. That's a savings of at least 13% off the cover price. It's quite a bargain! Shipping and handling is just 50¢ per book in the U.S. and 75¢ per book in Canada.* I understand that accepting the 2 free books and gifts places me under no obligation to buy anything. I can always return a shipment and cancel at any time. Even if I never buy another book, the two free books and gifts are mine to keep forever.

102/302 IDN GLQG

Name	(PLEASE PRINT)	
Address		Apt. #
City	State/Prov.	Zip/Postal Code

Signature (if under 18, a parent or guardian must sign)

Mail to the Reader Service:
IN U.S.A.: P.O. Box 1867, Buffalo, NY 14240-1867
IN CANADA: P.O. Box 611, Fort Erie, Ontario L2A 9Z9

Want to try two free books from another series?
Call 1-800-873-8635 or visit www.ReaderService.com.

* Terms and prices subject to change without notice. Prices do not include applicable taxes. Sales tax applicable in N.Y. Canadian residents will be charged applicable taxes. Offer not valid in Quebec. This offer is limited to one order per household. Books received may not be as shown. Not valid for current subscribers to Love Inspired Historical books. All orders subject to credit approval. Credit or debit balances in a customer's account(s) may be offset by any other outstanding balance owed by or to the customer. Please allow 4 to 6 weeks for delivery. Offer available while quantities last.

Your Privacy—The Reader Service is committed to protecting your privacy. Our Privacy Policy is available online at www.ReaderService.com or upon request from the Reader Service.

We make a portion of our mailing list available to reputable third parties that offer products we believe may interest you. If you prefer that we not exchange your name with third parties, or if you wish to clarify or modify your communication preferences, please visit us at www.ReaderService.com/consumerschoice or write to us at Reader Service Preference Service, P.O. Box 9062, Buffalo, NY 14240-9062. Include your complete name and address.

LIH17R

SPECIAL EXCERPT FROM

Love Inspired **HISTORICAL**

*Cowboy Conner Marshall doesn't know the first thing
about fatherhood, but he's determined to do right by the
abandoned baby left on his doorstep. As the doctor's
daughter, Kate Baker, helps him care for the sick baby,
they forge a bond that has him wondering if Kate
and baby Ellie belong on his ranch forever!*

Read on for a sneak preview of
MONTANA COWBOY'S BABY by **Linda Ford**,
available July 2017 from Love Inspired Historical!

"Did anything you tried last night get Ellie's attention?" Kate
asked Conner.

"She seemed to like to hear me sing." Heat swept over his
chest at how foolish he felt admitting it.

"Well, then, I suggest you sing to her."

"You're bossy. Did you know that?" It was his turn to
chuckle as pink blossomed in her cheeks.

She gave a little toss of her head. "I'm simply speaking
with authority. You did ask me to stay and help. I assumed you
wanted my medical assistance."

No mistaking the challenge in her voice.

"Your medical assistance, yes, of course." He humbled his
voice and did his best to look contrite.

"You sing to her and I'll try to get more sugar water into
her."

He cleared his throat. "'Sleep, my love, and peace attend
thee. All through the night; Guardian angels God will lend
thee, All through the night.'"

Ellie blinked and brought her gaze to him.

"Excellent," Kate whispered and leaned over Conner's arm
to ease the syringe between Ellie's lips. The baby swallowed
three times and then her eyes closed.

"Sleep is good, too," Kate murmured, leaning back. "I think she likes your voice."

He stopped himself from meeting Kate's eyes. Warmth filled them and he allowed himself a little glow of victory. "Thelma hated my singing." He hadn't meant to say that. Certainly not aloud.

Kate's eyes cooled considerably. "You're referring to Ellie's mother?"

"That's right." No need to say more.

"Do you mind me asking where she is?"

"'Fraid I can't answer that."

She waited.

"I don't know. I haven't seen her in over a year."

"I see."

Only it was obvious she didn't. But he wasn't going to explain. Not until he figured out what Thelma was up to.

Kate pushed to her feet.

"How long before we wake her to feed her again?" he asked.

"Fifteen minutes. You hold her and rest. I don't suppose you got much sleep last night."

There she went being bossy and authoritative again. Not that he truly minded. It was nice to know someone cared how tired he was and also knew how to deal with Ellie.

Don't miss
MONTANA COWBOY'S BABY by Linda Ford,
available July 2017 wherever
Love Inspired® Historical books and ebooks are sold.

www.LoveInspired.com

Copyright © 2017 by Linda Ford

LIHEXP0617